A Deadly Paradise

A Deadly Paradise

GRACE BROPHY

SOHO
CRIME

Published by
Soho Press, Inc.
853 Broadway
New York, NY 10003

Library of Congress Cataloging-in-Publication Data
Brophy, Grace, 1941–
A deadly paradise / Grace Brophy.
    p. cm.
ISBN 978-1-56947-491-4 (hardcover)
1. Diplomats—Crimes against—Fiction.
2. Police—Italy—Fiction. 3. Bank notes—Forgeries—Fiction.
4. World War, 1939-1945—Italy—Venice—Fiction.
5. Umbria (Italy)—Fiction. I. Title.
S3602.R6463D43 2008
13'.6—dc22
2007041137

10 9 8 7 6 5 4 3 2 1

For Miguel

Author's Note

DURING WORLD WAR II, near-perfect forgeries of Bank of England pound notes were produced by prisoners in a German concentration camp, an event now referred to as Operation Bernhard. Hitler's intention was to ruin the British economy by flooding the financial markets with the counterfeit notes. One of the subplots in this novel is based on this event. I should note, however, that all characters, living and dead, are wholly imaginary and that all other events and many of the institutions and place names, including the German Cultural Institute and the town of Paradiso, are fictional.

Her lips were red, *her* looks were free,
Her locks were yellow as gold:
Her skin was as white as leprosy,
The Night-mare LIFE-IN-DEATH was she,
Who thicks man's blood with cold.

THE RIME OF THE ANCIENT MARINER
Samuel Taylor Coleridge

Contents

PROLOGUE

Venice 1945

THE BOATMAN REMOVED the cigarette from his shirt pocket. Tomorrow was his day off, and he sighed with anticipation as he unrolled the cigarette from its greasy brown wrapper and passed it under his nose, inhaling deeply. He'd smoke half of it with a grappa in the café and the other half later in the evening, in front of the fire. He thought with satisfaction of the pile of driftwood that he had collected during his delivery rounds. Anna would be pleased, and when she was pleased she didn't complain if he shared a drink and a smoke with his mates. There was no shortage of grappa in wartime Venice. He sighed again and gathered his wool vest closer to his chest. The rain had started falling three days ago, the beginning of *acqua alta,* and the damp penetrated everything, even the newspapers that lined his shoes.

Only one person was on the esplanade, a schoolgirl in uniform. She stood some twenty feet from him, in full view of his barge, sheltering from the rain beneath the archway that separates the Cannaregio canal from the Ghetto. She lighted a cigarette, and he watched with desire as wisps of smoke drifted out toward the canal and mingled with the mist. Perhaps he would ask her for a cigarette. Foreigners were more generous than Venetians, and he often bummed cigarettes from them. But this schoolgirl was no ordinary foreigner, and he decided against it.

She was scantily dressed, just a light jacket thrown over her dark blue school uniform, and he wondered again why she was lurking there. She didn't live in the Ghetto, not among the Jews. And the Germans didn't employ school-girls as spies when they had so many willing Venetians to act for them. He knew for sure she was German. He'd seen her many times before, when the convent school at the end of the canal let out for the day. She had fat yellow pig-tails, wore an iron leg brace, and always followed behind the other girls, dragging her left leg at an awkward angle. At first, his natural kindness had colored his feelings and he'd felt sorry for her. But later, he heard her speaking in rapid-fire German to one of the nuns who accompanied the girls, and he had withdrawn his sympathy. She could go to hell with the rest of them.

He spat into the canal, consigning the crippled fräulein to her misery. She had nothing to do with him. One more load and he was finished for the day. He started the engine, waiting for its black smoke to foul the air, and then quickly turned it off again when he heard the warning blare of a police foghorn in the distance. He held his breath, waiting for the wake of the larger boat to push his barge against the pilings; but instead of the police proceeding up the canal, they docked directly across from him, in front of the Palazzo Molin. Four men exited the launch after it was secured, two in German uniform and two in plain clothes. The launch bobbled and rocked against the moss-covered steps, and one of the men slipped and almost fell. He let out a loud oath and the others laughed. A shutter was thrown open on the second floor of the palazzo, and an orange light sent a vaporous glow across the murky waters.

He spat again into the canal and watched as the men banged vigorously on the iron gates enclosing the palazzo. No one answered, and the men banged again, shouting loudly this time for someone to open up. Finally, a woman unlocked the gates and let the Germans inside. The wait for them to return seemed interminable to the boatman, and he thought longingly of the cigarette in his shirt pocket. But, in truth, the wait was shorter than he imagined—five minutes, no more, until the men returned, with a fifth man in lockstep between them. The fading afternoon light threw deep shadows across the water, but even in the shadows he recognized the fifth man. The boatman often delivered household items to the palazzo, and its owner, Count Molin, had once helped him pull a heavy crate onto the dock. But even without this personal encounter, the boatman would have known the count anywhere. He was tall, even for a northerner, and he dwarfed the Germans who assisted him into the launch.

The schoolgirl, who had stayed out of sight while the drama unfolded, waited until the launch had pulled away before she emerged from the depths of the archway. She approached the canal and stared across at the palazzo, standing so close to the edge that the boatman feared she might lose her footing. The iron brace would drag her to the bottom of the canal. He coughed discreetly in warning. But she ignored him and continued to peer intently at the palazzo. The falling darkness amplified the sounds of water lapping against cement, and a piercing cry from inside the palazzo drifted across the water. What the girl did next puzzled the boatman, so much so that he spoke of it incessantly to Anna until she stopped listening, then later to total strangers. The girl bent her right knee as though curtsying to a queen, turned, and headed toward the Strada Nova.

A Deadly Paradise

Book One

Paradise Lost

I

LORENZO WAS SURE he'd heard a soft mew coming from the garden next door. Normally he could see Tommaso quite clearly even when he was trying to hide. He was black as midnight and large even for an unaltered tomcat. The veterinarian said he was overfed and then, of course, he'd slip Tommaso treats whenever he passed him in the street. Lorenzo didn't usually worry when Tommaso was missing for a day, but since *la tedesca* had moved next door, he was keeping a close watch on him. The German had a flirtatious little female, and Tommaso had gone after her more than once.

He climbed the stone wall that separated the properties and caught his foot in one of the vines that sprawled exuberantly over his neighbor's garden. "Disgusting! It's a wonder every cat in town hasn't moved in," he muttered to himself as he untangled the vine to release his foot. "Tommaso, *vieni qui,*" he called softly, spreading the foot-high weeds apart as he moved through the garden. He heard another mew, softer and more plaintive, and he knew that Tommaso was in trouble. What's the little devil up to now, he thought, as he searched frantically under a pile of dead leaves. That's when he saw the hole in the basement window, just big enough for a gutter rat to crawl through; but Tommaso, the magician, had gotten himself into even smaller spaces in the past.

If he knocked on the German's door and told her that Tommaso was in her basement, she'd make a huge fuss, maybe call the carabinieri again. Lorenzo had played in that basement many times as a child and knew that once Tommaso went through the window, he had no way of getting back out. He tried to peer in, but the window was encrusted with dirt. "Tommaso," he called again, and was rewarded with another plaintive mew. Nothing for it, Lorenzo decided, reaching through the hole in the window to unhook the latch. He hadn't seen the German or her car that afternoon; he would be safe.

The window frame, which was stiff from grime and disuse, cracked loudly as he pushed it inward. He hesitated a moment, holding his breath, but, hearing no thunderbolts in German, he climbed through, dropping four feet to the basement floor. "Bad cat," he whispered as soon as Tomasso began circling his feet and pushing up against his legs. "*Andiamo a casa,*" he said, tenderly lifting the black cat onto his shoulder. Then he shuddered in disgust. Tommaso was covered in blood.

2

QUESTORE CARLO TOGNI, commander of the Perugia Questura, knew himself to be an even-tempered man, but sometimes his favorite commissario would try the patience of a saint. Alessandro Cenni was staring off into space, not listening to a word Togni was saying.

"Did you hear me, Alex? It's your chance to redeem yourself. If all goes well, I can bring you back to Perugia with a promotion. What do you say to vice questore?"

"I don't think being a vice questore would suit my temperament," Cenni replied, smiling wickedly, "particularly now, just when I'm beginning to like Foligno. Fewer politics and more police work."

"Don't be ridiculous! And don't try my patience, Alex. I'll put you in for vice questore, and you'll take it and be happy!" Why he indulged Alex Cenni was beyond him, but his talent helped. Cenni was the best he'd ever worked with—*none better,* he'd often tell his wife, Romina, when no one else was around. Until Cenni's transfer from Perugia to Foligno two years ago, the Perugia Questura had had the best arrest record in Italy. It was also one of the best run, and for that Carlo had Alex to thank. He leaned over the desk and dropped his voice. "Listen, Alex, a success here would all but guarantee me a transfer to Rome and you a promotion."

Alex laughed out loud. "I surrender. Whatever you say, *capo.* Besides, I'm bored! Beyond the pickpockets and the family feuds, Foligno is amazingly dull these days. This recession seems to have everyone in the dumps; even the crooks are conserving their energy. *Dimmi!*"

"It's what I already told you while you were gazing out the window!" Carlo snapped. "A German diplomat was murdered in the village of Paradiso. They found her body yesterday in the wine cellar. It's worse than murder!" He dropped his voice. "Mutilated! And that's between us, Alex, at least until the press gets hold of it, which may have already happened. I saw that clown from *La Repubblica* downstairs when I parked my car. You know the one I mean. You'd better not be the one responsible for him hanging around," he added ungraciously.

Cenni laughed again, still in good humor. "No problem, *capo*. If this murder is so hush-hush, why me? I'm *persona non grata!*"

The questore ignored the sarcasm. "You speak German; you're my best detective!" He tacked the last bit on with a generous smile and waited for the thank-you, but Cenni stared back without changing expression.

"How many times have I told you not to call me *capo!*" he snapped. "You know, Alex, things are very different in Rome these days, with the left back in power. The PM is anxious to get on the good side of the Germans. He'll show his appreciation if this murder is solved quickly—and quietly! It's your chance to have the Casati fiasco wiped off your record."

"Careful, Carlo. You're treading on one of my favorite memories. I'd do the same again." Cenni had arrested the fiancée of a senator (a very rich senator) against Carlo's specific orders. The charge of murder hadn't stuck; the senator had had far too many strings he could pull. And for his troubles, Cenni had been sent to Foligno, where he'd been rotting for the last two years. Of course he wanted to return to Perugia, Umbria's capital city and his hometown; but why give the power brokers the satisfaction of seeing him eat crow?

As much as he protested to the contrary, Togni was a paid-up member of that club. He'd cook his wife in Sunday's meat sauce if it would guarantee him a promotion, Alex thought with some regret. He liked Romina Togni.

The questore winced, almost as though he'd been reading Cenni's thoughts. "I know you'd do the same again, Alex. Don't remind me! You're too damned independent for your own good. Perhaps you should reflect that not all of us have Cenni Chocolates to back us up. Some of us need our jobs."

Alex hooted in genuine delight. "Good Lord, Carlo, Romina's family has far more money than mine. You two live like the Medici!"

Carlo smiled serenely. "True, but it's not my money," he said piously. "Besides, my bank balance has nothing to do with this discussion. Just do yourself a favor, Alex: cooperate on this one. The security officer from the German Embassy is outside. I'll send him in." Just before he reached the door, he turned and bestowed on Cenni one of his full-wattage smiles. "Be nice, Alex," he pleaded. "I want this promotion."

ALEX STOOD AT the questore's window looking down at his car below. He had parked it between the guard's shed and the fence, his permanently assigned space until two

year's ago, soon to be his again. It would be good to return
to Perugia, although in the two years since he'd left, his two
most reliable inspectors had married and one of them had
moved on. Piero was now in Assisi: Commissario Piero Tonni!
Elena Ottaviani, Piero's wife, was still in Perugia but currently on medical leave, recovering from a gunshot wound.

When Carlo had first mentioned vice questore, Alex
had perked up. I guess I'm not that different, he conceded to himself, secretly amused at his own vanity. We Italians love our titles. But now he wasn't certain that he should
accept. If he agreed, the opportunity to do nuts-and-bolts
policing would quickly disappear. Administration and
politics would take over and his chances of ever finding
Chiara's killers would be lost. The higher up he went, the
fewer possibilities there were of dealing with those who
might help him—pimps, prostitutes, petty thieves, most of
whom knew each other by reputation, if not by name.
Someone knew something. Chiara had been kidnapped in
Perugia, in mid-afternoon, in front of her parents' home on
Via Maestà delle Volte, twenty years earlier. Eventually someone would talk, and Alex wanted to be around when it happened, even if he had to wait for a deathbed confession.

He knew that the world at large viewed his long search
for Chiara's kidnappers as an obsession, and perhaps it
was. Genine had finally walked out on him three months
earlier, to study police procedures in Munich. "I can't wait
any longer, Alex. You say you love me, but when we're
together you're thinking about Chiara. You're in love
with a ghost! I just happen to look like her." When he'd

protested, Genine had marched over to his nightstand and removed Chiara's picture from the top drawer. "Hiding it doesn't help, Alex. Look at us!" she said, holding the picture up close to her face. "Blondes, with blue eyes—we even have the same shape of mouth, although *è vero* I'm better looking," she said immodestly. "Not that it helps," she added tartly. "Every woman you fall for looks like Chiara. A year ago it was that Croatian iceberg. Now it's me."

He had protested again, and Genine listened quietly to his denials. Later that same evening they made love, but it was perfunctory and unsatisfying. At three in the morning he awoke to a noise and heard her moving around in the bathroom. He knew she was crying, but he stayed where he was, staring into the darkness. How could he help Genine when he couldn't help himself? Days later, she'd told him about the Munich assignment. He'd tried to talk her out of it, but half-heartedly. If she stayed, he'd have to relinquish his obsession. He wasn't ready.

The sight of a large tomcat jumping on the hood of his just-washed car rescued him from his thoughts. He knocked loudly on the windowpane until the cat looked up. It yawned, jumped again, this time onto the roof, curled its body into a tight ball, and settled in for a nap. Alex was amused, at the cat's disdain as well as at his own need to keep his car clean. The sun was shining directly onto the roof; on a sunny spring day it was the ideal spot for a snooze. Rachel, his own cat, would have done the same, and Alex would have been sorely put out if anyone had tried to stop her.

3

"*DOTTOR CENNI, MI sensi di averla fatta aspettare.*" The words of apology for keeping him waiting were in Italian, but the accent was decidedly German. Alex turned from the window to greet Dieter Reimann, the German security officer, and wondered, irritably, how long he had been in the room observing him; he hadn't heard the door open or close. Dieter Reimann was a small, spare man with an unusually large head, made even more noticeable by the wisps of gray hair combed across his balding pate. Getting along in years, sixty at least, Cenni observed, and dressed like a tourist on his first trip to Italy. He looks damned silly wearing those galoshes and carrying that oversized umbrella, Cenni concluded, mainly to relieve his irritation.

"Exceptionally fine weather for this time of year," Reimann began after they'd exchanged credentials and settled on first names. Cenni winced again at Reimann's guttural Italian.

"Perhaps we should speak in German, Dieter," he responded, smiling to show his appreciation of Reimann's efforts. He was rather smug about his fluency in German, having read all of Goethe while at university, and was completely unaware that his own awkward efforts might evoke a similar degree of suffering in Reimann.

THE STORY THAT Reimann told in their thirty minutes together lacked credibility, Cenni decided, as he watched the German get into his car to return to Perugia. Something wrong there! When Cenni had expressed his desire to visit

Rome to talk to the embassy staff, Reimann had insisted that such a visit was unnecessary:

"You have everything you need," Reimann said, pointing to the folder containing the police and postmortem reports. "All the evidence points to an enraged lover, if not directly to the woman she picked up when she was in Africa a year ago. She did that rather frequently, you know, picked up young women, especially so as she got older." His face clouded over. "My government needs to know what happened to the papers that Jarvinia Baudler stole from the embassy. Even if it's true that she was tortured before her death—although your medical examiner dismisses this as a possibility in the postmortem report—it couldn't have been for those papers. They're of no interest to anyone outside the German government."

"I still don't understand, Dieter. What's in these papers you keep harping on and, if they had nothing to do with her death, why are they so important? Who wants them? The Russians, perhaps?" he asked provocatively.

Reimann laughed nervously. "Sorry Alex, but there's only so much that I'm at liberty to share. This is strictly a German matter, nothing to do with anyone here in Italy, or anywhere else. It was an act of petty revenge, a protest against her forced retirement, no spies coming in from the cold, as you seem to be thinking. Only a very small number of people are aware of their contents. I'm not fully in the know myself," he added with reluctance. "My charge is simply to keep them out of the hands of the wrong people, and that's all I need to know—"

Cenni interrupted. "But not all that *I* need to know!

Italy's not at loggerheads with Germany. We're not in the business of embarrassing the German government. If we find the papers, we'll turn them over to you after we've examined them, but *first* we must examine them." He found himself tapping his fingers on his desk in annoyance. He stopped tapping and continued: "My job is to find and arrest the murderer of Jarvinia Baudler. If my officers locate these papers and if we conclude that they have nothing to do with her murder, we'll hand them over to the magistrate assigned to the case. I'll certainly do all I can to keep the contents private, but the German government must apply directly to the judiciary if they want the papers sealed."

After fifteen years working in homicide, Cenni was an astute reader of emotions. Reimann exhibited none of the expected signs of anger, not even a prick of irritation, when Cenni refused to go along with the program he had outlined.

"Of course, of course," the German responded goodnaturedly. "You have your job, dottore, and I have mine. Just keep me informed. I may need help in filling out the correct forms in applying to the judiciary. Italian bureaucracy, you know, has a certain reputation."

It may have been Alex's imagination, but a slight chill descended on the room after Reimann addressed him as dottore.

4

"WE HAVE A problem!" Reimann said, holding the telephone receiver a short distance from his mouth. His hotel in Perugia had a five-star rating, but he had an innate distrust of Italian germs. He sat on the edge of the bed with his back to the window, shielding his tired eyes from the sunlight streaming through the window, as he kept watch on the door.

"What now?" the voice on the Berlin end asked. Reimann heard a fat sigh of annoyance.

"Cenni. Uncooperative." Reimann responded crisply. "We should have insisted on working with the carabinieri. They're easier to deal with. Cenni's threatening to turn any papers he finds over to the presiding judge."

"Why is that a problem? Have someone from the PM's office call the presiding judge."

"Not very likely. The last government had no control over the judiciary, and I doubt this one does either. It's independent here—like Cenni!"

"I want those papers, Reimann. If the information in them gets out, we'll have serious problems. What about that African she imported? Isn't she the logical starting point?"

A bank of clouds moved across the horizon, blocking the sun and casting a long shadow into the room.

"Disappeared!" he responded.

Another fat sigh from Berlin. "I have to go. You know what to do. No excuses; just do it. And we don't need to know the details; but of course you know that."

Reimann sat holding the receiver until he heard the dial tone. He was sweating profusely in the unheated room, and he used the edge of the brocade bedspread to wipe his face and hands. He was thinking about the woman he'd been speaking with. *Brass balls!* A friend of the chancellor's, she was the first woman appointed to head the BND, Germany's secret service, but there was nothing womanly about her ambition or her directness in serving that ambition.

I'll lose my pension if I don't find those papers, he realized. She blames me for letting it reach this point, Reimann thought as he poured another scotch, a larger one than the two that he'd swallowed earlier. He walked over to the hotel window, carrying his glass and the bottle, to look out at Mount Subasio in the distance. Just beyond his window was a large olive grove. He watched as the sun came from behind a cloud, dappling the pruned treetops and coloring the leaves a burnished silvery gold, the color of Jarvinia's hair when he'd first met her. He thought about Jarvinia and the trouble she was causing him, that she'd always caused him. He was a decent man and he believed that no one should die as she had. But he was also a man who valued justice, and he knew that Jarvinia had brought it on herself.

5

A DISCERNING PERSON might call Dieter Reimann a good man. He had loved his wife, he seldom passed a beggar on the street without emptying his pockets of change, and on most Sundays he received communion. He never spoke of thieving Gypsies, drunken Irish, or conniving Jews, and he never looked down on others because they had darker skin or attended a different house of worship. No one who knew Dieter had ever heard him attribute his good fortune, a steady job, a nice house, and a comely wife to anything but luck. He was one of those rare individuals who live by the maxim that "There but for the grace of God go I."

And yet, with all this goodness to keep him safe, he'd conducted a long and torrid love affair with Jarvinia Baudler. It was one of those events in life that cannot be explained, and perhaps if Dieter had left it that way, unexplained, he might have survived its consequences. But the selfsame Dieter who believed in a higher power believed equally in a rational basis for human behavior. He needed to understand the nature of things in general and the moral disposition of mankind in particular, and unlike so many of his fellow Germans who dismissed their history without a backward glance, Dieter spent many hours thinking and worrying about where Germany had been and where it was going.

He was forty, Jarvinia fifty, when they began their affair. It wasn't that he didn't know of her past. The rumors had been rife before she arrived in Rome. Jarvinia had made a name for herself on her last assignment in Spain, not just for her sexual proclivities and the very famous Spanish actress with whom it was rumored she'd had an affair (although Jarvinia denied it to him when he brought it up), but also because of the changes she had wrought in the cultural-attaché domain. The embassy had been turned into a concert hall on those evenings when it wasn't serving as an art gallery. Her events had given so much cachet to the embassy that the ambassador had overlooked what he knew of her sexual activities. Her assignment to Rome had been a promotion. If Dieter had been your

normal security officer, he would have resented Jarvinia
and the burdens she placed on him. If she repeated her
successes in Rome, opening up the embassy to all and
sundry and to countless visiting artists and musicians, his
work would be more difficult. But he thought it a fine
thing that she was securing a reputation as a cultural
leader for Germany. Germany had not yet redeemed itself
in the eyes of the rest of Europe, and Dieter desperately
wanted such redemption.

He had seen Jarvinia's picture many times in the Foreign Service newsletter, and he was expecting to meet a big
woman with a fleshy face, large round eyes, and light hair.
As his mother would have said, nothing to write home
about. His mother would have been wrong. Jarvinia in
the flesh was a rare commodity in German womanhood:
intelligent, funny, flashy, sexy, charming, nasty, bold, self-
centered, and self-congratulatory. Every newsletter sent
out by the Consulate after Jarvinia arrived in Rome was
about Jarvinia. Of course, there were just as many things
she was not: meek, generous, modest, kind. But as she had
once pointed out when he had protested her unkindness
to one of his clerks, all the characteristics he said she was
missing added up to *boring*. "I am never boring," Jarvinia
had declared with her usual lack of modesty.

He remembered to the minute when their affair began.
She had asked his help to move some furniture in the
apartment provided her by the embassy. Huge, ugly Italian
stuff, she'd said. "I'd like to throw it into the Tiber, but it
probably wouldn't sink." She had a viperous tongue, and
he decided to go himself rather than send one of his men.

Up until then, he had never seen Jarvinia in anything but pants. Her medical file said that she'd had polio as a child and she walked with a slight limp, so he had assumed one of her legs was bowed. She met him at her door, barefoot, in a silk robe that came to the top of her knees. She had beautiful legs. He could see her nipples through the silk robe and realized that she was not wearing underwear. But what he remembered most about that evening was her hair streaming in thick waves down to the middle of her back. She'd told him once that when she was a schoolgirl her hair had been the color of pure gold. He was glad the color had changed as she aged. At fifty, it was a mixture of gold and silver strands, thousands of shimmering strands of light.

When they lay in bed together with her hair spread out over the pillow, he wondered if he were her *Rumpelstilzchen*, if she would betray him as the German queen had betrayed the misshapen dwarf once she'd had her gold. And, of course, with Jarvinia it was always about the gold. This seemed strange to him, as sex with Jarvinia was like nothing he had known with his wife. Lyse, a good woman, was horrified if he suggested anything that deviated from standard practice. Jarvinia had an engineer's respect for standard practice and a creative flair for every more innovative position. She read the Kama Sutra like Lyse read her catechism. Her moans and sighs were filled with passion and longing. There was nothing faked about Jarvinia's lovemaking.

"Why do you go with women?" he had asked her once after some particularly adventuresome sex on her balcony in clear view of her neighbors. She had laughed at first, but then took his question seriously.

"Men have to dominate. It's always about them: get me a cup of coffee; I'm going to the football game, you can go alone to my mother's; give up your career; stay home with the kids; look sexy for my friends; don't look sexy for my friends. In bed, it's even worse: get on top; move your ass; suck my cock; turn over, you're done. Men by nature are takers and women are givers. With some exceptions, of course. I've got a man's nature in a woman's body. I prefer men for friends and women for all else, but there's no reason not to enjoy both. And I do," she had said.

"So what does that make me?" Dieter had asked when they'd gone inside and he was dressed to leave. "If you're the dominator, what am I?"

"My slave, darling Dieter, what else?" she had responded. And he knew it was true.

Less than a month after they'd begun their affair, she began to use him. In the embassy, he had the authority to issue German passports without performing the usual security checks. The first time she had asked him to approve a passport, for a woman who claimed hers had been stolen, he had refused. The woman had a criminal record and it was her third lost passport in two years. He was sure she was selling them on the black market. Jarvinia had refused to have sex with him for two months.

The next time she asked, for a woman with a heavy Polish accent, a recent citizen, he had agreed. The woman was middle-aged and unattractive, and Jarvinia only enjoyed the company of younger women. From the moment he approved that passport, life, as he had known it, ended. She was circumspect and only asked him to approve passports four times in eleven years, apparently when the anticipated profit overrode the dangers. But other demands followed, some petty, one major. Nothing in the embassy was safe from her greed for beautiful things. Years into their affair, when they met rarely, he'd found a valuable Dresden vase in her bedroom. It had once adorned the ambassador's suite, and the ambassador's wife had accused one of the Albanian cleaning women of stealing it. The woman denied it, but the ambassador fired her anyway.

Jarvinia had laughed at his consternation when he'd accused her of stealing the vase. "A temporary loan," she'd said. "I'll return it when the Philistines leave. That wife of his wouldn't know real Dresden from that junk they sell along the Kurfürstendamm."

"What about the Albanian?" he had asked.

Jarvinia had shrugged and changed the subject.

She threatened him with exposure, to his wife and to the ambassador, until he gave her the combination to the master security files. From unsubstantiated rumors, he suspected that she had used information from those files to blackmail one of Germany's most prominent politicians. He didn't want to have his suspicions confirmed, so he ignored the rumors. Thoughts of suicide consumed him, and he stopped receiving communion. His wife of thirty-one years died of an aneurysm on a cold spring morning and he couldn't stop crying. Even during working hours, tears would fall at the most inauspicious moments.

He was embarrassing himself and the ambassador, and he was asked to take two months compassionate leave. Eleven years had passed since the start of their affair, and his passion for Jarvinia waned; hers for him had never really existed. He had been a minor diversion and an interesting experiment, she had admitted when they were arguing about the vase.

When he returned to Germany, he confessed everything to his parish priest, a true saver of souls. The priest gave him absolution under the condition that he stop sleeping with Jarvinia. About the blackmail and stealing, he was grave but practical. "Change the combination on the files but don't lose your job over something you can't remedy. The German government won't forgive you. God will," and he gave him absolution again.

After he returned from Germany, Jarvinia never again asked for what she'd always so brazenly termed "a favor." Another fourteen years passed—twenty-five in all from the time that Jarvinia had first arrived in Rome—and they settled into being nothing more than co-workers. They had drinks together like two old warhorses, and on a few occasions he accompanied her to one of the many cultural events in Rome. Her need for new and younger lovers never ceased, and he often wondered how she managed to keep them content—and, more often, how she managed to live so far above her income. Every week, he visited Lyse's grave in Rome's most famous cemetery, always with lilies, and waited patiently for Jarvinia's downfall, and his own.

6

"ALEX, DOWN HERE." The voice was Piero's. He was seated in the lower section of the Bar Sensi, well away from the crowd of workers gathered at the top having their midday coffees. Cenni shouted over the noise to Orlando, the bar's manager, that he needed a coffee before heading down the stairs.

The two policemen eyed each other silently. The last time they had been together was in January, to celebrate Piero's promotion, the day before Genine had left for Munich. Alex knew that Piero blamed him for Genine's decision to leave.

"Piero, *come stè?*" Alex finally asked in Umbrian dialect. Then with considerably more warmth, "Damn, Piero, but it's good to see you." He gathered his former lieutenant into a bearhug. The two of them sat and waited in awkward silence for their coffees to arrive and the noise to subside.

He looks tired, thought Piero, noticing the purple shadows under Alex's eyes and the deepened lines around his mouth. Genine made him happy. Why'd he let her go?

Piero looks happy, and thinner, thought Alex. No sign of an apple tart in sight. In the past, Piero could never pass the Bar Sensi without stopping for at least one pastry, usually two. Marriage agrees with him, Alex reflected, with a twinge of envy. Everyone around him was moving on; only he was standing still.

Orlando came down the stairs. He unloaded two coffees from the tray, as well as an apple tart for Piero. "It's wonderful to see the two of you together again. Welcome home, dottore," he said to Alex, giving him a friendly pat on the shoulder.

Alex grinned at Piero. "Elena's doing a bang-up job managing your diet. *Cin cin!*" he said, downing his caffè macchiato in one gulp. "Orlando, another one, *per favore.*"

After one o'clock, the place emptied out sufficiently for Alex and Piero to talk. Piero pulled a manila folder from his briefcase and slid it across the table. "Here's the information you wanted, Alex. Jarvinia Baudler! Not one of my favorites. She stirred up a considerable lot of trouble in Paradiso during the last year. Nasty woman. She was always causing trouble in bars and with the locals. Two denunciations against her next-door neighbor. His family's lived in Paradiso for hundreds of years, then this lesbian Kraut rents the house next door and bullies the local police into giving the neighbor a warning for letting his cat run free. She'd caught it trying to mount hers. Its name is Princess," Piero added disparagingly. "She even threatened to kill the neighbor's cat if it happened again."

"What's happened to Princess?" Cenni asked.

"The neighbor has it. I hear he's promising kittens all around for early summer. Say good-bye to the purity of that line," Piero replied. He started riffling through the papers in his folder until he found what he wanted. "Here, read this! Her first denunciation was sexual; the second is environmental. She says the cat peed on her dahlias, killing them. Who in Italy grows dahlias, anyway? Hardly surprising that someone cut off—"

Cenni interrupted. "You know! I thought only the medical examiner—"

"Of course I know." He grimaced. "I have a friend in the carabinieri. Shame having to see that. Must have been quite a shock."

"Even more of a shame that no one in this country can keep his mouth shut, apparently, not even the carabinieri. The postmortem report was sealed. Does anyone in this country know how to keep a secret?" he asked sarcastically, not realizing that Orlando was standing directly behind him.

"How about the followers of St. Francis? They hid his body in the Basilica and kept its location secret for hundreds of years," Orlando informed him, handing Cenni his second coffee and Piero another apple tart.

Cenni smiled, partly at Orlando's reference to Italy's favorite saint, but mainly at the sight of Piero's second pastry. "*È vero,* Orlando, Italy's only secret."

He waited until Orlando had gone back up the stairs before speaking again. "The CIA would never succeed here, not with every third cousin of every policeman's wife privy to state secrets."

"Come on, Alex, we're not that bad. And you should talk; you're the one who wanted to meet in a bar to discuss police business."

"The coffee at the station house isn't fit for human consumption." Cenni slid the folder back across the table.

"I have to get back," Piero said, standing.

Cenni looked up, puzzled. "Sit, Piero! I've got thirty minutes before my meeting with the medical examiner."

Piero sat again, too modest to assert his new status.

"Listen, Alex, keep the folder and talk to Orlando if you

want to know more about the German. She dropped in here whenever she was in Assisi, always drunk by the time she left. And now I have to get back. You never know what they're up to when the boss is away." It wasn't Piero's intention to belittle his officers; he'd just wanted to remind Alex that he had a different job these days. He added, "*È vero*, Alex, they're really a great group, except Staccioli."

"Staccioli! You mean that fat bastard's still around?" Alex responded. "Don't tell me he's sucking up to you these days?"

"Not a chance! Not me! I put him to filing residency applications. Genine'd love that. Remember how she despised him!"

AS ALEX WAS leaving the Bar Sensi, a gust of wind lifted one of the newspapers that had been left abandoned on an outside table and plastered it against his chest. He peeled it off and scanned the front page quickly. A single column and, miraculously, nothing about the manner in which the German had been murdered; but it wouldn't be long!

Cenni set off for his meeting with the medical examiner still somewhat in the dark regarding the character of Jarvinia Baudler. Piero had blasted her unmercifully, but his only knowledge of her was from the police blotter and a dispute over two cats in heat. Piero's obvious distaste for Baudler's nationality was understandable. His grandfather had died at the end of the Second World War, supposedly fighting the Germans. To Piero's mother, who had successfully indoctrinated her son, the Germans were to blame for everything that had gone wrong in her life.

Italians were an insular lot, and Piero had kept the habits and prejudices of his parents. Cenni also knew that Piero's distaste for the German had as much to do with Baudler's sexual habits as her origins. The rest of Europe was moving toward enlightenment with respect to sexuality, but even in the larger cities of Rome and Milan, particularly Rome where St. Peter's dominated the skyline, his countrymen continued to treat homosexuality as a moral disorder. In small hill towns like Assisi and Paradiso, it was rare for even the most courageous to live openly with a partner of the same sex.

Dieter Reimann had been of even less help in defining Baudler's character than Piero. He and Baudler had worked together in the Rome embassy for twenty-five years, and although Reimann had not said so directly, Cenni inferred from the security officer's reluctance to discuss his colleague that he and Jarvinia had been friends. Reimann might have sympathized with her refusal to retire in dignified silence, perhaps because his own retirement was imminent. Orlando had offered a bartender's view of the German: friendly and funny when she wasn't drunk, obnoxious when she was; and, drunk or sober, a lousy tipper.

He reflected on what else he'd learned from Orlando. Jarvinia Baudler's status as Germany's cultural attaché to Italy was no secret to Orlando or to anyone else with whom she'd come into contact. The only secret—hers—was that during the year she'd lived in Paradiso, she'd no longer been employed at the embassy and had no diplomatic status.

According to Orlando, Baudler had been a drunk and

she'd grown worse in the last few months. She always parked illegally in the plaza, and if the police complained, she'd demand they call the embassy. The police never checked on her claim of immunity—couldn't be bothered, according to Orlando. A few weeks before her murder, she'd thrown a drink into the face of the woman that she'd come in with, a tall good-looking black woman, more than forty years her junior. Orlando had attributed the worsening of the German's temper to this woman.

"A real looker, in her late twenties, I'd say, and very sexy. Copper color. On the few occasions they were in here together, the men standing at the bar couldn't stop drooling. She and the German were rumored to be lovers, which made her even more interesting to some of them." Orlando's description of the mysterious girlfriend had been slanted toward the sensual: tall, curvy, good legs, almond eyes, shoulder-length hair, great tits. "She had the German eating out of her hand," he said. "South African, I'd say from the accent. Not that she talked much; she let the German do the talking. A few of the regulars spoke of making a move on her if she ever came in alone."

"You too, Orlando?" Cenni had asked.

"Leave the young to the young, is what I say. I've worked too many years for this." He patted his paunch. "I prefer to share it with someone who knows what it's worth."

In one respect at least, Cenni had quibbled with Orlando's assessment of what was behind Baudler's increasingly bad temper.

"You realize, of course, that people in love normally improve in temperament."

"Not this one, dottore. On the last day Baudler was in here, she'd been hanging around the bar for nearly two hours waiting for the girlfriend, and drinking heavily. Trust me, dottore, she was a dog in heat without a bitch. She needed to bite someone."

7

ALL DAY LONG, Cenni had been happy. The sun was out, and tomorrow he would return to Perugia. It was an idyllic spring day, and he was putting off the inevitable demise of his happiness, taking the roundabout way to the mortuary. Fifteen years in homicide, and Cenni was not yet resigned to viewing murder victims cut open from chin to groin and plundered of their organs, which, all things considered, was inexplicable. He had entered a profession whose singular reason for being was that someone should die. His mother threw it up to him constantly: it would have been kinder to her if he'd become an undertaker. She was guided in all things by her social set, a group of moneyed matrons in competition with one another, and his profession embarrassed her. But his brother and grandmother, whose opinions he respected, had also voiced their surprise when he had chosen the police after graduating first in his law class.

Although uncomfortable with the mumbo-jumbo of psychiatry, he hadn't entirely disagreed with his friend Sandro, a Freudian, who had suggested a few years back that Cenni was at odds with the laws of nature, that he studied death as an enemy to be conquered. There was a kernel of truth there, but only a kernel. What Cenni looked to defeat was death before its time. He abhorred murder, which deprived its victims of their four score years and ten. For many of his colleagues—those still tied to the Church—death was a glorious beginning and God a benevolent accountant. When they arrived at the pearly gates (none of them ever considered an alternative destination), God would review his ledger: twenty points in the right column if they had loved their wives; ten points in the left if they'd kept a mistress; five points for every occasion they dined at their mother-in-law's; one point in the left for calling her *that old bag*. But for Cenni, dust-to-dust was not a biblical subtlety; it meant exactly that: final, inexorable oblivion.

It was a twenty-minute walk from the plaza to the hospital. He was humming to himself when he arrived at his destination. Two officers of the municipal police whom he passed along the way had greeted him enthusiastically, and tomorrow he'd be back in Perugia where he knew everyone and everyone knew him. But his joy in the day was extinguished as soon as he rang the bell for entrance to the mortuary. He was meeting the medical examiner there for the sole purpose of viewing the body of Jarvinia Baudler in her final degradation—a naked shell of decaying flesh: kidneys, liver, heart, and lungs thrown into a plastic bag on the steel autopsy table, her genitalia pitilessly exposed. In lowered voices they would discuss the preliminary postmortem findings: the manner of death (homicide), the number of broken bones (ten), the weapon (a log with a jagged edge), the length of the attack (approximately five minutes), the cause of death (acute myocardial infarction). At some point, they would stop talking, perhaps look away to avoid each other's eyes, or speak of some other aspect of the case, and then, finally, in hushed tones one or the other of them would speak the unspeakable, the reason for the sealed report: the excision of Jarvinia Baudler's clitoris with a pair of rusted pruning shears.

THE ELDERLY ATTENDANT greeted Cenni at the front door cheerfully. "Dottore, we thought you were gone for good, and here you are back again." Cenni wondered if he knew the man. Surely he should remember him. The attendant had no lashes and the tissue around both his eyes was red and weeping. It appeared to be diseased. Not someone he would easily forget. He nodded in response to the old man's greeting, but instinctively kept some distance between them as they walked down the windowless narrow hallway. The stagnant air, reeking with noxious smells, he remembered very well: Lysol, formaldehyde, and sodium hydrochloride, overlaid with a sickening flowery scent. The hospital's subbasement had originally been designed as a storage area for medical records, but an ambitious city official had had it converted into a mortuary. It lacked an adequate filtering system, and the Department of Forensic Pathology had been trying for years to shut it down, but the same city official, or maybe another, had managed to keep it open for the ten or fewer autopsies performed there every year. Probably to keep the old man employed, Cenni surmised. Someone's cousin or in-law. It was an Italian phenomenon, keeping one's family working in unnecessary jobs, and only fools wasted their time railing against it.

The door to the main autopsy room was open, and the old man walked directly over to the steel table in the center of the room, swept his hand over the plastic bag and its occupant as though he were introducing a distinguished personage, and pulled down the zipper. He turned to Cenni, who had stopped short at the doorway, and indicated with a hand gesture and a broad smile that Cenni should take a look.

The senior medical examiner, the replacement for Marcello Batori, who had finally retired kicking and screaming in protest, had agreed to meet Cenni at the hospital at three o'clock, and he was annoyed that she had not yet arrived. He would have preferred to view the body with the pathologist, but he was also reluctant to hurt the old man's feelings, so he stepped forward, ignoring the sign above the door that read DANGER! NO ENTRY EXCEPT AUTHORIZED PERSONNEL. Cenni had read the preliminary report carefully, yet he was still surprised at the extent of the bruises that covered Jarvinia Baudler's upper torso. The preliminary postmortem, which Batori's replacement had completed in record time (and that in itself was a record), stated that she had been pummeled repeatedly with the jagged end of a piece of firewood, perhaps as many as ten times, and that both arms and shoulders had been broken in multiple places.

"Looks quite peaceful, don't she, dottore, if you don't go below the neck. Her hair is especially beautiful; I just combed it."

"Please step away from the body now!" came a new voice.

Cenni, who had been deep in thought wondering if the old man were all there, jumped when he heard himself spoken to so rudely. The voice that had accosted him was loud and high-pitched, a woman for sure. When he turned to give her a piece of his mind, he thought she was a midget. The woman standing in the doorway was fully rigged out in protective clothing, head to toe: rubber boots and gloves, surgical gown and apron, high-tech respirator, and an ugly green cap hiding her hair.

"Commissario, you must leave the room immediately. There's a risk of contagion." Cenni jumped a second time, this time away from the body. When he got to the doorway, the woman had already turned and begun to walk away. Cenni followed her down the hallway until she entered a door to the right and motioned him inside.

"Surely you know the rules," she said, rounding on him. "No one is permitted in the autopsy room without express permission from the medical examiner, and then only if properly clothed. I've finally gotten a go-ahead from Rome to shut this one down. It's so loaded with infectious matter, it could start the next bubonic plague."

If she hadn't laughed when she saw the panic register on his face, Cenni might have gone screaming out the front door searching frantically for a vat of antiseptic. "Sorry," he responded sheepishly. He knew the rules of the autopsy room as well as anyone, but like most of his fellow officers he rarely observed them, mainly because Batori had never enforced them. In his own defense, he added, "I've been in there before dressed in street clothes. With *Dottor* Batori. He was okay with it."

"That idiot! He should have contracted an infectious disease twenty years ago. Tuberculosis, rabies, plague, anthrax, hepatitis, smallpox, herpes, Creutzfeldt-Jakob—mad cow to you—every disease agent known to man is probably lurking in the corners of that autopsy room. We haven't actually met, have we?" she asked, interrupting her diatribe against Batori to pull off her right glove. "I'm the medical examiner, Dottoressa Falchi," she said in a conciliatory tone, extending her hand.

Cenni hesitated before taking it, and she laughed. "I donned this space outfit to meet with you. I'm clean." They were standing side by side, and she didn't quite reach his shoulder. Not quite a midget, he reflected, but certainly not more than five feet tall.

She closed the door and then removed her respirator and cap.

Cenni finally saw her face. A vast improvement over Batori! A small delicate nose, deep-set black eyes, and a sensuous mouth that owed nothing to the current rage for silicone injections. A small voice in the back of his head scolded him for being a chauvinist, but he ignored it and gave the petite medical examiner his most winning smile. Better than an improvement, he decided. Her last name was Italian but her physiognomy suggested that she was part something else. Maybe the better part, he thought disloyally, admiring her delicate bones.

"You're putting me on, I hope, about all those diseases," Cenni asked, not quite sure.

She laughed again. "Well maybe about mad cow. We haven't yet had a recorded case of it in Umbria. But to answer your question seriously, the Angel of Death, or Malak al-Maut as my mother calls him, would flee from this place. It stinks of formaldehyde. The attendant who let you in, Claudio, has allergic dermatitis from its overuse. The smell hangs in the air; and for what, I ask you? We rarely embalm bodies in Italy, yet Batori ordered it by the keg. Probably from a brother-in-law," she added sarcastically. "And don't get me started on Claudio. He breaks every rule in the book. The day I came here to perform the autopsy on the German, I found him in the autopsy room drinking coffee and eating a sandwich. My God, think of it! Eating in the autopsy room! But enough. If you want to review Baudler's postmortem in the autopsy room, you need to be properly outfitted. Or . . ." and she smiled charmingly, "if you'd rather, we can do it outside in the sunshine and get the stink of this place out of our nostrils. And have a smoke."

I like her, Cenni thought. She's not as young as she looks, which is about twenty. From her position as head of forensic pathology in Perugia, he knew she had to be at least thirty, probably older. Yet she still has passion, still believes the system can work for her if she yells loud enough. Her reference to Malak al-Maut, the Angel of Death in Islam, could account for that other part of her and also perhaps for her passion. No full-blooded Italian working in a government job still believed in the possibilities of change.

Cenni had some ten minutes to think about how he would begin his discussion of the German's postmortem, and its delicate nature, with this good-looking woman. He wasn't even sure if it was because she was good-looking or because she was a woman that he was so uncomfortable, although he knew that either one probably meant he was a chauvinist. He'd ask Elena about it the next time he saw her.

Cenni and his twin brother had moved forward professionally in the old Italy, a male-dominated world, he as a senior police officer and Renato as a bishop in the Catholic Church, but the old Italy was rapidly disappearing. Women had crowded into all the professions except the church, and the church had lost its relevance. The birth rate in Italy was the lowest in Western Europe, and women no longer accepted their priests' admonition that their job was to stay at home and breed. Abortion, especially among married women, was now considered a sacred right. Cenni recognized that his comfort level in working with a female pathologist was of no consequence; he had no recourse but to adapt.

He was seated on one of the benches that lined the pedestrian walk to the hospital's front entrance, waiting for Dottoressa Falchi (or Tahany, as she had asked him to call her) to change out of her space outfit into street clothes. He leafed through the postmortem report again, trying to frame his questions in a way to avoid embarrassing either of them. He realized it was going to be worse than he feared when he saw her approaching. She had been hiding a very trim figure under that surgical gown, and the rubber boots had been replaced with sling-back spike heels, about three inches' worth, he estimated, as he watched her struggling on the cobblestone walkway.

She plopped down next to him, emitting a large sigh of

relief before lighting a cigarette. "I hate that place and I hope to God—yours and mine—that this is the last time I'll have to work in there. I wonder what *la tedesca* would say if she knew how she was spending her last days above ground. She was quite snotty, I've heard. I don't think she'd be too happy at the way Claudio exhibits her to all comers. You'd think she was Madonna or the Queen of England, for Christ's sake," she said, exhaling a long stream of smoke at the end of her speech.

Now how did she do that, Cenni wondered, watching the smoke rise above their heads and disappear into a shaft of sunlight. She must have the lungs of a deep-sea diver. He couldn't contain himself any longer.

"You know, Tahany, I don't generally interfere in anyone's pleasure, so long as it's not a felony. But inside the mortuary you were so concerned that you might contract an infectious disease and outside, in the fresh air, you're smoking yourself into an early cancer."

"Yeah, yeah. I know. I'm planning to stop," she replied, tossing her spent cigarette into the bushes. "In the meantime, care to join me?" she asked, proffering the open pack.

After she had lighted both their cigarettes, she looked straight at him. "Let's get it out of the way. Her clitoris was hacked off. There, it's said! *Excised,* I suppose is the word I should use, more genteel. But there was nothing genteel about what was done to Baudler, although, thank God, it was done after she was dead. If the killer were trying to make a statement, it's not particularly clear from anything at the crime scene exactly what it was. It was a sloppy job, certainly nothing even close to a Sunna circumcision or

any of the other forms of female genital mutilation prac-
ticed in Africa—where I was born, in case you've been
wondering. Even those horribly botched jobs performed
in secret in Italy and in other parts of Europe are executed
better than this one. If I had to call it, I'd say the person
who killed the German is mad as a hatter. Not someone
you'd want on the loose."

8

THE NARROW CROOKED house, the smallest and some
said the oldest house in town, held upright by the clock
tower on one side and the deconsecrated chapel on the
other, was at last covered in paint. The pink house, Anita
said to herself twice. She liked the sound of it so much,
she said it again a third time, and then out loud. She had
petitioned the town council for more than a year for
permission to paint her house pink. It wasn't saturated
color that they objected to, just the color pink. They
counterproposed with yellow, initially a mellow light-
toned yellow, and, later, a hard bright gold. When she
rejected yellow, they moved on to green, five different
shades of green, and then finally to blue. They were
persistent in pushing blue: peacock, indigo, azure, gen-
tian, sapphire, aquamarine, and turquoise, so she finally
offered a compromise. She suggested lavender. But they
objected to lavender even more than they did to pink.
Each month for over a year, the council sent around a
workman to apply another patch of color to the house.
Live with it, they said to her, try it out, they begged, let it

speak to you, they suggested, until Anita's house took on
the appearance of a gaudy clown. She rejected all their
offerings, firmly. It was her house and she wanted it pink:
a glowing, vibrant, rosy pink.

In the days when the fountain across from the house
had provided water for the town's annual flower procession held every June to honor the feast of Corpus Christi,
Anita had played inside, in the dungeons where prisoners
had been tortured. It was a different time back then, when
men routinely inflicted pain on their enemies before
killing them, not to extract information, but simply
because they liked it. The house wasn't pink back then,
according to the town council; but how could they know
that for sure, Anita had argued. And it wasn't pink when
she played there as a child, when her uncle Orazio had
lived there; it was the color of pewter, dull peeling pewter.

Marta, Anita's mother, had grown up in the house, but
she'd left it when her parents died, when Anita was three
years old. They had gone to live in an apartment on the
other side of Paradiso. The house was half her mother's,
and Anita couldn't understand why her mother didn't
live there, but this was just one of the many subjects that
Marta refused to discuss with her daughter. She also
refused to talk about Anita's father, who had left Marta
when Anita was still an infant. Orazio, Anita's uncle, had
stayed in the house but Anita always knew that one day it
would be hers. It was the only sure thing in her life. Her
mother said Anita would never have children, that no
man would want her because of her deformity, so the
house was her compensation.

Orazio, who hadn't married, died suddenly in 2000, after eating poisonous mushrooms, and his half-share of the house came to her mother by default. When her mother died two years later, of a fall from the fourth floor balcony of the selfsame house, it had passed to Anita, her only child. In the thirty-five years that Orazio had lived in the house alone, with no woman to tidy up after him, it had deteriorated, and Anita set about restoring it. Perhaps "restoring" isn't the right word, as she had the modern Italian's desire for marble floors and elaborate plumbing. Orazio had lived with pitted brick floors and one small bathroom with a handheld shower on the first floor. Her love of expensive materials and American plumbing meant that Anita had to plan wisely. Anita's mother had left her only child a bequest (a very large bequest, according to the town's notary), but Anita knew one should never spend foolishly. She would fix the house slowly, and when it was finished, painted inside and out, she would move in. So she rented it for four years, but never to the same tenant for more than a year at a time. When each tenant moved out, Anita would bring in the workmen and they would replace a floor here, add a bathroom there. The house, which had four stories and a cellar, was ten feet in width and twenty feet in length, so it took a good bit of imagination and architectural sleight-of-hand to squeeze three bathrooms, a marble-enhanced kitchen (with dishwasher), two bedrooms, and a room in which to watch TV into the smallest house in town.

Jarvinia Baudler, a German diplomat, had been Anita's

most recent tenant. Anita knew that renting to Italians was fraught with danger. The government gave them rights that Anita didn't want them to have, so she'd rented her house only to *stranieri,* and when possible to Americans. Americans paid in advance, never disputed their utility bills, replaced all the spent light bulbs when they left, and added considerably to Anita's stock of household furnishings. When they couldn't find what they needed in the house, they purchased it, and often left it behind. The cobbled-together set of chipped and cracked dishes that Anita provided had been supplemented by one of her American tenants with a full set of china handpainted with blue periwinkles. When the tenant left, Anita individually wrapped each of the blue periwinkle dishes in newspaper and stored them in the basement.

Jarvinia Baudler was the first German Anita had rented to. She would also be the last. Anita, who was never finagled by anyone out of anything, had been finagled by the German into signing a two-year lease; not just any lease, either, but an official stamped document, prepared by the town's only notary, covered in wax seals, and in the end paid for by Anita. After the lease was recorded in the town hall, Jarvinia refused to compensate her. "Why should I pay?" she asked when Anita presented the bill. "It's your house."

"She's nothing but a criminal," Anita told Lorenzo, her cousin and confidant, particularly after Jarvinia followed her initial transgression with others equally shameless and costly. "I'm not paying for garbage pickup," constituted their second skirmish. Jarvinia won that one also, although Anita planned to recoup the twelve euros by padding the water bill. Then came the dispute about the wine glasses. Jarvinia had expected Anita to provide glasses with stems. Anita had been drinking wine for thirty years and didn't own a single glass with a stem. The last straw, Anita told Lorenzo, was the German's comments regarding the quality of the cutlery. "Do you really expect me to eat my peas with this?" Jarvinia had asked caustically, holding up a knife that had been a wedding gift to Anita's mother. Was she implying that Italians ate their peas with a knife? In the past, on the few occasions when tenants had complained, Anita had had her way. Most of them spoke Italian poorly, and after a few shrugs of Anita's shoulders, or a few blank stares, the complainants would walk away in confusion. And if they didn't, she would assault them in rapid-fire Italian. Jarvinia Baudler spoke perfect Italian and she never walked away.

The real difficulty began a month after the German moved in, when her women friends arrived, some for short visits and others for lengthy stays. And then one of them, a young black woman, moved in and didn't leave. All those who gathered in the town's only café discussed her advent from early morning until late at night, particularly the old-age pensioners, who were the most prolific gossipers. One of them, old Enzo, approached Anita at the bar one day and asked if she'd ever joined in their games. Anita smelled the grappa on his breath and heard the others snickering in the background. She slapped him hard across the face. The other men in the café gasped in excitement, and the two carabinieri who were having a coffee at the bar escaped through the front door. Enzo apologized to Anita the next day when no one else was around.

The talk died down after a while as other gossip took its place. Giorgio Moroni was arrested for beating his wife about the head with a pasta pot. Angela Ricci left town in a huff after she was caught *in flagrante delicto* with her employer's husband. The notary accused the mayor of falsifying his monthly expenses, although this latter bit of gossip was no surprise to most of the town.

Jarvinia eventually made friends among the old men. She entertained them with stories of the former prime minister's lechery at various banquets given at the German embassy, occasionally bought a round of grappa in the mornings when most of the regulars were drinking coffee, and judiciously frequented the local butcher, baker, and candlestick maker rather than shopping at the large super-markets in Bastia.

With respect to Jarvinia, the town had settled into a compromise of sorts. The town never compromised where Anita was concerned. The whispers, which had died down after her mother's death, started up again. Anita's defor-mity, an open secret, fueled the town's insatiable appetite for sexual innuendo. Wherever she went, to the kiosk for her morning newspaper, to the café, or the pharmacy, peo-ple whispered behind her back.

Anita hadn't fully understood the tenor of Enzo's remark, but she'd known instinctively when she slapped his face that it was dirty and that it implied something dirty about her. When her request to paint the house pink was denied, and the council refused to give Anita a reason, other than to say it wasn't appropriate, she consulted Lorenzo. He'd been her science teacher in high school and was a cousin of her mother's. He was also the only pensioner in town who didn't frequent the café. His explanation confounded her even further. "They're afraid if the house is painted pink, its flamboyance will draw attention to what goes on inside," he'd said.

"But pink is my favorite color," was Anita's response. She didn't understand why the town associated her with the German and those other women, and she was too proud to defend herself against spiteful calumnies. Now, when Anita closed her eyes at night seeking the relief of sleep, she would see her mother's ghostly presence standing at the foot of her bed, ramrod-straight as she had been in life, lips blackened by death, mumbling invocations to the Virgin to free her daughter from the evils of temptation. The temptations were always those of the flesh! Anita was beginning to hate Jarvinia.

Life in Paradiso became unbearable for Anita on the day she walked into the café and saw Jarvinia at the card table with three of the pensioners. They were playing briscola and the German was dealing. They were laughing uproariously at something Jarvinia had just said, but they stopped immediately when they saw Anita. Enzo broke the awkward silence that followed by offering to buy her a coffee. Anita experienced a spasm of guilt as though it were she in the wrong. Her family had settled Paradiso in the eleventh century, and *she* was now *la straniera*. *La lesbica* was one of them.

She was determined to rid herself of the German before the lease was up. She consulted a lawyer in Perugia, an octogenarian, who agreed not to charge her unless he could guarantee results. "Dear me," the *avvocato* repeated several times as he perused the lease. "This is a well drawn-up document, Signora. Iron-clad, unless your tenant is a public nuisance? Is she?" he asked.

Anita hesitated. She wasn't entirely sure what he meant by a "public nuisance," but mainly she was reluctant to talk about what was really bothering her. If she said the word out loud, maybe he would think she was one of them. Her need was so great that she finally told him everything, even about Jarvinia's refusal to pay for garbage pickup. Other than that brief twitch of his lips, he seemed to be taking her case seriously, and once or twice he shook his head in sympathy.

"Unless this woman is running a brothel or charging clients to have sex, she's within her rights to entertain whomever she wants. It's her house during the term of the lease. What's more, she's a diplomat, so she has some rights even we don't have," he added. Anita left his office sorely disappointed, but at least he hadn't charged her. He even advised her to get tough with the town's council. "Paint your house pink," he said. "There's nothing they can do to you." Have some gumption, he seemed to imply.

In the end, it resolved itself. The rental agent with whom Anita listed her apartments told her less than a week after she'd hired a painter and purchased the paint that Jarvinia was looking for another house to rent, one with most of the rooms on the same floor. "She can't do all those stairs any more," he said. "She had polio as a child and she's having a recurrence."

Anita took one more very long look at the pink house and exhaled a sigh of happiness. The carabinieri who had been guarding the square had disappeared. She decided that the police wouldn't care if she let herself inside to check on the furnishings. The last time she'd been inside, she'd spied deep scratches on the legs of one of her mother's chairs. No more tenants with cats, she said to herself as she approached the house, and definitely no more Germans.

9

SOME MIGHT SAY that Paradiso is like any other hill town in Umbria, but anyone who has lived there knows this is not true. Some towns are reached by steeper climbs, some have better views, and some, like Gubbio, have preserved their medieval architecture with no pink houses in sight. Even the flower festival held every year to honor the feast of Corpus Christi is not unique to Paradiso, and if you ask any tourist which town creates the most beautiful and elaborate flower paintings, you can be sure they'll say Spello. Nonetheless, Paradiso is famous throughout Umbria, and even throughout Italy.

In 1978 a mother and her child were murdered there. The mother was found dead in bed, with the weapon of execution, an ax for chopping firewood, embedded in her skull. The child was found on the floor of her bedroom, where it appeared she had been playing with her doll, her head sliced open from front to back. The local doctor, who also served as the coroner, said that he'd never seen such destruction of human flesh or such an abandonment of humanity. Other people had been murdered in Italy, but the Paradiso murders attracted the country's attention because of the way the bodies were found. A nine-year-old playmate of the murdered child wandered into the house looking for her friend and found *death and blood all around her,* or at least that's how one of the newspapers put it. Childhood is sacred to Italians, and the horror of this little girl finding the mutilated body of her friend plunged the nation into grief.

Almost always, family murders are committed by one of its members, so the police naturally looked to the husband first. But he had the perfect alibi. He and his brother-in-law, also a likely suspect, were working in Switzerland. The police combed the woods that surrounded Paradiso at the time looking for vagrants, but none were found, and no one was ever arrested for the murders. Some of the newspapers played off the name of the town in their headlines: one of the more literary ran

the headline PARADISE LOST. Another headline screamed
out OBSCENE PARADISE, but the headline that stuck in the
minds of the town's inhabitants was A DEADLY PARADISE.
At the first town meeting held two months after the murders, one of the inhabitants suggested that they change the
town's name. It won by two votes, but after three years of
submissions and rejections, arguing and name-calling, the
matter rested.

Although Cenni had been a child at the time of the
murders, he was familiar with the case. It was still listed on
the police blotter as *open* and had been passed to him five
years earlier when the original case officer retired. It was
one of seven files that were still open, and this was the oldest of them. He'd read up on the murders a few years ago,
but that was the extent of his involvement until now. He
did wonder, when the questore was describing the sheer
brutality of the German's murder, if there might not be an
association between the two cases. They were different in
choice of weapon, but the same uncontrollable rage was
evident in both. The police, with the help of a local psy-
chiatrist, had concluded in 1978 that they were looking for
someone who was mentally unhinged. Thirty years was
not such a length of time. The murderer could still be alive
and residing locally. He'd asked one of the clerks to leave
the case file on his desk.

The questore had left a message on his cell phone that
he'd assigned Cenni a very reliable officer. She would
meet him in Paradiso at four o'clock, at the German's
house. He was glad it was a woman and could only hope

she was half as good as Elena. He was afraid no one would ever measure up to Piero and Elena. Elena had provided the team with an extra dimension. She had an instinct about motives, particularly where women were concerned, that he and Piero lacked. It was ironic, he thought, that she would have protested this evaluation as chauvinistic, insulted at any hint that women were in any way different as police officers, even if the observation were offered in praise.

The streets of Paradiso are narrow and steep, narrower than most, Cenni realized when he found himself slowing to a crawl to avoid scraping his side-view mirror against a blue Ape that was parked streetside. He made one last sharp turn and entered a tiny square at the top of the town. Carabinieri were posted at both ends of the square. He showed his identification to a sergeant, who waved him through, indicating that he should park at the north end of the square, adjacent to the open belvedere that looked down on the valley below. Within the belvedere a church pew faced the view. On its other side were parking spaces, identified by six unevenly spaced white lines. Numbers were painted within each space, from one to five, matching the number of each residence in Piazza Garibaldi. Very efficient, Cenni decided, and very American in its blatant declaration of private property. He wondered if anyone in town actually respected this assertion. Probably not, he concluded.

He parked in the last space, which he assumed belonged to the murder house. No. 5 Piazza Garibaldi was a narrow structure squeezed between two public buildings, a clock tower with the hour hand missing and a falling-down chapel with flaking stuccowork. The house was painted an incongruous throbbing pink. In the blinding sun bouncing off the square, it assaulted the eyes. Only one day had passed since the German's body had been discovered, and no curious crowds or reporters were congregating outside the house. Cenni was grateful that the finer points of Baudler's murder had not yet reached the press, but realized it was just as likely that it had already dropped into the category of old news.

The door was unlocked, and Cenni entered directly into the main sitting room, which was narrow and minimally furnished with a faded purple couch, two wicker chairs, and a wicker basket filled with art books. No TV, he noted. The floor was marble and completely out of place in this small peasant house. The sitting room led into a small kitchen with highly polished marble countertops and a large fireplace at the far end. Both rooms were empty, and he wondered what'd happened to the questore's "reliable" officer.

"So you've finally arrived. I was getting bored counting my fingers and toes."

Cenni whipped around to find Elena standing behind him.

"Where did you come from?" was his unfriendly response to his favorite inspector. But he really did want to know where she'd been hiding.

She pointed to a small doorway located between the two rooms.

"Stairway," she responded. "And I'm doing very well, thank you. Nice to see you too," she said, but with a wide grin of affection.

"Sorry Elena, but you startled me. How are you? And what are you doing here? Piero told me that you're still recovering from your gunshot wound, and the questore insisted that you're on medical leave. I did request you, you know."

"Piero treats me like a baby, although I love every minute of it," she added, still grinning. "Marinella called"—Cenni smiled when Elena mentioned the name of the office gossip—"to tell me you're back. I phoned the questore and told him I wanted to return early, to work with you on this case. He agreed, although he also said that the rules you impose as to those you'll work with are ridiculous. And my shoulder is healing nicely. Thank you for asking! Would you like to see me do some pushups?"

Cenni hesitated about how to express his pleasure that Elena was back. She was adamant about women's rights and an advocate of doing things American style, so he was never sure if he was allowed to kiss her on the cheek or even give her a collegial pat on the back. This time she made it easy on him.

Abandoning all foreign influences, she kissed him on both cheeks and smiled in delight. "Look what I found," she said, holding up a yellowing sheet of paper. "Very interesting stuff!"

CENNI SPENT THREE hours in the house going over the postmortem, the crime-scene photos, and, finally, the evidence that Elena had found. He had already discussed the crime-scene photos and the postmortem at length with Tahany Falchi while she smoked half a pack of Players. The body, she'd said, had been moved after Baudler was dead, dragged ten feet from where she had fallen and positioned against the first cellar step. The German had been standing near the stacked firewood when she was first struck with a jagged piece of firewood. The police found the piece of wood that had been used, lying apart from the other firewood. A sliver had lodged in the dead woman's right arm. It was a long, unwieldy log, some three feet in length. It was difficult, according to the forensic report, to get clean fingerprints. A number of partials were found, including those of the victim. Perhaps she had stacked the wood herself, Falchi suggested. The other two sets might include those of the murderer, or were those of the person or persons who had delivered and stacked the wood. The initial blow had broken her elbow and must have hurt like the dickens, according to Falchi.

"The first blow was the hardest and also the one that resulted in her heart attack. The other blows, some ten at least, were struck by someone standing over her, most of them landing on the right side of the body and none of them, oddly enough, directed at her head. There was very little blood, as only a few of the blows broke the skin. We found a small pool of blood near the stack of firewood; but most of it was on the steps, from the excision of her clitoris. There were also light smears of blood on the floor between the firewood and the steps, caused by the killer dragging the body. I should also add that the subsequent blows, after the one that broke her elbow, were superficial, and of surprisingly little force."

"What do you mean?" Cenni had asked, surprised at her conclusion, considering the extensive bruising on Baudler's upper body.

"Yes, I was surprised as well. From the number of blows and the mutilation, you'd think her assailant was outraged and that the blows would have been more frantic, but that's not the case. Given the same injuries without the heart attack, my guess is she'd be in the hospital today and not the morgue."

When Cenni asked if a woman could have inflicted the first blow, Falchi said:

"Of course. Countrywomen in Umbria are often as strong as the men. How often do you see a woman in her eighties walking a mile uphill carrying two huge baskets of groceries? You or I would give up before we made it halfway to the top. Sure, it could be a woman, or one of those wily little men, half your size, who hang out in the café playing briscola. I imagine the German wasn't expecting the attack, which is why she was so defenseless."

And before he could ask, she'd added that she had no idea what was behind the mutilation, although her guess was that it had been easier to perform with the body in a half-sitting position, which may have explained the reason it had been dragged to the steps. She did have one supposition: she explained that, in some cultures, one of the many reasons for performing a clitoridectomy was the belief that an unmodified clitoris could lead to masturbation or lesbianism.

Elena had listened silently while Cenni had reviewed the postmortem's finding with her, jumping in just once to add that the pruning shears had also been found, stuck in a clay planting pot, but they'd been cleaned first. No evidence of prints or clinging flesh. When he had finished going over Falchi's findings, Elena hesitated a moment, then spoke up.

"What about the letters? I didn't find them in the house, and they're not in the folders of evidence that the carabinieri gave us."

"What letters?" Cenni asked, puzzled.

She froze, and Cenni knew that she'd let someone's cat out of the bag, probably Piero's.

"Tell me, Elena," he said, holding her gaze.

"Piero didn't tell you?"

"No. You tell me."

She sighed. "I may be misremembering, but a few months ago Piero told me that the carabinieri had had a number of complaints from Baudler about anonymous letters; one of them actually suggested she should have her clitoris removed, 'Just like that African bitch you're living with'—I'm quoting from the letter," she added. "Shortly afterward, Piero told me that the local police knew who was sending the letters and put a stop to it. The usual jerks with nothing better to do, Piero said."

"So you think Piero just forgot?" he asked, searching her face.

"Don't, Alex. Piero and I are married. If you think he should have told you, talk to him yourself. Just keep me out of it, please." She rose from the purple sofa and walked into the kitchen. "The carabinieri left some bottled water in the fridge. The only thing they didn't trash, apparently. Do you want some?" she called out.

Cenni knew when Elena walked away that she wouldn't discuss the matter further. It was now between him and Piero. He replied, "Yes, thanks. Water would be great, and now let's talk about that document you found."

If he'd ever doubted his reasons for preferring Elena to others in the Perugia Questura, the letter she'd found that five carabinieri had missed in their wild search of the murder house was an excellent reminder. In the hour that Elena had spent waiting for him, she'd searched the house, looking in all the places that had been searched before, and in one place that she knew women often hid secrets, their clothing. And she'd found Baudler's secret, a single sheet of paper, hidden inside the lining of her winter jacket.

It was in Swedish, a language that Cenni did not know well, despite having a Swedish grandmother. It was written on what appeared to be letterhead paper, although the top of the letter had been partially torn off. There was no date to indicate when it had been typed. The small bit of engraving remaining on the top indicated that it had been sent from Skandinaviska Nordea Banken in Stockholm. It was signed by Jacob Lagerskjöld, a name that Cenni recognized immediately. The Lagerskjölds were distant cousins of his grandmother. There were two other references in the text that he also recognized: Banca Centrale Venezia and Count Molin. The Molin name was well known in Italy; the Countess Molin was one of the richest women in the country. He knew the letter was important, but he had no idea why. He stuck it in his wallet. His grandmother, his favorite person in the world and sharp as a tack at eighty-nine, would translate it. He had no idea how it might relate to Baudler's murder; nonetheless, he was still sure it was the document that Dieter Reimann was seeking.

"They threw her clothes on top of the bed and some of them had slipped to the floor," Elena explained. "I was hanging them back on their hangers when I felt this crinkle. I could see right away that the lining had been ripped and repaired. She even used a different color of thread, navy blue instead of black. I used my nail clippers to open the seam and my little sewing kit to stitch it back together. Only this time with black thread."

"What else?"

"Well, if that's not enough, take a look at her bank statements. In a credenza upstairs I found statements and bills going back twelve months. The first nine months, she was living way above her means. Her pension of seventeen hundred thirty-nine euros is deposited to her account once a month. That was the only deposit, yet her bills far exceed that amount. Then three months ago, there was a single deposit of ten thousand euros, and after that a deposit each month of three thousand euros, all transferred from the same account number. One month ago, another deposit was made of five thousand euros, but get this: the account number this time was different. Strange, don't you think? That's a pile of money for a good little fräulein. Maybe she was blackmailing someone."

*   *   *

THEY SPENT THE remaining two hours searching the
five floors of the murder house looking for additional evidence. Cenni agreed silently with Elena that the carabinieri had trashed the place during their search. Dirty
laundry, bed and table linens, bath towels, and Baudler's
clothes and shoes were tossed everywhere. Surprisingly,
they had made just a cursory examination of Baudler's
papers, so her bank statements and receipts were still in
the house. After putting on gloves, Cenni looked through
the papers quickly before dumping them all into a plastic
grocery bag that he'd found in the kitchen, while Elena
kept up a running commentary on the shoddy work of the
competition.

"It doesn't really matter, Elena, since we're doing a
search now. Maybe the officer in charge resented our taking over and decided to leave the grunt work for us. Who
can blame him?"

Cenni felt strongly that the competition between the
military and civilian arms of the police was ridiculous and
that an overhaul of police functions was long overdue.
Every second year, the public heard about new procedures and new responsibilities, but nothing ever really
changed. *"For things to stay the same, everything must change,"*
Tancredi Falconeri says in Visconti's *The Leopard*. Sadly, it
was true. He also had a great deal of sympathy for the carabinieri who provided the day-to-day policing of Italy and at
the same time were the butt of every lame joke about stupid policemen. The glamour bits went to the state police,
so he restrained himself in front of his officers when it

came to assigning blame. But Elena was right, the place was a mess!

"I know, I know. I've heard your lectures before. But look at this! They searched the rag bin and missed the obvious." She reached down to the floor and picked up two pairs of panties. "Very different sizes! I found two different size bras as well, in that stack over there," she said, pointing to a pile of underwear on the floor. "Baudler had a skinny friend, but it looks like she must have moved out, as most of the stuff here is in Baudler's size. Sixteen," she added, and grinned maliciously.

After searching through everything on the four floors and in the cellar, they climbed to the top floor, which consisted of one room and a terrace. The room was empty, except for a few boxes of books, which Elena went through, complaining the whole time about the dust and the owner's poor choice of reading material.

"Whoever owns this place is a religious nut. All these books are religious, and some of them are centuries old. Look at this one," she said, holding up a book for Cenni to see: *Padre Pio: The Priest Who Wears the Wounds of Christ.* My grandmother owns this one!"

Not mine, Cenni thought, opening the door to the terrace. His grandmother, Hanna Falkenberg, was a rabble-rousing atheist, and he rather enjoyed the irony that her favorite grandson was a bishop in the Catholic Church. Of course, she'd deny it, that Renato was her favorite, but Alex knew that Hanna, as she insisted they call her, preferred his brother to him. He didn't really mind, as he was pretty sure that, given the choice, he'd prefer his brother as well. Renato was the nice twin.

The terrace commanded a 180-degree view of the Umbrian countryside. The view was magnificent, but he also noted that it was a long drop from the terrace to the valley below. The house had been built against the original town wall, and he estimated that the distance from where he was standing to terra firma was a hundred and twenty feet. The terrace wall was just waist-high, and he assumed that whatever conditions Baudler may have suffered from, she'd been exempt from acrophobia.

He went back inside to find Elena reading one of the books. She looked up and frowned. "Strange to find something like this among all those religious books. It's a medical dictionary, and it opened without any help to a section on sexual deformities—almost like a bookmark."

"Any particular deformity?" Cenni asked.

"There's a faint pencil mark under *hermaphrodite*."

"Curiosity, I suppose. Teenagers are always checking out their sexuality, afraid they're different from their friends. When we were thirteen, Renato and I searched through every book in the house looking for information on male sexuality."

"And. . . ?"

Cenni laughed. "Ask Piero if you need enlightenment on what every boy needs to know. Now stop looking at dirty pictures and put those books back in the box. I want to check the basement door again. There's a huge spider web across the door opening. If a web that size takes more than two days to spin, we can be fairly sure the murderer came through the front door. Not that it makes much difference either way. Too many people in these small towns leave their doors unlocked during the day—and night. Maybe Baudler was in the habit of leaving her door unlocked. Make a note of that. We also need to know how many people had keys to the front door. Make a note of that too. And see if you can find out how long it takes a spider to spin a web of that size."

"How do you expect me to do that?"

"Call a spider expert, Google it, or ask Piero. He never had problems with any of my requests. And he never complained!"

"Lovely, how he throws Piero at me," Elena murmured.

Cenni ignored her grumbling and continued his observations. "The only other way in is through the basement window, which is how the neighbor and his cat got in. But the neighbor's traces are the only ones the carabinieri found on the ledge and the floor, and the cat's, of course. Must have been quite a shock to the poor cat."

Elena, who hated cats, was nonplussed. "The 'poor cat'! What about the poor *neighbor?*"

"I think we should quit now," Cenni told Elena when they'd finished searching the murder house. "It's after six, and you don't want to wear yourself out your first day back. We can interview the owner of the house and the neighbors tomorrow. And I also want you to find out who's been sending Baudler money, as soon as possible. That looks promising."

"And you'll want to go to your grandmother's and have that letter translated," Elena responded, reading his mind.

10

ALEX REACHED HIS grandmother's apartment in Perugia shortly after seven. She immediately sent Lucia off for a bottle of champagne. "And bring three glasses," she shouted after her.

"I thought the doctor told you no more champagne," he admonished her.

"Don't be ridiculous," Hanna responded. "I plan to go out in style—*my* style, not your mother's. But what brings you here at seven o'clock? Isn't there a playoff game tonight? Something brings you here besides love and duty."

"You always could read my mind," Alex said, leaning over and kissing her on the forehead. "I have a letter in Swedish that I need you to translate. It's connected to a case."

"I wish you and your brother would remember that you're one quarter Swedish. Neither of you knows more than ten words of the language, and most of those can't be repeated in company."

"And whose fault is that?" he asked affectionately.

In the time that it took his grandmother to find her glasses and read the letter, he observed her closely and had a heart-rending moment of profound sadness. Her hands shook noticeably from what her doctor claimed was the beginning of Parkinson's disease, and her once substantial Swedish frame was shrunken and bent, more so since his last visit a month ago. In July, she'd be ninety, and Renato was planning a great surprise. He was bringing her three very eccentric Swedish nephews to Italy for the celebration. Alex tried hard never to think of her death, but he realized for the first time that it might not be so very far away.

She finished the letter, removed her glasses, and stared off into space. Alex waited for what seemed an age, until his impatience broke through.

"What does it say? Does it provide a motive for murder?"

"I suppose it does," she replied quietly. "And for some shame as well."

Hanna Falkenberg was a cousin of Jacob Lagerskjöld, who had signed the letter, so Alex waited for her to respond in her own time.

She began slowly, looking down at her hands: "The letter is cryptic, but I'll give you my interpretation: Jacob is writing to Count Molin to let him know that ten million pounds, in twenty-pound notes, is on its way to Banca Centrale Venezia, presumably for distribution. The date is missing, but from another reference within the letter, I'd say it was written in 1945, and in 1945 it's highly doubtful that the Bank of England would send large sums of money to Skandinaviska Nordea for distribution, not when Jacob and his brother Marcus were viewed by both the British and the Americans as German sympathizers." She looked up and gave him a wry smile. "I suppose it sounds hypocritical for a naturalized Italian to be complaining about the neutral Swedes, but you know my position on the war and the Swedish government's decision to remain neutral."

Alex nodded. He'd heard it many times before.

"Are you suggesting that this letter may have a connection to Operation Bernhard?" He drew in his breath at the possibility of a murder tied to the most infamous counterfeiting scheme of the last century.

"Yes, and I'm not at all surprised. Who else would the Germans turn to but the neutral nations, Sweden and Switzerland in particular? Laundering hundreds of millions of counterfeit British pounds is not easy. They had to find legitimate avenues for distribution. There's just so much money you can launder by using it to pay off your spies. You know the story, I suppose, of the German spy whose codename was Cicero?"

"No, tell me."

"Elyesa Bazna was valet to the British ambassador in Ankara. He leaked important information to the Germans, for which they paid him £300,000, but in counterfeit pounds. After the war he sued the German government for outstanding pay and won. Those delightful Turks!" she said laughing. "And some Italians don't want Turkey in the European Community. Brothers under the skin, I'd say. Think of it, Alex; it's believed that the Germans printed the equivalent in today's currency of $4.5 billion in British pounds."

"But they found the money in the early sixties at the bottom of an Austrian lake," Alex replied. "So even if it's true that Jacob Lagerskjöld laundered money for the Germans, or was attempting to launder money through a Venetian bank, what does it matter today, and how could it justify murder? Jacob Lagerskjöld's dead, isn't he? And so, probably, is Count Molin. And if I remember correctly, the Bank of England made changes to its currency some time after the war to ensure that none of the counterfeit pounds could be used as legal tender."

"Don't be naïve, Alex," Hanna said, more sharply than she'd intended. She was aware immediately that she had offended her grandson, and reached out and patted his knee. "Sorry, love, but you know me on this subject. Consider the countries that don't want this scandal dragged back out into the sunlight: Germany, Sweden, Switzerland, Italy, England, and that's just for starters. Anything that reminds the Germans of their history is uncomfortable, and if this letter is just surfacing now and in a murder case, it has some relevance. Perhaps the money never reached its destination, and the Germans used it for petty cash after the war, maybe in Italy. It would have come in handy. They wouldn't want that publicized. And the Swedes, you've heard me often enough on their pathetic war. They collaborated with the Germans and everyone else for money, but don't remind them. They've been in denial for sixty years. And Italy! Two minutes after its citizens hanged Mussolini upside down by his toes, they buried their Fascist past. It never happened! Is there any family in this country who lost someone during the war that doesn't claim he was a partisan fighting with the resistance? Nobody wants reminders."

"The English?

"As much as the others. This was a huge embarrassment to the British. The pound in those days was what the dollar is today, the world's prime currency. Even the Bank of England couldn't tell the difference between the counterfeit bank notes and the real ones. It was only when a bank clerk found herself holding two bank notes with the same serial number that the Bank of England realized it had a problem. Believe me, they all have a stake in keeping this quiet."

"Does it say in the letter that the money was actually shipped to Venice?"

"I'll read it to you." It took her a minute to find her glasses, which had slipped down between the chair and the cushion, and while Cenni was waiting, he reflected on the implications of what his grandmother had just told him. Italy's left-leaning government was working on a number of projects with Germany's right-leaning government. Neither would welcome revelations about their Fascist pasts. But his instincts told him that whatever game Baudler had been playing, it was on an individual level. He doubted that her murderer was a state-hired executioner. Hired hands killed with cold efficiency, and they generally disliked messes. He wouldn't put it past any of the governments his grandmother had mentioned, Italy included, to get rid of Baudler if it was expedient, but not in this particular manner.

"Here they are. I was sitting on them," Hanna said. "I'll read you the sentence: *Please let our agent know if the boxes were received in good order.* You can decide what that means, but it says to me that the money had already been shipped

and he's trying to find out where it is. And since the
agent's name is not mentioned, it seems likely that Count
Molin knew who the agent was and had worked with him
before. Possibly the money was diverted by some interested
parties. Maybe Count Molin received the money and
stored it for safekeeping and then the war ended. He
would have had ten million British pounds, undetectable
as counterfeits. There's a whole lot one can do with money
like that at the end of a war with the country in turmoil. Is
this count any relation to Marcella Molin, the one who
owns all those vineyards?"

"I don't know. Elena is researching it, probably at this
very moment, so I won't know anything until tomorrow."

"*Caro,* you've picked my brain long enough. No more
politics tonight. I'm rusty from watching all this reality TV.
Where's Lucia with our champagne?" She lowered her
voice. "Make sure you invite her to join us. Your mother
snubbed her the other day and hurt her feelings. Lucia, by
the way, was the best birthday present you've ever given
me. Renato is still trying to top it." She smiled sweetly.
"Sven wrote and told me about the birthday celebration,
but please don't tell Renato that I know."

II

HIS GRANDMOTHER FED him on French country pâté,
spinach ravioli with a butter and, sage sauce, and afterward, Belgian chocolates. Alex accused her, very gently, of
being a traitor. Cenni Chocolates is the second largest
manufacturer of chocolate in Perugia, and Hanna was

one of its founders. "But Belgian chocolates are better," she'd responded, while searching through the assortment for a champagne truffle. For all her talk of carousing to all hours of the night, he noticed that she hadn't finished half her glass of champagne before she nodded off in her chair.

After Hanna had gone off to bed, Alex had stayed talking to Lucia, while finishing up the champagne, until after ten. Lucia had been working as a maid in Assisi for a family involved in one of his more notorious cases and had been fired for spreading lies—or, as Lucia described her offense, "Telling it like it is." He'd felt somewhat responsible, having encouraged her to reveal family secrets, and he liked her, despite her disposition to gossip. He had introduced her to his grandmother, who also loved to gossip, as a possible companion two years ago, and they had been together ever since. Hanna's previous companions, all of them chosen by his mother, had been prissy women in their fifties who thought his grandmother outrageous. Lucia accompanied Hanna everywhere, and they had frequently been seen dining in Perugia's better restaurants, until a few months ago when Hanna had been diagnosed with Parkinson's.

Cenni skirted around what was bothering him by first offering up compliments.

"That was a delicious, Lucia. I had two helpings of ravioli. But I noticed Hanna barely touched hers, although she finished her pâté and had five chocolates afterward. I was wondering if she perhaps she should be getting more protein and vegetables in her diet."

"Pâté is protein," Lucia responded defensively.

"It is, but I was thinking more in the line of a piece of fish or a lamb chop with a vegetable, and a nice salad: lettuce, tomatoes, onions, maybe some zucchini. They're all excellent this time of year. And perhaps fruit to finish." Even to himself, he sounded lame, and he had to suppress a smile.

Tears welled in Lucia's eyes. "Oh, dottore, I'm sorry, really I am. I love Hanna; she's been so good to me. She's my friend, and she's also like a mother to me. I can tell her anything. I really do love her, but she won't touch any of those foods you mentioned. Every night, except when we go out to eat, which is not often any more, she wants exactly the same things. She lives on that awful French pâté. In the morning she has it on a croissant, and it has to be a croissant from the French bakery on Corso Vannucci, and for lunch it's pâté on a baguette. And it has to be with only one type of pickle and one type of mustard."

"Have you mentioned this to my mother?"

"Oh, no. I would never do that. Hanna would consider that squealing. Your mother is very bossy and Hanna hates it. But I did talk to her doctor, twice now."

"What did he say?"

"That old people often have peculiar tastes in food. He said it's more important that she's eating and staying strong, and that the French are a healthy people and they eat pâté all the time. I'm really sorry, dottore, I'll do whatever you think best."

Cenni thought for a minute before acknowledging that the doctor was probably right. He was also a little horrified at himself; he'd almost involved his mother in his grandmother's affairs. Hanna would go back to Sweden before she'd let anyone tell her what to do, particularly his mother.

"You know, dottore, I have an idea. If you could come by a few nights a week for dinner and insist on a vegetable with fish or lamb, Hanna will order what you like. She loves it when you visit."

Cenni squirmed inwardly at this reminder that he'd been derelict in his duty for more than a month, but he had to admire Lucia for the clever way in which she'd turned his lecture to her into a reminder that it was he who was neglecting his grandmother.

HALF AN HOUR after climbing into bed, he was still wide awake. His conscience was clean, so that wasn't the problem. He'd promised Lucia he'd come for dinner twice a week, more often if he could manage it. A clean conscience is usually a guarantee of a good night's sleep; but it wasn't his own conscience that was keeping him awake, it was Piero's. He had pushed Piero's promotion to *commissario* using what leverage he could muster, which had been sadly depleted after the Casati case. Had he made a mistake? Was Piero too inexperienced? Even experienced officers find it difficult not to succumb to political pressure. Piero was a good policeman but a novice in politics; without someone at hand to guide him, he would have found it difficult to stand firm against pressure from his superiors. In the past, Alex had been Piero's mentor, but that was before he'd been sent down to Foligno. The questore was no help; he might even be the one applying the pressure. Perhaps the questore had brought him back from Foligno strictly for show. Alex hated to acknowledge it, but he was now the elder statesman in the Perugia Questura. To the Germans, he would have been the obvious choice to lead this investigation. Alex never knew what the questore was up to.

After a few more turns of his pillow, he reached a conclusion. There were two possible reasons for Piero not to have told him about the threatening letters: he'd been told not to by the questore for reasons as yet unknown, or he was protecting someone for personal reasons. There was nothing for it; tomorrow he'd have to visit Piero in Assisi, and that decision put quit to the wonderful day he had planned for himself. So turns the world, he thought, and promptly fell asleep.

12

EVERY EVENING ALEX set his alarm for seven; and every morning exactly at six, his cat, Rachel, would jump on his chest and lick his chin until she woke him. In the beginning, when he'd first rescued her from a murder scene, he'd tried closing the bedroom door, but she'd scratch all night until he had to let her in. He'd tried ignoring the licks, but she was insistent. He'd tried scolding, but that was equally ineffective. Every cat lover is positive that his cat has human qualities, and Alessandro Cenni was no exception. The expression of wounded sensibility that Rachel affected when he gently chided her was surely an act, but it worked. So at ten minutes after six each day, he got out of bed to fill her bowl with food, and at six fifteen he was wide awake. So, as on every other morning since he'd adopted Rachel, Commissario Cenni was the first to arrive at the Perugia Questura.

He began his second day of the Baudler investigation by reviewing the file on the 1978 murders in Paradiso. He'd read the file a few years earlier but was still surprised at the enormous changes in police practices between then and now. The police had collected very little crime scene evidence in 1978, and what they had collected had been discarded ten years ago during a cleanup of storage facilities. But he doubted that what had been discarded would be of any help. The ax handle had been checked for fingerprints, with the conclusion that it had been cleaned while it was still embedded in the mother's skull, or else that the killer had worn gloves. The house had been dusted for prints, but no comparisons were made against suspects' prints, as none had been collected. As soon as the police realized that the father and the brother had been in Switzerland at the time of the killings, they jumped, rather absurdly, Cenni thought, to the conclusion that a passing vagrant was the killer. The house was located outside the town wall with no immediate neighbors, and the mother was known to have usually left the door unlocked. The husband and brother, who returned home for the funeral, looked through the contents of the house, and both said nothing was missing. They also said they'd kept the ax in a shed behind the house, and that the shed was never locked. The assumption by the officer in charge that the killer was unhinged seemed reasonable. What was not reasonable to Cenni's thinking was the accompanying assumption that the killer was a vagrant.

The chief investigating officer, now retired, hadn't kept the file updated, and there were no records of either the father or brother's later addresses, although there was a lone magazine clipping dated six months after the murders stapled to the front of the folder. It was an interview of the father, obviously paid for, in which he claimed that his wife and daughter had been raped. The coroner had been explicit in that regard: "No evidence of sexual molestation of mother or child." He looked through the file trying to find any indication as to which of them had been murdered first, the mother or the child, but could find nothing. The time of death was listed as between nine and noon. The bodies were found by the dead child's playmate shortly after midday.

What did excite Cenni was the interview with the child who'd found the bodies. Her name was Anita Tangassi, which was the name of the current owner of the pink house. She was nine and a playmate of the child who was killed. He was a bit surprised at the difference in ages, as the murdered child, Bianca Lanese, had just turned seven. The interview had taken place in the local barracks. Three people were in the room in addition to the police and the child: Marta Vannicelli Tangassi, the child's mother; a neighbor, Lorenzo Vannicelli; and the local priest, Father Alberto Lacrimosa. A stenographer had taken most of it down verbatim, even the bickering between the mother, the priest, and the neighbor. The interviewer was the chief investigating officer, Commissario Giuseppe Landi. Cenni highlighted the parts that were of particular significance:

COMMISSARIO LANDI: Anita, what made you decide to visit your friend's house instead of going home for lunch as you usually do?

ANITA TANGASSI: Bianca's father sent her a doll with blonde curls. The curls grow if you wind a key in her back. We were going to play dolls after school. She wasn't at school, so I went to her house.

COMMISSARIO LANDI: When you rang the bell and no one answered, why didn't you go home? Why did you go inside?

ANITA TANGASSI: The door was unlocked.

SIGNOR VANNICELLI: You've done that before, haven't you, Anita, gone inside without being asked?

ANITA TANGASSI: *(Nods her head "yes" in response.)*

COMMISSARIO LANDI: When you went into Bianca's room and saw her lying on the floor, did you touch anything?

ANITA TANGASSI: I touched her head. It was red with blood. It was sticky and I wiped my hands on my dress.

SIGNORA TANGASSI: You should have washed your hands in the sink. You can never get bloodstains out.

(Child began to cry and Commissario Landi offered her a chocolate bar.)

COMMISSARIO LANDI: Anita, did you go into Signora Lanese's room?

(Child hesitated; looked over at Signor Vannicelli, before answering.)

ANITA TANGASSI: *(Shakes her head "no.")*

COMMISSARIO LANDI: Anita, why didn't you look for Bianca's mother to tell her your friend was hurt?

ANITA TANGASSI: The house was scary. I was afraid.

SIGNOR VANNICELLI: That makes sense. Or are you expecting a nine-year-old child to do your job and go search for the killer?

(Exchange of words between Commissario Landi and Signor Vannicelli.)

COMMISSARIO LANDI: Anita, why did you go home after that? You had to pass by the carabinieri. Why didn't you stop at the station and tell a policeman about Bianca?

(Child hesitated before answering.)

ANITA TANGASSI: The police take bad children away and put them in jail. I'm supposed to go right home from school for my lunch.

(A footnote was added that Signora Tangassi worked in the family's grocery store during the day and left her daughter's lunch prepared for her at home.)

SIGNOR VANNICELLI *(addressing the child's mother)*: Now, do you realize how ridiculous it is to threaten Anita with the police if she doesn't eat her vegetables?

FATHER LACRIMOSA: Children need instruction and discipline. Marta is an excellent mother, and she doesn't need criticism, certainly not from a Godless atheist like you!

(Argument between the mother, the neighbor, and the priest, with everyone talking at once.)

COMMISSARIO LANDI: Where did you and Bianca usually play together?

ANITA TANGASSI: My uncle lets me play house in his cellar. We played there sometimes, and yesterday we played dolls at the back of Bianca's house. We used the woodshed for a dollhouse.

COMMISSARIO LANDI: Did you or Bianca ever see any strange men hanging around when you were playing together?

(Child hesitated; looked over at Father Lacrimosa and then at Signor Vannicelli before answering.)

ANITA TANGASSI: No.

CENNI WAS SURPRISED at how thoroughly documented the interview had been. It was six pages long, and in many ways better than the tape-recorded interviews they currently conducted. The stenographer had actually noted the child's gestures and had recorded the sidebars between the adults in the room. When Anita began to cry, the stenographer had even written down the mother's response to the proffered chocolate bar. "Remember your manners, Anita, and say thank you."

Nonetheless, he was disappointed at the number of opportunities Landi had missed. Questioning a young child who's just seen her best friend's head cracked open by an ax is not an easy task, but the child's responses were unusual and should have been scrutinized with more care. She'd cried only once, and that was because her mother scolded her for having blood on her dress. He also wondered how Anita knew her friend was not at school that day. When Cenni had been in school, lunch-hour dismissals were at different times for different classes. Presumably, a child of nine would be in a different class from

a child of seven. No doubt there was a reasonable explanation, but Landi hadn't even asked.

And why did the girl hesitate when Landi asked about
strange men hanging about their play areas? She'd looked at
the priest and then at the neighbor before answering. There
were certainly lots of strange priests in this world (*Mi dispi-
ace*, he said mentally, apologizing to his brother the bishop).
And who was this neighbor, with the same last name as the
mother's? Why was he in the interview room? Why was he
acting as the child's defender? Wasn't that the mother's job?

Alex and Renato had been ten when *The Bad Seed* had
finally reached Perugia's only movie theater. Their grandmother had taken them to see it. It had been the only
argument between Hanna and his mother with respect to
which he had to acknowledge—although by hindsight—
that his mother had been right: she had said the twins
were far too young to see horror films. Renato had night-
mares for weeks afterwards. Alex did too, but he never told
his parents about them.

Children do kill, even very young children. The girl in
the film was eight. Leaving aside fiction, there were many
recorded cases of murders by children in Italy, although
he couldn't think of one in which the child cold-bloodedly
axed its victims to death. Was a girl of nine even capable
of lifting an ax to the height needed to strike a lethal
blow? Lots of open questions, but later this afternoon he
would interview Anita Tangassi and the neighbor who'd
found Baudler's body, the same neighbor who had defended Anita in 1978. He might actually get some answers.

13

"EUREKA! I'VE FOUND IT."

"Isn't that redundant?" Cenni asked, not looking up from the document he was perusing.

"My God, Alex, but you're getting pedantic. And gray! Yesterday, I noticed a few gray hairs along the sides of your head."

Cenni was relieved to hear Elena address him by his first name. It had taken four years. When they'd first worked together, she'd been very formal, addressing him as commissario or dottore, and occasionally as *signore*. And then, later, when she'd wanted to annoy him, *capo,* a trick he'd adopted and now used on the questore. Marriage, he decided, was agreeing with her as well as Piero.

He looked up and smiled to show that her references to his pedantry, and in particular to his gray hair, had missed their mark.

"Sit and tell me what you've found."

"Lots of the credit goes to Marinella. I asked her yesterday to research the bank account stuff. She was here last night until ten and back in this morning at seven, claims she beat you in by ten minutes. Don't forget to say *grazie* when you go by her desk. She still has a huge crush on you, which, considering that you've been in Foligno for two years, is nothing to sneeze at. A kind word from you will keep her on air for a month."

"You want me to encourage her!"

"She doesn't need encouragement."

"Forget Marinella," Cenni said abruptly, afraid he was beginning to blush. "Tell me what you have."

"Good stuff. The big deposits to the German's account were made by a Marcella Molin, a/k/a *the Contessa Molin.*" Elena had intended to follow up the a/k/a with her usual speech on the bloodsucking aristocrats who refused to give up their titles, but realized from a twitch in Cenni's forehead that it wasn't the right time. She read his moods better than she did Piero's.

"*Si,* I know who she is. That's particularly significant when coupled with what I learned last night. Continue. I'll tell you about it later."

"The other deposit was made by Marcella Molin's first cousin, a Saverio Volpe. They both live in Venice. And . . . drum roll, please!"

"Go on."

"Molin's last deposit was made before the German's death. She cancelled the automatic deposit order yesterday. Highly significant, I'd say."

"Maybe, maybe not. She could have heard about Baudler's murder on the news and cancelled the deposit. What about the cousin?"

"Just the one deposit, and it was done manually. No automatic deposits scheduled."

Cenni pushed back his chair and removed his glasses, which he insisted, to anyone who asked, were for reading only.

"Is there any news on the German's car, or did she even have a car?"

"She definitely had a car: a 2004 Volkswagen Jetta. Not

very posh for a German diplomat! I'd have expected a BMW or a Mercedes. She re-registered it six months ago, without the diplomatic plates, to her address in Paradiso. But where it is now is anyone's guess. Marinella ran it through the stolen-car registry. Nothing. Later this morning, she'll check with the local garages. Maybe Fräulein Baudler lent it to the girlfriend with the size-four panties."

"So speaks the feminist," Cenni said.

"Sorry," Elena responded.

THEY AGREED TO meet later in the afternoon, in Paradiso, to talk to Anita Tangassi and Lorenzo Vannicelli, the neighbor who'd found the body. Elena would go ahead to canvass the neighborhood. Perhaps someone had noticed unusual activity on the day of the murder: a stranger in the piazza, a delivery truck, loud voices coming from the victim's house. The carabinieri had already talked to everyone who lived in Piazza Garibaldi, and Cenni had reviewed their notes. Nothing suspicious had been reported, which was suspicious in itself. Something untoward was always happening in village squares. But the carabinieri were local, and although this helped in day-to-day policing, in cases like murder it could also have drawbacks. They knew the town and its inhabitants well, perhaps too well. Unintentionally, they had formed certain biases that might influence the questions they asked, how they asked them, or who they believed. A fresh viewpoint always helped, and Elena was particularly skilled in getting witnesses to open up.

In the meantime, he was on his way to Assisi to see Piero concerning the threatening letters to Baudler. It promised to be an awkward meeting. Piero and Elena were not just his colleagues, they were his friends; and if his friendship with Piero ended, he could no longer work closely with Elena. She was loyal to her husband, and she had no talent for hiding her resentments. He phoned down for a driver, and, just before he left, ducked into the bathroom. Elena had been putting him on, he decided. Not a single gray hair in sight.

14

CENNI TOOK THE stairs two at a time until he remembered what lay before him. By the time he reached the garage three floors down, he was walking slowly and scowling. He looked around for Mario, his usual driver, but couldn't see him anywhere.

"Alex, over here."

Piero was standing to the side of the garage, the motor of his car idling, and Mario was nowhere in sight. Cenni wondered why Piero was in Perugia.

"I was coming to see you. I was at the desk when you called down for a driver. I hope you don't mind, but I told Mario I'd drive you to Paradiso. Elena is already there, and she can bring you back. I have to talk to you, Alex. I thought we could do it in the car."

"And Elena, she agreed to this meeting?" Cenni asked.

"Elena has no idea I'm here," Piero said, puzzled. "This has nothing to do with her."

That's what you think, Cenni thought to himself, but he knew from Piero's face that he was telling the truth. He'd often wondered how Piero had happened to be born Italian. Not only did he *not* resemble the vast majority of his countrymen with his green eyes, red hair, and Irish freckled skin, he lacked their God-given ability to say what they didn't mean with every appearance of sincerity, or, as Cenni referred to it, their gift for flattery. Piero would never have made it alive through his twenties in medieval Italy, and the rack would have been wasted on him. Cenni, on the other hand, would have thrived.

"Then perhaps I should drive," Cenni said. Piero had no respect for stop signs or traffic lights, which would have been okay if he had had any of the instincts of a good driver, which he did not.

"*Dimmi,*" Cenni said after they were on the highway. He was wondering what Piero was waiting for.

"It's kind of awkward, Alex. I don't know where to start."

"At the beginning, where else?"

"You know about my mother's older brother, Enzo."

"Not a thing; this is the first time you've ever mentioned him. What about him?"

"He's an alcoholic. My mother stopped talking to him years ago. Says he's a disgrace to the family." He hesitated, and Cenni could see in the mirror that Piero was blushing. "I don't feel that way. He's my uncle, and after my father died when I was nine, he took me to football games and sometimes in the summers to the beach in San Benedetto. And when I was fifteen and he'd won big on the World Cup, he gave me money to go away with my friends for a week. My mother didn't have the money, but if she had, she probably wouldn't have given it to me. You know my mother."

Piero had been on his way to becoming the classic *mam-mone* when Elena rescued him. He'd spent all his vacations with his mother, and she'd call him at work three times a day, and even on his cell phone when he was out working a case. Yes, he did know Piero's mother.

"Enzo lives in Paradiso. Years ago, there was a pasta fac-tory outside the town and he worked there. When the factory closed, he stayed on in the village. He mainly lives on his old-age pension and money that I give him. My mother says he just uses my money to buy drinks, but I don't care. He's family."

"And Elena, what does she think about you giving him money?" Cenni asked.

"She's with me. To quote her, 'He likes to drink, so what?'"

"I'm with you both so far—your uncle drinks, my grand-mother drinks, so what? But why do I need to know all this?"

Piero sighed loudly. "Yesterday I left something impor-tant out when we were discussing the Jarvinia Baudler case."

"*Si*," Cenni said. He kept his eyes on traffic.

"Six months ago, she received four anonymous letters, poison-pen stuff. They were mainly about her sexual activ-ities, with a string of quotations from the bible. One said that it's better to lose a part of one's body than for the whole to be thrown into hell. The reference was to having her clitoris removed, like they do to women in Africa. It added that if Baudler didn't stop doing what she was doing (I don't think the writers even knew what that was), they'd remove it for her. It was ugly stuff, Alex, and when I read the letters, I was ashamed."

"Why should you be ashamed?" Cenni asked, knowing already where Piero was headed.

"Because Enzo was involved."

"I guess I understand. Is there more?"

"Yes. I have a good friend in the carabinieri in Paradiso. We went to school together and he knows Enzo very well. He usually calls me if he thinks Enzo is getting into more trouble than usual. By luck, Baudler turned the letters over to Gianluca, and he called me. One of the neighbors directly across from where Baudler lived had seen Enzo slip the letters under the front door. Gianluca said it was best if I talked to my uncle to find out what was going on, and he also agreed not to show the letters to anyone else in the carabinieri. Gianluca and I were very close in high school, and Enzo would take us both to the football games."

Cenni knew the story immediately. The rest of Europe was quick to criticize Italians for their faults, as they perceived them: corrupt, duplicitous, and even, on occasion, lazy. The latter contention Cenni thought particularly contemptible, considering the contributions Italians had made to the world in the course of two thousand years. It was the old maxim: what have you done for me lately. But they rarely give us credit for our virtues, he reflected, the primary one being loyalty to family and friends.

"So how did it turn out?" he asked. "And why don't you think I should call your uncle in for questioning? I'm assuming you don't think Enzo murdered the German."

"Absolutely not! He didn't even write the letters. A few of the old-age pensioners who hang around in the café were responsible. The worst of them, a retired cara-biniere, started the letter-writing campaign. They bribed my uncle with drinks to slip them under the German's door. After I spoke to Enzo, I went to see each of the three men individually and scared them shitless. The policeman—he was the one who wrote the letter about removing her clitoris—died two months ago from a heart attack. Listen, Alex, I know what Enzo did was wrong. I know what I did in not telling you was wrong. But I didn't want him dragged into a police station and to have his face splashed all over the dailies. The shame would kill my mother."

Not that old bird.

"Where are the letters now?" he asked, turning to look at Piero.

Piero signed, even louder this time. "You're not going to like this, Alex. We burned them. Gianluca and I decided they were too nasty to keep in a file."

"And Baudler. What'd you tell her?"

"That the person who'd written them had left town, and that she wouldn't be getting any more letters. We also told her that the law required us to keep them on file, so we couldn't return them."

Cenni pulled into one of the larger gas stations along the highway.

"I need a coffee, and I want to think about this."

After two coffees for him and an apple tart for Piero, they came to an understanding: Piero would never do anything like this again, at least not without first consulting Cenni. "Once something like this gets out, you're a target for anyone who needs a favor."

Then they talked about damage control. In the carabinieri, only his friend knew about the letters, and Piero said he'd stake his life on Gianluca's discretion. Cenni was more of a cynic, but he was comfortable with the knowledge that Gianluca had just as many reasons to stay quiet as Piero.

"How many other people know about the letters besides Enzo and his two pals?"

"Normally, I would say at least their wives. But in this case, I don't think so. The ringleader was a widower. The other two were very embarrassed—and ashamed—and each of them insisted on being interviewed alone. There's Baudler, who's dead, and the woman she was living with at the time, who's since disappeared."

"Nobody else? You're sure?"

"Elena, but she'd never say anything. Oh, and one more. Baudler's neighbor, the one who found the body. The German insisted to Gianluca that the neighbor must have sent the letters, for revenge. And Gianluca was present when she accused the neighbor directly. They'd had two fights about his cat jumping her cat. I told you about it."

Cenni responded, "That's a problem. You realize, of course, that the person who killed her may have cut off her clitoris in the hope of diverting attention to the letter writer. Fortunately, the person who actually wrote that letter is dead, or we'd *never* be able to cover this up."

Cenni threw the car keys to Piero. "You drive; I want

to think about this some more. Oh, and Piero, at stop signs. . . ."

Piero smiled broadly, hugely relieved to have absolution. "I know, at stop signs, stop. What about at red lights?"

THE TWO CARABINIERI who'd been guarding the square the previous day were gone, replaced by two junior officers from the Perugia Questura, when they reached Paradiso.

"Elena took care of that quickly enough," Cenni remarked to Piero. "I hope it wasn't your friend she replaced."

"Don't worry. She would have blamed you: *damned territorial senior officers,* she'd have said."

Elena must have heard the car pull up: she met them in the middle of the square.

"You here!" she exclaimed, when she saw Piero walking toward her. She looked from her husband to Cenni and back again, scrutinizing their faces, and then smiled. "This is very nice, two men to take me to lunch. I'm starved."

"And our interviews?" Cenni asked.

"Not until two. Signora Tangassi claims a prior appointment with her realtor, and the neighbor has a doctor's appointment. I thought it best if we begin as friends, so I didn't insist that we meet at noon. And besides, I have some things to report first. A café at the bottom of the town serves decent pizza, or at least that's what Enzo tells me."

"You saw Enzo," Piero interrupted. "Where?"

"Sleeping on that bench over there," she said, pointing to the church pew that faced the view. "I gather from

Gianluca that he starts drinking early in the morning, and by noon he's ready for his nap. On nice days, he sometimes naps there to enjoy the view."

Piero started to walk over toward the bench, but Elena grabbed his arm. "He's gone home. I think he was embarrassed to have me see him in that condition. Don't worry about it, Piero. He drinks a little. So what?"

The café Elena took them to at the bottom of Paradiso, located just inside the town walls, could have been any café in any small town in Umbria. A few scrubby plastic tables and chairs were distributed unevenly outside the café on a cement patio. Immediately inside the double glass doors was a display case filled with various types of panini, and one tramezzino (not shrimp and egg, Cenni noted), stale cornetti and assorted pastries (no apple tarts, Piero noted), and square slices of cold pizza to be warmed up in the microwave. Next to the food case was the steel-topped bar, and to the right of the bar was a gelato case with just the basic three flavors. The height of the summer season had not yet arrived. On the top of the bar to one side were opened boxes of candy bars—the box advertising Cenni chocolate was empty—and a large jar of peppermint sticks. At the other end were little wire stands filled with various types of lottery tickets, and behind the bar was the ubiquitous coffee machine. The patrons could also have been found in any café in any small town in Umbria. Two boys, fourteen or fifteen years of age, were in the back of the bar betting on two of the three slot machines; four pensioners, all male, were playing briscola at one of the tables set along the side of the bar. Two men stood behind the

dealer, providing commentary on the players' skill or lack
of it. The briscola players looked up when Cenni, Piero,
and Elena walked in, probably because Piero was in uniform. The boys at the slot machines were too busy losing
their allowances to turn around.

Cenni, after one quick look in the food cases, wondered
if alcohol had freeze-dried Enzo's taste buds. The pizza on
display was dried-out and unappetizing; the lettuce sticking
out from the lone tramezzino was decidedly wilted.

"I think we go through there," Elena said, pointing to
an undecorated door at the back of the room.

This is definitely not like every other small-town café,
Cenni thought, when they had passed through the door.
It was just minutes after twelve, and the room, with ten or
twelve tables, was already crowded with customers. Some
of them looked like truckers, which explained the five or
so large trucks he'd seen parked across from the restaurant in the public lot. Elena walked to a table in the corner
of the large room, and Piero and Cenni followed.

Their waiter gave Piero a worried look before reading off
the lunch offerings from his order pad: four choices in
pizza; Margherita, mushroom, basil, and four-cheese; two
choices in pasta: penne alla primavera and ravioli with a
meat sauce; and one meat entrée: coniglio alla cacciatore;
for a side dish, green salad or potatoes roasted with rosemary. Pork or lamb were the usual meat entrées in small
Umbrian restaurants, and Cenni hesitated before ordering
the rabbit, although it was one of his favorite dishes.

"Ask one of those truckers," Elena suggested, which
he did.

"Can't go wrong in here, *signore,* no matter what you eat. I stop for lunch whenever I'm in this part of Umbria. Food is good, plenty of it, and reasonable." He pointed to his own dish of rabbit: "Delicious."

They began and finished in complete silence. The rabbit was tender and young, falling off the bone. Cenni used all the bread, even Piero's portion, to sop up the brown sauce. Piero ordered soup and ravioli, and Elena ordered a mushroom pizza and shared half of it with her husband.

"Coffee all around," Cenni said when the waiter came to clear the dishes.

"And a tiramisu for me," Piero added.

Elena frowned.

Cenni jumped in before she could say anything. "So, tell me what you have to report."

She hesitated a moment, apparently thought better of what she'd planned to say to Piero, and launched into her report. "Really good stuff. The first person I interviewed, an old lady who lives across from the house, was at her sister's the day of the murder and didn't see anything. But every other day she's like a pillar of salt in front of her window. She complained about all the strangers that went in and out, mainly women, but one older man in particular. Three times in the last month alone, she says she saw a black Mercedes parked in her spot. She took down the license number and reported it to the carabinieri."

"Gianluca must have loved that," Piero interjected.

"Gianluca is her major complaint. She's mainly annoyed at him. He told her there's no law against cars parking in any of the spots along the belvedere, and particularly in her spot, as she doesn't *even* own a car. She took great exception to his use of the word *even*. She wrote it down and showed it to me. She thinks he was suggesting that she's too poor to own a car. She wants to know if I can reprimand him. I promised I'd put a note in his file."

"Elena, you didn't!" Piero said.

"Keep'em happy, is my motto. Anyway, I couldn't if I wanted to. He's carabinieri, remember. I'm surprised Gianluca hasn't wrung her neck by now."

"Did you get the license number?" Cenni asked.

"I certainly did, and I had Marinella run it through the computer. Veneto plates. The owner is the infamous Marcella Molin."

SIGNORA CECCHETTI, ELENA'S pillar of salt, had provided more than just information on the black Mercedes. Elena had called on her at ten in the morning and finally found her way back to the front door of No. 3 Piazza Garibaldi shortly before noon. What prolonged the visit was Elena's agreement to reprimand Gianluca, the carabiniere, or at least that's how Signora Cecchetti had interpreted Elena's response. The signora had been born in Paradiso and, as she loudly told Elena (she was deaf in her right ear), she would die in Paradiso. She knew everyone, and everything about everyone, and, if Elena hadn't prevented her, she would have started at the beginning. Elena, of course, wanted to know what had happened in the square within the last few days, or weeks.

It took an hour, a coffee, and two biscotti for Elena to

drag the signora back to the present day, but when she finally managed to do so, she got an earful. The German had been a Jezebel, and nasty to boot. She once gave Signora Cecchetti the finger, simply because of the few complaints she'd made to the carabinieri about the company she was keeping. "You have to remember," she told Elena, "that she was living next door to a chapel. The things those women got up to in there were an offense in God's eyes. I even spoke to the priest about it."

Elena was tempted to ask about the priest's response, but a digression of that magnitude would've taken too much time.

"The woman keeps notes," Elena told Cenni. "She has it all written down, license-plate numbers, times of coming, times of going. It's hard to believe she's not the one in the morgue. And just one day a month she leaves her house for five hours to visit her sister in Spello, takes a taxi 'for an exorbitant sum.' What kind of luck is it that on the one day she's out, the German is murdered? Otherwise, she'd have given us the name and address of the killer, maybe even a confession."

"Perhaps luck had nothing to do with it."

Elena jumped on Cenni's suggestion. "We'd have to assume the killer is someone who lives in the square and knows Signora Cecchetti's schedule. That would eliminate Molin"—Elena refused to grant her a title—"and anyone else who doesn't live here. That's too easy."

"Not necessarily. Baudler's lived here for more than a year. She would have seen her neighbor leave the last

Wednesday of every month, dressed to kill. From what I've learned of Baudler, she made it a habit to laugh at her neighbors. She probably told everyone she knew about the spy who loved her, and the single day a month that she was free of her. I don't think the signora's visiting schedule will help us find the killer; it was just an observation."

"Here's something else she told me which should be of use. The German was having trouble with her car. On Tuesday, it wouldn't start, and the pillar of salt says Baudler gave her car the finger before giving up and returning to her house. I guess that was her primary mode of expression."

Cenni laughed. "I may yet get to like her. At least she knew how to express herself in style."

"Some style! Anyway, the signora claims that the German didn't leave the house again on Tuesday, and that her Volkswagen was still in the same place when the taxi picked the old lady up at eleven to take her to her sister's."

"The neighbor found the body at five o'clock on Wednesday afternoon. The postmortem indicates that Baudler had been dead some five hours, give or take an hour, when Falchi examined the body at eight. Counting back, let's say Baudler was killed between two and four in the afternoon. So what happened to her car? Did she drive it somewhere, say a garage, and leave it there? And if so, how did she get back home? Or did the garage pick it up after the old lady left at eleven? We should have heard something by now from one of the garages in the area. Ask around if there are any local mechanics who fix cars on the side. When you have time," he added, noting

Elena's raised eyebrows "What about the other people living in the square? Nobody saw anything?"

"Nothing, according to the carabinieri. In addition to the German, the old lady, and the neighbor who found the body, there are two couples living in the square: a man and his wife who work in Perugia in the same law office; and an accountant, who also works in Perugia, and his wife, who works in a shop in Assisi. The husband drops her off every morning and picks her up at night. They're all out of their houses by nine and none of them returns until after six."

"And the German's other visitors in the last few weeks: did the history of the world take down their license plate numbers as well?"

"Oh, yeah. An elderly gentleman, very distinguished-looking according to the signora. She likes him because he bows to her when he sees her sitting at the window, but mainly because he never parks in her spot. BMW, German plates. I called it in to Marinella two hours ago."

"So, what else did she tell you?"

"Remember the medical book yesterday, the page that fell open to a description of hermaphrodites!"

"Elena, I wish you'd stop doing drum rolls every time you have something new to tell me. Just get on with it."

"All right, then. Anita Tangassi is the hermaphrodite; and, according to Signora Cecchetti, she killed her mother, and maybe even her uncle. Is that sufficiently direct for you, Dottor Cenni?"

15

ANITA TANGASSI WAS inside the kitchen of the pink house checking through the cabinets when Cenni and Elena arrived back from lunch. She was fifteen minutes early and, from Elena's point of view, shouldn't have been in the house in the first place. She found it impossible to hide her displeasure:

"Signora, who let you inside?"

"I let myself in with my own key. It's my house."

Cenni was inclined to agree, and he also didn't want to antagonize her at the beginning of the interview—plenty of time for that later—so he asked if she'd found everything in order. That was a mistake. She snatched up the green-and-white-checkered cloth that had been covering the kitchen table and flung it to the floor.

"There, ring marks! I warned her about using coasters. And look at the scratches on the table legs. It's that cat of hers. I hope there's no one expecting me to return her deposit."

While she was throwing a minor tantrum, Cenni had a chance to observe her. She was thirty-nine, but seemed younger, perhaps because of the tantrum. She had strong, attractive features: long nose, full lips, white straight teeth, and dark eyes set wide apart. Her hair, which was black and curly, framed her face nicely. She was taller than average and had large bones. Her dress was simple, straight black skirt and white cotton shirt, sensible shoes. She had very shapely legs. As he observed her, he realized that he was looking for telltale signs that she was a hermaphrodite. He also realized that he was a fool. He'd always objected to putting labels on people, and here he was doing it to Anita Tangassi. The term *hermaphrodite* was outmoded, a way of describing a dozen or more different genital or reproductive abnormalities. He'd recently read a long article in one of the more erudite magazines about the surprising number of people who were born each year with ambiguous genitals: one of every two-thousand births, the article had said. In a small town like Paradiso with everyone's life at the disposal of every malicious gossip, where the slightest difference could be cause for ostracism, Anita Tangassi's life must have been pure hell. He wasn't surprised at the tantrum.

When they finally began the interview, Cenni was quick to reassure the woman that the purpose of "their talk" was to help the police understand more about Signora Baudler so they could find her killer. In no way did he mean to suggest that she was implicated in her tenant's murder. He also informed her that they were taping the interview.

"Standard practice," he said, reassuringly.

"*Certo!*" Tangassi replied, seemingly at ease with the police if a bit defensive about their commandeering her house: "Three days now! And I need to prepare it for another tenant. She's only paid up through May and this is already the first of June."

Elena jumped in, stopping Cenni before he could begin, to ask about the keys. "How many are there besides the one you let yourself in with?"

"Four in total. I have two and I gave her two, unless she

had some new ones made, but I doubt it. You need a card to make replacements, and I don't give that to anyone. And I want her keys back. They're expensive."

Elena noticed the frown on Cenni's face—he hated interruptions—and she spoke up again, this time to him:

"You told me last night to make a note about the keys."

"So I did. How many keys do the police have?"

"Just the one."

"Let's see if we can come up with the other one for Signora Tangassi," he said, and began again:

"Signora Tangassi, after we finish talking, I'd appreciate it if you'd accompany Inspector Ottaviani and me through the house to indicate if anything is missing or if you notice anything out of place."

"But I did that with the carabinieri on Wednesday evening," she protested.

"Yes, I know, but it would help us as well. I'd like to focus on the cellar where she was killed. But before we do that, I have a few questions". Cenni, in his long career in homicide, had encountered many different types of personality—in actuality, as many as the total number of witnesses and suspects he had interviewed in those years. Each demanded a different approach; and, within a few minutes of meeting Anita Tangassi, he'd decided to try shock. It didn't work.

"Lorenzo Vannicelli, the neighbor who found the body, did he kill her?" Cenni began.

"I don't think so," she responded, phlegmatically. "They didn't like each other's cats. But wouldn't it be easier to kill the cat?"

"We're talking about her, not her cat."

She shrugged. "No reason to kill her that I know of."

"And you, signora, did you kill her?"

She pursed her lips. "You said just a minute ago that I wasn't implicated."

"I ask this question of everyone concerned in a murder case."

"The exact opposite. Because of this murder, I can't get into my own house. My realtor told me a week ago that the German was planning to find another place to live, and I was delighted. You can ask him if you don't believe me. She refused to pay for garbage pickup, and you can see what *she* did to my furniture."

Garbage pickup, her furniture! Cenni was amazed at Signora Tangassi's ability to focus strictly on her own concerns.

"If I were to tell you that we have witnesses who claim to have seen you two arguing, what would you say?"

"That nasty old bat across the street probably told you that. She sits at her front window all day and minds everyone else's business but her own. If she doesn't see something interesting to talk about, she makes it up. I haven't been inside my own house since the month after *she* moved in. *She* mailed me the rent on the first day of every month, and when I had utility bills, I'd put them in the mail. Every now and then, if I were walking by the house, I'd slip them under the door."

"You're saying you haven't been inside your house in more than a year?" Cenni responded incredulously.

"I pass by a few times a week, particularly in spring. It's

the shortest distance between where I live and my grove of
olive trees. And sometimes I visit Lorenzo. But if that old
bat across the square says I've been inside this house, she's
lying!"

Cenni had to admire the way in which she'd skirted
around his statement that she'd been seen arguing with
the German. He tried another tack:

"Signora Cecchetti was away on the day of the murder.
It's rather a coincidence that someone murdered Signora
Baudler on the only day that your neighbor was not sitting
at her window. Perhaps the killer was someone who knew
that Signora Cecchetti was not at home the last Wednesday
of every month."

"Which is everyone. She's been doing it since I was a
child, and she makes a production of it too, let me tell
you. You'd have to be deaf, dumb, and blind not to
notice."

"What about the back door, signora? Do you have keys
for that as well?"

"The door's locked, and the key's been missing for
years. I told her if she wanted the lock changed, I'd take
care of it, but it would cost a hundred euros. She refused!
And if you've seen the jungle out back, you'd know she
never used that door. There's a dirt road in the back of the
house, but it's been overgrown for years. Nobody uses it
any more."

"And there's a large spider web over the door at the
moment," Cenni commented, looking at Elena as he said it.

Elena, grinning, responded with a prepared speech:
"Spiders are well known to spin their webs quickly and with

great diligence. Two, maybe three hours to spin a web the size we found down in the cellar. If, however, the web has bugs and flies in it, this may indicate it's been there for a while. Or, it may not."

"You've been doing your spider homework, Inspector," Cenni said, smiling. "How many bugs does a spider eat in a day?"

For the first time since they'd found her in the kitchen checking out the cabinets, Anita Tangassi showed some softening of expression, even, he thought, a hint of a smile. He'd been waiting for just such a moment:

"Signora, your name is very familiar to me. Are you the Anita Tangassi who found the body of her best friend in 1978?"

Tangassi's body stiffened. The look she gave Cenni was venomous. "I don't want to talk about that, and I don't have to. Lorenzo said I never had to talk about it again." She sounded and looked very much like a recalcitrant child.

Cenni decided it would be unwise to continue this line of questioning, although he was even more convinced that Anita Tangassi knew something about the Lanese murders beyond what she'd admitted to in her original interview in 1978. He asked her a few more questions about Jarvinia Baudler.

"Did Signora Baudler leave her door unlocked when she was at home?"

"I don't know."

"Did Signora Baudler have many visitors?"

"I don't know. Ask the nosy bat across the street."

"Did Signora Baudler pay her bills on time?"

"The ones she paid, she paid on time."

"Did Signora Baudler tell you why she was leaving?"

"*She* didn't tell me; she told my realtor."

"Did Signora Baudler have anyone living with her?"

With this question, he touched a chord.

"When I rented the house to her, she claimed she was alone. Then, as soon as I signed a lease, she brought in another woman. Black, too. Probably illegal. Going around telling everyone *she* was a diplomat to impress them. A criminal, more likely!"

"Did she get on with the people in town?" he asked, fairly sure the answer would be *no*. He was surprised.

"With the old men she did; she was always buttering them up, buying them grappa. Even the drunks, telling dirty jokes, making up lies."

He'd kept the delicate question to last. "Signora Baudler's clitoris was removed after her death. What do you think about that?" he asked, phrasing the question to elicit some type of response beyond her usual abbreviated answer.

"It's disgusting! Filthy-minded! I don't want to talk about it," she said, and turned away from his gaze.

He concluded from her response that she'd already known about the mutilation. Her reaction was one of disgust, not of surprise. Whether she was the person responsible was still to be determined.

The significant facts that Cenni had elicited from Anita Tangassi were her obvious dislike of Jarvinia Baudler and her extreme reluctance to talk about the earlier murders.

He found the latter unusual. Most people can't shut up about the crimes they've witnessed, and the more grue-some the crime, the more they need to talk. But his expe-rience with children was limited, and he acknowledged to himself that children might react differently, even thirty years later as adults.

Touring the house with Signora Tangassi was a lesson in parsimony. No matter which floor they visited, she had a complaint, and it always involved money and what it would cost her to repair the damage, none of which was apparent to either Cenni or Elena. In the cellar she really let loose. Every empty bottle and dirty jam jar was counted; every half-empty can of paint was lifted to measure its contents; and every box was checked for tampering.

"Someone's been into my periwinkle dishes," Tangassi exclaimed while examining one of the boxes. She spent the next ten minutes kneeling on the dirty floor, unwrap-ping each dish from its protective covering and holding it up to the light. Elena spent the same ten minutes making strangling gestures behind the signora's back, while the commissario devoted his time to examining the back door. The spider web that had covered it the previous day had been rent in two and the bolt was open. Someone besides the police had recently visited the murder site.

16

SIGNOR VANNICELLI ARRIVED promptly at three o'clock, as Elena had instructed. Even though the door was unlocked, he waited for Elena to let him in, and that pleased her. As she told Piero later that evening, "He has respect for the police." Anita Tangassi had annoyed Elena just enough to make Signor Vannicelli appear cooperative, even before he demonstrated it.

Lorenzo Vannicelli, the neighbor who'd discovered Jarvinia Baudler's body, was a retired science teacher. He was sixty-five, of medium build, with dark wavy hair and a pleasant manner; and, as Cenni was to find out in short order, he also headed the *Rifondazione Comunista* party in Paradiso. It wasn't that *il professore* advertised his politics to whomever he met at the moment he met them, but rather that they crowded into his every sentence, whether he wanted them to or not.

While Elena was in the kitchen setting up the recorder before the interview began, Cenni asked Vannicelli to accompany him to the cellar to show him where he'd found the body. The cellar was on two levels: the larger level, the one in which Jarvinia Baudler had been killed, occupied the length and width of the house, with a stone stairway at the front end which led to a cave located under the street. The lower level, the cave, had once been part of the catacombs that ran under the streets of the old part of Paradiso. It had been sealed off from the main tunnel in the early part of the last century.

"The bank is in this part of the town, and I've often thought how easy it would be to get into the bank's vault with some quiet explosives by going through the catacombs. But then maybe I watch too many films," Vannicelli said, forgetting for the moment that Cenni was a commissario in the civil police.

"Do you know for sure that the bank has its vault in the basement?" Cenni asked. "Nowadays a good many banks have their vaults on the street floor, although I don't suppose it would be that difficult to get to the street floor from the basement, but then you'd still have to blast through the vault door. I really think it's easier to just come in through the street, a lot less digging. And at one or two o'clock in the morning, who's looking out their windows?"

"Signora Cecchetti!" they both said simultaneously.

"Good point that, about going in through the front door," Vannicelli said when they'd stopped laughing. "I'll have to remember it."

"Try to wait until I've retired," Cenni responded. "Otherwise I might have to remember this conversation."

Their discussion about where Baudler had been killed was more serious and at one point quite testy. Cenni asked Vannicelli about Signora Cecchetti's assertion that Anita Tangassi had killed her mother and maybe even her uncle.

"The police are all Fascists under the skin," Vannicelli responded in anger. "You can't help it, can you? We'll shake you all out of your trees as soon as we're really back in power." Mixing his metaphors, Cenni thought. He never took offense at such talk; it was, after all, just talk. The Left in Italy, with its hundred or so parties, couldn't even agree on a name, let alone policy. And besides, he himself had voted *L'Ulivo* in the last election.

"I wouldn't let Inspector Ottaviani hear you talk like that. She might take offense," Cenni responded. "Let's just say that Signora Cecchetti is a gossip, and I want to put her insinuations to rest."

"Anita was with me when it happened, out in the garden. We were cutting some basil. We both saw her mother, Marta, fall. She suffered from vertigo and shouldn't have been out on the terrace. Her doctor had warned her often enough, but she was a fanatic about cleaning."

"And the uncle. What's that all about?"

"Orazio ate some bad mushrooms. He was always out in the woods looking for new varieties. He fancied himself a naturalist and was convinced that he could distinguish edibles from those that were poisonous. He had some strange theories, as well; he claimed it was possible to develop an immunity to even the most lethal mushrooms if eaten in minuscule amounts over a period of time. And he would search the woods for hallucinogenic mushrooms. He took far too many chances. I'm the one who found his body. He'd been dead for at least twenty-four hours. The carabinieri found a basket of little brown mushrooms of the genus *Galerina* in the cellar. There was a postmortem, and the finding was death by misadventure, or, more specifically, death by the toxin *amanitin*. All of this is documented, by the way."

"And Signora Tangassi? Where was she when all this was happening?"

"Anita was in Rome, in the hospital. That also is documented."

"I'm sorry if I offended you, Signor Vannicelli. Any time the police are investigating a murder, we're also dealing with rumors, vendettas, insinuations, what have you. We'd like to ignore the busybodies of the world, but in murder cases we don't have that luxury."

At the end of Vannicelli's interview, he and Cenni were friendly enemies. Vannicelli answered all questions concerning his part in finding the body of Jarvinia Baudler willingly, without hesitation.

"I heard Tommaso crying close to four-thirty, which is when I crawled through the window and found her body. I took Tommaso home and called the carabinieri from my house, about five o'clock, give or take a few minutes." Concerning the way she was dressed, he was very specific. "Whenever I saw her in the square or outside watering her plants, she had on pants and sensible, low-heeled shoes. When I found her body, she was wearing a dress and high heels. I don't think she wore those around the house. She must have been either coming or going."

When Cenni asked why it was necessary to climb through the cellar window to reclaim his cat, he was very direct.

"When she first came to live here, we became friends. On the really hot evenings last summer, we'd sit out on the wall of the fountain to cool off and share a bottle of wine. She spoke beautiful Italian, was intelligent and very funny. I liked her. And then my cat Tommaso jumped her female, and the friendship evaporated. What she thought would happen to a female in heat in the streets of Paradiso is beyond me, but she actually called the carabinieri to complain. And she was always throwing her weight around, claiming to be a diplomat, demanding extras, including discounts from the local stores. You name it. If I'd told her that Tommaso was trapped inside, she'd have made a huge fuss. I couldn't be bothered, and her car was gone from the front, so I decided to climb through the window."

"You must have had a shock," Cenni said, letting Vannicelli respond as he wished.

He frowned. "Very ugly that, very ugly! I hate seeing people humiliated and degraded, even bad people. Positioning her like that, sitting her up leaning against the stairs, with her dress wrapped around her waist and her legs spread apart, totally exposed, was degrading. I'll help you if possible, although I don't imagine there's much I can do."

"What about visitors? And the woman she was living with? Anything you can tell us there?"

"In the beginning she had quite a few visitors, mostly women; but after the black woman moved in, it was mainly the two of them. Occasionally I'd see a man visiting her. Not Italian. German probably, an older man. He drove a BMW. He was around less than a week ago, if I remember correctly. But you can always ask Signora Cecchetti. She keeps a ledger."

"What about the black woman? Did they fight? Do you know when and why she moved out?"

"If I saw her outside the house and she was alone, she'd always smile and say hello. When she was with Baudler, she kept her eyes down and acted as if she didn't see me. She seemed nice enough and was a real looker. It's hard to figure out what she was doing with a woman in her seventies. I last saw her maybe three weeks ago. But I don't think she was still living with the German. Before that, I hadn't seen her in months. I was outside in the front pruning plants, and their front door was open. Their voices were loud, but they were yelling in English, so I had no idea what they were saying. The black woman got into a black Mercedes that was parked over by the belvedere. I didn't get a good look at the driver as they left by the back road, but it was definitely a man. Oddly enough, she got into the back seat, not the front, as if he was a hired driver."

"What about the back door? You have access to that from the back garden. Did you let yourself in yesterday or today, perhaps to look for your cat?"

"Tommaso has too much to occupy him at home these days to go wandering. I took the German's cat home with me. Besides, the police boarded up the hole in the window, so there's no way he can get in."

"So you weren't in here late yesterday or today?"

"No. And I was out in the garden today until I left for my doctor's appointment. I would have seen if anyone went inside. Why, has someone been using the back door?"

Cenni didn't reply, but he was convinced that Vannicelli was telling the truth.

"Have you seen anyone using the back entrance since the German moved in?"

"No, and if I had I would have warned them off. That road has been off-limits to traffic, car and foot, for more than ten years now."

Cenni knew his next question would trigger an explosion, so he'd waited until the end of the interview. "About Signora Tangassi, is she the same woman who was involved in the murders of a mother and a child in 1978?" He had used the word *involved* deliberately.

"There you go again. Give an inch, take a mile! Anita wasn't involved in any murders. She found the bodies, a horrific experience for a nine-year-old. And don't you go talking about it to her, or I'll use whatever influence the party has to get you written up. The Right was voted out of office this year, or didn't you notice?"

"*Calmati,* Signore," Elena said, turning off the recorder. "The commissario didn't mean anything offensive by his question."

Cenni still hadn't figured out the relationship between Vannicelli and Anita Tangassi. He decided to send Elena back to visit Signora Cecchetti.

Before Vannicelli could walk out the door in a huff, he asked him one last question. "Signore, how are the cats?"

"Early days yet, but I think we'll be having a litter in August. Shall I save one for you?" he asked, turning to look directly at Elena.

Book Two

The Sparrow and the Peacock

I

THE SPASM OF coughing stopped and Queenie returned to her previous activity, counting her money. The vineyards had been particularly successful in the past two years, and she reaffirmed her previous decision. She would sell to *Marchesi Antinori*. She no longer had the energy to oversee operations, and who knew better than she that absentee ownership never worked. She had tried it forty years earlier, and it had been a disaster. All employees steal money given the opportunity, human nature being what it is. And Italians are particularly skilled at it, given their extensive experience in cheating the government of taxes. Not that Queenie blamed them; she did the same herself. In October, she had rented the attic apartment to an American couple, the trusting kind who'd never dream that the Countess Molin, a descendant of the Medici, would cheat the government of a few hundred euros in taxes. But the euros add up no matter how many you may already have, and Queenie had always preferred addition to subtraction.

She laughed out loud thinking of the American couple, particularly the woman. They were so anxious to please, *delighted, so happy, thrilled,* to rent an apartment from a countess. Queenie helped it along, as she always did, playing the great lady to perfection, even inviting them to afternoon tea. That invitation alone ensured another two hundred euros a month for the tiny rooms in the attic, and although they'd looked a bit surprised when her realtor explained that the lease was written for five hundred euros less than the actual rent, they'd signed it quickly enough. The husband looked as though he might protest, but the wife grabbed his hand and squeezed it hard. Queenie knew her pigeons.

Compound interest, rates of return, yields, relative risk, coupons, the vocabulary of investing was as music to her ears. When the doctors, four of them, told Queenie that her lung cancer had advanced, that with aggressive treatment and some luck she might last another six months, her greatest pleasure had become her greatest regret. So much money and property, accumulated with such devotion, and no one that she cared to leave it to. A sacrificial waste, she thought, taking another drag on her cigarette, realizing perhaps for the first time in seventy-seven years that she *really* would have to leave it behind. Even now as she lay encapsulated within a cocoon of pillows and bed hangings, she had daydreams of taking it with her, like the Pharaohs.

For a full week she had retired completely from the world, abed in her seventeenth-century four-poster with velvet hangings, legal and financial documents piled high around her. The first three days of that fateful week had

been devoted to mourning, something no one would do
when Queenie was dead. In the next three days she ran the
household staff off their feet, not to mention her Italian
bankers and American brokers, mailing and faxing and
posting bank statements, financial reports, contracts,
prospectuses, codicils, and testaments. On the seventh
day, Queenie made her decision. She would divest herself
of all her property, other than the Palazzo Molin. In his
will, her father had affirmed over all other affirmations
that the palazzo must stay within the family. Saverio Volpe,
her do-gooder cousin on her mother's side and her only
remaining family, would inherit the palazzo unless she
could find a loophole. Queenie had never begrudged
spending money when the outcome was important, so
she'd asked Carlo Fabretti, the wiliest lawyer in Venice, to
devise a plan. And he had, a magnificent plan. After her
death, Palazzo Molin would house a foundation to honor
Queenie's father for his bravery during the war. Saverio
would have a difficult time getting that bequest overturned
by the courts. Venetians love war memorials, and they
love even more the drama of seeing one of their own get
done out of money. The foundation would be the largest
in the Veneto, and she would be the talk of Venice. She
took a last skimpy drag on her cigarette, now burned
down to the filter, and sighed with pleasure.

She fingered a long strand of natural pearls, perfectly
matched, a family heirloom that appeared in Grazia
Molin's wedding portrait, painted in 1680 by Bombelli,
and not worn since Queenie's mother was a bride. She
admired the delicate ovals of light and thought of Juliet,

who loved the pearls and who always asked to try them on whenever they were out of the safe. Just this once, Juliet had begged a month ago when they had attended the opera, but Queenie had refused. The pearls were priceless, not for the likes of Juliet. All of Queenie's lovers had had their price, and Juliet's was higher than most. Of the scores that had passed through her life, some lasting weeks, others years, just two had loved Queenie. Queenie had loved only one in return.

2

"THE SPARROW" AND "the peacock" is what Queenie's father had called them. She had been the sparrow, of course, Jarvinia the peacock. "Sparrow" was the nickname her father had given her, as he'd never liked her baptismal name of Marcella; and until he had called her best friend "peacock," she'd been very pleased. She had been devoted to her father.

After Marcella was born, her mother had been very sick. Nannetta, who'd nursed Marcella when she was a baby and who'd stayed on, and on, told Marcella when she was seven that her mother had once tried to throw her into the Cannaregio Canal. She'd been crying for more than an hour when her mother lifted her out of her crib. Her father, who had been in the room at the time, thought her mother was finally coming out of her depression, and he watched with love as she walked out onto the *loggia* with their infant daughter. He stopped her just as she was about to fling Marcella into the canal. Her mother never did emerge from her depression, and Marcella never did learn to love her.

It was always, and only, Marcella and her father, until Jarvinia came along. Every Sunday, father and daughter would begin the day at the Caffè Inglese. Her father would drink a *caffè corretto,* and she would have a *caffè latte* and a cream puff. Afterward they would take long walks through Venice, and he would tell her stories about the families that had made Venice the greatest seafaring city-state in the world, pointing out the various *palazzi* in which they had lived and describing each of the buildings and its style of architecture in detail. He'd also talk incessantly about honor and Marcella's obligation to keep Palazzo Molin and herself within the Venetian family. He had already decided that she should marry Saverio Volpe, her second cousin on her mother's side. He would finish by reminding her that Palazzo Molin and the Molin family, with the arms of four doges on its escutcheon, were without equal. He never mentioned their Spanish blood or that Grazia, the Spanish upstart, had purchased her way into the Venetian nobility, and Marcella, wisely, never brought it up. Their walks were long and exhausting, and she loved them and worshipped him.

Their solitary walks ended soon after the peacock came into their lives. Jarvinia was one of several Germans at Marcella's school, but she preferred to mix with Venetians. When Jarvinia first enrolled, when she was twelve, she wore a heavy brace and dragged her left leg at an awkward angle. She said it was the result of an automobile accident, but Marcella found out later that it was actually caused by polio. Other girls of Jarvinia's age were ashamed of their smallest blemishes, imagined or real, but Jarvinia treated hers as a badge of privilege and if the other girls left her behind during their walks, she'd scream after them, "Hold up, you bitches." Any other student would have spent days in detention for using foul language, but even the nuns seemed to favor Jarvinia. She wasn't beautiful but she had something special and everyone knew it. So Marcella felt particularly sought-after when Jarvinia chose her as her best friend. They were both at the top of their class, but in different subjects. Marcella excelled in mathematics and the sciences, Jarvinia in languages and art. Art was Jarvinia's grand passion.

When did the sparrow sense that she was losing her father's love to the peacock? Probably not at first. Jarvinia charmed everyone when she wasn't cursing them, and Marcella's father was as easily charmed as the next man or woman. Then, of course, there was Jarvinia's passion for the Tiepolo frescoes. No person of any importance ever entered Palazzo Molin who was not given the grand tour of America, Europe, Asia, and Africa by the Count. The four public rooms off the grand salon on the *piano nobile* were famous throughout Europe for their frescoed ceilings. Marcella was rightfully proud that they adorned the Palazzo Molin, but to herself alone she acknowledged that they bored her. There was no science in them, and thus no truth, and that irritated her. Jarvinia would gaze at them for hours and then talk to Marcella's father about them at length.

Three days before Jarvinia's thirteenth birthday, the doctors agreed that she could go without her brace once or twice a week, and the count decided to take his daughter and her best friend to a celebratory lunch at the Caffè Florian. Jarvinia was well developed, even at thirteen. She borrowed one of her mother's outfits, including a pair of open-toed sandals. She wore a green straw hat with white peonies decorating the brim, and a green print dress, flared at the hem and cut low and tight across the bosom. She wobbled when she walked, and whenever she thought she was going to topple over she'd laugh and grab hold of the count's arm. That was the day that the count bestowed the nickname "peacock" on her. It was also the day that both father and daughter fell in love.

ON THE DAY that Jarvinia had overheard Marcella instruct Nannetta to address her as *contessa,* she had begun calling Marcella "Queen of the Adriatic." Soon, she had shortened it to Queenie until all their school friends, and even Marcella, forgot her real name.

"So, that's the full unbridled story, sex in all its lovely and unlovely aspects." That was how Jarvinia wound up her lecture to Marcella on the glories and pitfalls of married sex. Marcella had just turned fourteen and Jarvinia, who was a month younger, knew everything there was to know about begetting babies. Marcella had used the word "beget" and Jarvinia had rolled around on Marcella's bed laughing. "'Beget'! Oh, my dear Queenie, there's no begetting about it, just a whole lot of fucking."

Queenie was horrified by Jarvinia's description of the wedding night and said she'd refuse even if it meant never having babies. Jarvinia had laughed at her. "There's more than one way to have sex, and it's not always so gruesome. Do you want me to show you?" she asked, pushing Queenie down on the bed. Queenie held her breath. "Go ahead," she said.

Jarvinia jumped off the bed. "You little hypocrite. You're willing, so long as you get to play obedient victim. Go ahead yourself! I bet you do all the time, and you'd do it quick enough with Papa if he asked."

The aftermath of that exchange was that the friends stopped speaking, but that didn't stop Jarvinia from visiting the palazzo, the frescoes, or Queenie's father. The count didn't seem to notice, or didn't care, that his daughter was not speaking to her best friend. Queenie could hear them talking together for hours in the America room. Her father had decided that the frescoes needed refurbishing, and he was consulting his daughter's thirteen-year-old friend as to the method. On Jarvinia's fourteenth birthday, the count took her to the Caffè Florian, but this time for dinner. Queenie was left at home.

Felicia, another friend from school, also at the Florian for a family celebration, had seen them together and told every girl in the fourth form and even some of the nuns about it. Jarvinia walked around school as though she owned the world, and Queenie hid in the bathroom and cried. Felicia said that her parents were disgusted, that they'd almost chided the count for his behavior but decided not to. Of course they decided not to. The count was on the board of the oldest bank in Venice, and his business interests were considerable. Queenie tried not to hear Felicia's stories, but how could she not?

The count had chosen a table lit by candles in a far cor-ner of the main dining room looking out on San Marco. They drank champagne and Jarvinia spoke very loudly. She had taken off her brace and was wearing high heels. Felicia said Jarvinia looked ridiculous. "She could have passed for twenty in all that makeup. And she didn't have her hair pulled back at her neck as she usually does—it was hanging down to her waist. She's so vain about her hair. My mother said it's probably dyed, just like her mother's. Her mother lives with a man who's half English and half German. My father says he'll work for anyone with the right price and that her mother will do the same." Every-one in school knew what that meant.

Queenie knew it was true about her father and Jarvinia. Her mother was in the hospital again, but even when she came home for a few odd months every year, she had no real presence in their lives. Queenie wondered sometimes if her mother even knew who she was. Nannetta hated Jarvinia, mainly because Jarvinia made fun of her.

It was Nannetta who told Queenie that Jarvinia had been to her father's bedroom, four times. "She's the devil's spawn. We need a priest in here to fumigate."

3

DEATH IS A waiting game, Queenie thought philosophi-cally. The waiting is just more intense when you have a penciled-in appointment. She turned off the light, pushed aside some papers, and slid down under the covers. She couldn't see the ceiling directly above her, but her favorite section of the America fresco was visible. Of the four frescoes, this had been Jarvinia's favorite, the reason Queenie had chosen to move her bed into this room when she could no longer climb stairs. It had taken Queenie sixty years to understand why Jarvinia would gaze at it for hours, but she understood now. Jarvinia had imagined herself as the woman in the feathered headdress riding a crocodile, her passions wild and free in the natural, unfettered New World.

She stared into the fire at the other end of the room. Just a few flickering blue flames. The fire would die down soon if Nannetta didn't bring in more logs. Jarvinia had always loved a ferocious fire. She had been the only person who could talk the count into building one in the America room. He was afraid smoke would damage the ceiling. Strange, she thought, how oddly we shape our destinies; he who lives by the sword dies by the sword. She pulled the covers up to her chin, knocking papers to the floor, and wondered if tonight she'd dream again of eating cream puffs at the Caffè Inglese.

Book Three

Venice 2007

I

THE TRAIN JERKED forward a short distance, then stopped, causing Cenni to spill his thimbleful of coffee. "*Vaffanculo!*" he uttered, just loud enough for the matron sitting across from him to overhear. She looked up from her magazine in surprise. "*Scusi,* Signora," he said, "but I really needed that coffee."

Another twenty minutes at least before the food trolley makes its return trip, Cenni thought mournfully, as he settled back into his seat and smiled again at the woman seated across from him. Milanese, he decided, judging from her clothes (expensive) and her expression (haughty). Husband is probably a fan of Milan, not cock of the walk this week, though, not after Juve scored the winning goal on Sunday in extra time, he thought vindictively. The woman smiled back and shyly looked away. He watched as she twisted her wedding band around her finger. Maybe he was wrong about her. Maybe she was just nervous. She probably needs a coffee as much as I do, he decided, and smiled in sympathy.

Another forward jerk and the train started up again, and this time it kept going. He checked his watch. They had waited in the station for the train from Milan to arrive and had departed Bologna ten minutes late, but with any luck they'd arrive in Venice no later than four, and he'd still have time to interview Marcella Molin and Saverio Volpe and get back to Bologna for the night. He'd return to Perugia in the morning. It'd been a long two days, with a particularly tedious start this morning. The questore had insisted on a meeting at nine o'clock, even though Alex had informed him that he had nothing new to report. Then the mad rush to catch the 9:58 train from Perugia to Venice, and the main business of the day was still before him. The countryside flashed by, and he drifted back some thirty-odd years, to his first solo train ride.

IT HAD BEEN a hot, dreary, aimless summer. He and Renato had been stuck in Perugia since school let out, mainly because their mother was quarreling with their grandmother and had refused to let the twins spend any time with her at the family's farm on the outskirts of Bevagna. Then Renato got the mumps and was put to bed, and Alex was packed off for two weeks to his mother's uncle in Bologna.

Zio Riccardo, who refused to answer to "uncle," lived in the center of Bologna, in a cavernous apartment on the third floor of a converted palazzo. He was a writer of inflammatory pamphlets, an implacable Leftist, which had apparently escaped his mother's notice, perhaps because her uncle belonged to no registered political party and echoed no official party line, or more likely because he had money and no wife or child to leave it to. "Your mother's a throwback to the Neanderthals," Riccardo had told Alex when the nine-year-old had piously quoted his mother on the importance of personal hygiene. Riccardo never washed his hands after he flushed, when he could flush, as the three toilets in the apartment were almost always backed up. Alex had pictured his mother in a leopard skin wielding a club and laughed. Another day, Alex had quoted his mother on the evils of cursing, and Riccardo responded by calling her "a frustrated nun and a courtesan of the pope," a paradox too complicated for a ten-year-old to grasp. Alex had pictured his mother in a nun's habit wielding a crucifix and hadn't laughed.

"You're here to secure my money when I kick off," Riccardo had told Alex amicably a few days later, asking his great-nephew if he wanted another coffee. They were sitting in the corner café where Riccardo spent most of his days and nights debating all comers on sex, politics, and religion. At the end of one of those debates, Alex, who'd not yet learned *not* to echo other people when he had something to say for himself, had quoted his paternal grandmother on the evils of religion. "Now, there's a woman who likes to sweat in bed," Riccardo had responded, grinning. "I love those Swedes." Riccardo had met Hanna Falkenberg only once, at the wedding of his niece ten years earlier, but he worshipped Anita Ekberg, and therefore all Swedish women. He had a poster of the

Swedish movie star, wading in a Roman fountain, pinned above his bed. When Alex left Bologna to return to Perugia at the end of the two weeks, he was carrying a fistful of lire to spend on the train. "On nothing sensible, mind you," his uncle had warned, "just coffee and sweets." Riccardo had totaled up a thousand lire each time Alex said *vaffanculo* on their last day together. "That'll teach your mother to treat me like a babysitter," he'd said when he handed Alex the money.

His uncle died four years later, but the visit had achieved something of his mother's purpose. Riccardo left his apartment, his money, and his inflammatory pamphlets to his great-nephew, in trust until he turned thirty. "It's not exactly what I had in mind, but at least it stayed in the family," Alex overheard his mother say to a friend after the funeral.

"*Scusi,* Signore." Alex looked up and saw the matron that he'd slandered in his thoughts standing over him. He had fallen asleep. "We're here," she said, smiling. They alighted together, and he offered to buy her a coffee in the station bar, but she refused graciously. As she walked away, he called out to her. "*Scusi,* Signora, but who does your husband root for?" She turned, looked puzzled for a moment, and then said, "You mean football, I assume. Milan usually, but I'm a Juve fan myself."

HE DOWNED TWO coffees at the station bar instead of the usual short one. It was surprisingly good coffee and the first positive thing he could remember about Venice since a school trip there at the age of seven. He and Renato had detached themselves from their class to ride the *vaporetti* for four hours, terrorizing passengers, changing lines whenever a deck hand threatened to throw them overboard. They had finally become bored and disembarked at San Marco where, after climbing to the top of the bell tower twice and screaming at the top of their lungs to those below, they had settled into chasing pigeons from one end of the square to the other. An officer in the carabinieri had collared them late in the afternoon and dragged them to the police station, where Signor Lancioli was waiting. He had stayed behind to look for them while the rest of the class went on to Milan.

The fun they'd had that day lost its flavor when they were grounded for a month. By listening through the heating grate, he'd heard his mother abusing him to his father: "I think we should send Alex to military school. Renato only does these things when Alex drags him along. He broke his leg last summer jumping off the barn roof because Alex dared him." She never lets anything go, he remembered thinking. That might also have been the occasion on which he resolved never to marry, a resolution he abandoned less than a month after meeting Chiara in their first year at university.

Chiara had dragged him to Venice the second time, in lieu of going to Elbe to scuba-dive with friends, and he'd made her pay dearly. His complaints were incessant and petty: the lamb, the polenta, and the wine were vastly inferior to anything you'd get in Umbria, and vastly overpriced. He hated fish and refused to try any Venetian specialties, and their pension had bedbugs, although

Chiara insisted that he'd made that up. He had saved the
bill from the Caffè Florian for two coffees and an ice
cream. "A family of ten could live on this for two months,"
he told anyone who'd listen. He still hated Venice, but for
a different reason: that had been their last trip together,
and it could have been his warmest memory of Chiara.
Instead, it was her last memory of him, a selfish sodding
bastard.

THE CROWDS WERE exactly as he remembered, loud,
pushy, and self-advertising. One woman, with an Oxford
accent, was particularly audible. "Definitely Cannaregio.
San Marco is strictly for the tourists," she shouted back at
the hàrried woman who followed in her wake. "We want
Linea Quaranta Due," she added, throwing in the Italian to
impress her friend. It wouldn't impress the natives, as her
accent made Cenni wince. Can't afford San Marco, Cenni
concluded, as he gracefully dodged the hustlers pushing
cheap hotels, visits to glass factories, and boat rides around
the lagoon. He was headed to *Ponte delle Guglie,* a stop on
the same line, and observed that the woman doing the talking carried a small weekend case while her companion
inexpertly balanced two huge suitcases mounted on a roller
cart. A porter offered his services, but the imperious one
dismissed him and said *sotto voce* to the other, "They steal
you blind," a remark he found unreasonably irritating,
considering that he had made it often enough to Chiara.

They reached their destination just after the deck crew
had closed the gates. The waterbus was about to depart.
Cenni pushed ahead of the two women.

"*Polizia,*" he said.

The mariner shrugged his shoulders as though he didn't believe it but didn't really care and opened the gate so Cenni could enter. He tried to close the gate again but the English women pushed right past him. He shrugged and let them board.

Cenni's destination was just one stop from the station, so he remained on the open deck and thought again of Chiara, who had refused to shelter in the cabin no matter how ferocious the weather. He and Renato had loved riding the boats when they were seven, but Chiara had been twenty-two when they'd visited Venice, and she had loved the *vaporetti* more than the most excitable child. Even during a squall, she'd lean precipitously into the wind, calling out the names of poets and painters and pointing to the buildings in which they had lived.

"I'm going to live in Venice before I die," she'd said on their last day.

"Not as my wife," he had replied.

"I never heard anything so outrageous! What about him?" Cenni tried to ignore the autocratic tones of the English woman who was standing behind him until he realized that she was quarreling with one of the crew and referring to him.

"*Che cosa c'è?*" Cenni asked the man.

"The English ladies don't want to pay their fares and they keep pointing to you, but I don't know what they're saying."

Cenni addressed the two women: "Is there a problem?" The companion seemed relieved when Cenni spoke to them in English, but the leader seemed to consider it her right.

"He wants eighteen euros for traveling one stop: six for me, six for my friend, and six for our luggage. Now I ask—"

Cenni stopped listening when he realized that the *vaporetto* had halted in mid-canal just a few hundred yards from the Ponte delle Guglie. An unusually wide transport barge was approaching from the opposite direction, and all traffic in the canal had to wait for it to pass under the bridge. Another waterbus, also traveling north, was idling some ten meters from theirs, and many of its passengers had crowded against the rails to see what was happening. Policemen have a notorious dislike of gawkers, so Alex was amused to find that, without thinking, he had joined the other passengers at the railing. Directly across from him on the adjacent vessel, tightly pressed between two men, a woman leaned into the wind. She had straight black hair cut to her shoulders and a face that was etched in sorrow. It was twenty years since he'd last seen Chiara, and he would have known her anywhere.

2

HE HEARD A muffled shout behind him and the whirring of the engine, and they began to move. The *vaporetto* that had idled next to theirs was already under the bridge, headed toward its next stop. Years ago, in a gunfight with car thieves, Cenni had seen a rookie cop freeze for fewer than fifteen seconds, just long enough for him to die, and

Piero had once described to him a condition called sleep paralysis, where a person wakes from a deep sleep to find that he can't move any of his limbs. Cenni wasn't sure what had just happened to him, but he had looked at Chiara for a minute, perhaps longer, and been unable to say or do anything, not even raise his hand or call out. And then she was gone from the railing, and so were the two men in the dark suits who had surrounded her.

They were drawing near to the landing dock. Cenni grabbed the sailor by his arm and demanded to know where the other boat was going.

"You mean the DM?" the crewman asked, shaking him off.

Cenni nodded yes, remembering the two large black letters painted within an orange circle.

"*Diretto Murano*. No stops before Murano."

"And this boat, where does it go?" Cenni demanded, with no attempt at civility.

"Here," he said motioning to the dock and the passengers waiting to board. "After that: Crea, Sant'Alvise, Madonna dell'Orto, Fundamente Nove, Cimitero San Michele, Murano Colonna, Murano Serenella, Murano Venier, Murano Museo," he said, calling out names as though reciting a litany to the Virgin. "Five stops between here and Murano," he added, just in case his interlocutor couldn't count.

"Don't let those people board, and tell the other passengers this is the last stop," Cenni said with some heat. "I need to get to Murano now."

The mariner who'd begun throwing ropes around the

steel beams on the dock turned and looked at Cenni in disgust.

"Signore, I was very patient when you pushed your way onto my boat at the Ferrovia playing policeman, but now you go too far." He nodded toward the front cabin. "I will call my captain!"

"*Polizia di Stato,*" Cenni snapped, this time pulling out his wallet and displaying his badge, "and I'm commandeering this boat for police use."

Three passengers were lined up to disembark and one of them, an elderly woman carrying a small dog in a basket, said something in dialect that sounded nasty.

"'*Cosa?*"

Cenni turned to find a giant of a man in a stained captain's hat standing behind him. Before he could reply, the old lady repeated her nasty comment, this time to the giant.

"*Calmati, calmati,* Signora," the giant responded, and then, to Cenni, "Why are you harassing my crew?"

Cenni repeated what he had just told the sailor.

The giant looked at Cenni, then at his credentials, and then to the heavens. He didn't bless himself, which under the circumstances was fortunate, as Cenni was about to explode.

"Commissario, even empty of passengers, this old tub could never catch the DM. Come," he said pointing to his cabin. "We'll call ahead to the police on Murano. They'll meet the DM when it docks and arrest your criminal. We can also call ahead for a police launch to meet you at Sant'Alvise. With luck, you might get to Murano before the DM docks."

To the sailor, in Veneziano, he said, "Let the signora's doggie go home to his dinner and board the passengers. We're behind schedule."

The captain's admonition to the signora to calm herself worked on Cenni as well. The commissario enjoyed a reputation among his colleagues for judicious, reasoned policing, and his reason had returned. In the seconds it took them to walk to the cabin, Cenni rethought his first wild attempt at doing something, anything. What if the woman at the rail was an illusion, a reflection of his longing for Chiara? No! Chiara's hair had been the color of corn silk. The mind plays subtle tricks, but he could never have imagined Chiara with black hair.

Where had she been? Who were the two men standing next to her? Twenty years had passed since she had disappeared; she'd made no claims on her inheritance, or on him. What if the kidnapping had been a ruse, a desperate attempt to escape obsessively doting parents and a lover too selfish to give her a few happy days in Venice? He shook his head in disbelief. No sane person cuts off her own finger to convince her parents or her lover that she's been kidnapped. If the two men on the *vaporetto* were her original captors, they might kill her if the police came at them with guns. Anyone monstrous enough to cut off a young girl's finger and post it to her parents wouldn't stick at murder. And although his mind didn't want to go there, he was forced to acknowledge that she might have her own reasons for not being found.

He decided on a plan while the captain was ringing the police. Two officers dressed in plain clothes would station themselves at the first stop. If she got off, they would follow her and her companions, discreetly. If she stayed on the *vaporetto,* they would board with the other passengers and follow her when she did get off. He would remain in the background so as not to scare her, although the one thing that stood out in his mind was that while he was standing at the rail she'd shown no reaction to him. He would decide on the next step when he had time to study the situation. Perhaps her destination would provide some answers.

Cenni realized that the police were not falling into lockstep as swiftly as the captain had expected. The giant's tone was becoming combative. Cenni signaled to him to hand over the telephone. Before speaking, he pressed the receiver against his chest. "Carabinieri or civil police?" he asked.

"Carabinieri," the giant replied and laughed silently when Cenni rolled his eyes.

"*Capitano,*" Cenni began, giving the officer at the other end a higher rank than he was likely to hold. "Oh, I see. Sorry, *Maresciallo,*" Cenni said, correcting himself. "Alessandro Cenni here, *Polizia di Stato,* UIT. What's the UIT?" he said, repeating the question that had been asked at the other end. "*Unità della Investigazione del Terrorismo.*" Cenni replied, a level of irritation with a hint of condescension creeping into his voice. Cenni was quite sure that if such a unit existed, it would be called the UIT. He then proceeded to explain his purpose for being in Venice, with an artful twist, and ended with, "Good, excellent—ten minutes, at Sant'Alvise. *Grazie, Maresciallo.*"

The marshal had become very cooperative as soon as Cenni explained that he was following a woman who could lead the UIT to a particularly dangerous cell of terrorists working out of the Veneto. He had emphasized that she was an invaluable lead and no one—"and I mean no one"—should approach her or put her in any danger. "Be discreet," he warned. "Better to lose her than put her on the alert," were his last words after providing the suspect's description. It was perhaps the most comprehensive description of a beautiful spy the marshal would ever receive.

Twelve passengers disembarked at Murano Colonna. None of them looked anything like the woman the UIT officer had described. The marshal knew this case could be the making of him; he'd assigned four men to the task of following the woman instead of the two requested by the commissario. Two of them had reported to work in uniform and had to borrow civvies from the glass sellers in an adjacent shop. The marshal directed two of his men to wait behind the yellow line with the passengers who would board the *vaporetto* and two to wait where the passengers would disembark. Of the passengers disembarking at Colonna, four were men—"certainly men," the two carabinieri later protested to the commissario—two were children, and six were women. One woman, clearly not a tourist, held the hand of one of the children, and in her other hand she carried a wicker basket from which two large loafs of bread protruded. When Cenni asked them her hair color, they were quick to respond that her hair was hidden by a scarf. "What color eyes?" he asked. "Well, she was looking down, talking to the child, so I never really saw her eyes or her face," the other explained. "I remember something unusual, though," the second carabiniere piped up. "She had four fingers on her right hand. The index finger was missing."

WITH A SENSE almost of despair, Cenni checked into the Hotel Da Mula at eight o'clock that evening. Chiara *had* seen him on the *vaporetto,* yet she had chosen to stay in hiding. Murano is a small island with a large population, nearly six thousand residents, he learned from the marshal, and that number didn't include those who worked on the island during the day and left at night for home, in Venice or Mestre, or on one of the other islands in the lagoon, or the thousands of tourists that visited the glass museum, the factories, and the hundreds of little shops that line the quays. Fishing boats, taxis, *vaporetti*, sightseeing cruises, yachts, gondolas, hundreds of opportunities for her to leave, if she hadn't left already. There was no way he could continue to tie up the Murano police in a sham spy chase to assist in the search. The carabinieri officers working on Murano were clearly not trained to do plainclothes work, and he should have known this before he got them involved. But they had helped in one respect. Two of the four men who had gotten off at Colonna were heavyset businessmen in dark suits. Both were well known on the island, a father and a son, highly respected glass merchants, and Cenni had interviewed them in their offices less than an hour ago. As soon as he'd entered their shop, he knew immediately they were the two men who had stood with Chiara at the railing.

The son had noticed her while they were waiting in line for the DM. He followed her to the rail, and his father followed him. He had struck up a conversation. He lived on Murano, he'd told her, and hadn't seen her before. He wondered if she were going there to buy glass and offered his assistance. "My father and I know everyone in the glass business," he explained to Cenni. She'd been friendly but hadn't responded to his advances, he said sheepishly, looking over at his father, who made a joke about his son, the Murano Casanova.

"She said she was visiting an elderly woman, a relative who was very sick, and she wouldn't have time to socialize, but she said it nicely, not like some beautiful women who think they're too good to date fat men," he said with some bitterness. She had intrigued him, he said, a beautiful woman with a sad smile.

Cenni questioned the glass merchant carefully as to what he and the woman had talked about but avoided any mention of why the police were looking for her. "She's very beautiful," the glass man said again. "Her eyes are the intense blue of one of those goblets, cobalt blue." He pointed to some wine glasses on display. "It's too bad about her face and her hand," he added as an afterthought. "Must have been a horrific accident," he said.

The man's comment about Chiara's face took Cenni's breath away and he couldn't respond.

The father, thinking his son might have offended the commissario, added, "It's not that bad, really, her hair covers most of it. A scar, like any other. She's lucky that whatever caused it missed the eye. Starts at the cheek-bone and runs all the way down past the chin."

CHIARA'S FACE, HER beautiful, perfectly formed face. That's why she had never returned. Somehow, in some way, she had escaped from her captors but was ashamed to come home. She had to have known that her parents were dead. It had been in all the papers when her father died, and then again when her mother committed suicide. Her kidnapping had been front-page news for months. The guilt that he'd experienced earlier in the day was nothing to what he was now feeling. There was no one else to blame for her reluctance to return home. He had wor-shipped Chiara's beauty without considering how such worship might affect her. He knew the moment the glass merchant mentioned the scar that it didn't matter, and wouldn't have mattered twenty years ago, that he loved Chiara for her laughter, her irreverence toward every-thing pompous, her wit, and her gift of loving, in particu-lar of loving him. But how could she have known? His praise had always centered on her external beauty, never on the essentials, perhaps because he'd been jealous. Some of their professors, the important ones, preferred her thoughtfulness and depth to his flashy, impulsive solu-tion to every problem. If they had graduated together, she would have preceded him to the podium.

She must have been aware of his jealousy; she was too intelligent not to have known. Even today, she had outwit-ted him. The merchant said they'd been talking about the need to change the transportation system if Venice were going to save its canals when she'd abruptly excused herself. He and his father had left the rail at the same time, wondering if she was unwell. A few minutes later, he had seen her approach a woman sitting inside the cabin. He assumed the woman was local, as she was carrying a market basket filled with groceries and was accompanied by two school-age boys, both wearing football jerseys and carrying book bags. He saw the two women exchange parcels, and later, when they were disembarking, he noticed that the woman with the sad smile was talking animatedly to one of the young boys. They were discussing last Sunday's game.

3

HE GOT BLIND drunk that night, the kind of drunkenness that comes only with age, depleted blood cells, and a completely jaundiced view of the world. When he awoke the next morning in a tiny single bed, on its foam-rubber mattress, he had no idea where he was, what had poisoned him, or whether it was true that life was worth living. At the moment it wasn't, and he groaned loudly as he got out of bed. The bathroom was so small that he had to go inside and close the door before he could climb into the shower. Never, never stay in a cheap hotel if you plan to get drunk the night before, he resolved, as he danced under tepid water trying to catch a few drops. The towels only added to his suffering: two thin scratchy pieces of cloth, two feet long, with the hotel's name written in indelible ink along the hem. Ordinarily, he'd feel compassion for anyone who had to steal towels from the Hotel Da Mula, but he had none left after succoring his own misery.

With one hand shielding his eyes, he unlatched the shutters, opened the window, and looked out upon the day. "Beautiful," he groaned and sat down on the bed to reflect on the previous evening. He'd begun his descent into Dante's Third Circle at the trattoria next to his hotel. He vaguely recalled ordering two carafes of local wine with his meal. It had continued in a bar frequented by locals in Campo San Bernardo where he drank gin for two hours, but it was in an after-hours dive on Fondamenta Vetrai that he'd finally gone under. An elderly fisherman decided to teach him how to drink grappa as it's drunk on the lagoon. The questore was always affronted by Cenni's capacity for strong liquor. He'd have been pleased to learn—not that Cenni planned to enlighten him—that his future vice-questore had feet of clay. "Grappa, 120 proof, clear un-aged alcohol, not that aged sugar water you call grappa in Umbria," the fisherman said when calling for their last round, at least Cenni hoped it had been their last round. He always dealt better with hangovers when he was unaware of actual numbers.

Reason had deserted him the previous evening, and it appeared not to have returned. He was hearing voices: "*Signor Poliziotto . . . Signor Commissario . . . dottore. . . .*" In general, at least in Italy, civilians don't scream at—or for—senior police officials. They present themselves and their bona fides at the front desk and wait for admittance to *l'onorevole's* office. But someone was definitely calling him from the street.

He pulled himself up gently from the bed, returned to the window, and looked out and down. An old man, dressed in a tattered windbreaker and knee-high rubber boots, was standing below, looking up and smiling. Cenni took a long look at the old man and groaned again. It was his drinking buddy from the previous evening. The man's name came slowly, but it did finally come:

"*Si, Signor Dolfin. Che Cosa c'è?*"

"I found her, your beautiful signorina."

Always discreet, Cenni hesitated before responding. "I don't understand. What signorina?"

"The beautiful signorina with the four fingers. Dottore, I've found her!"

Cenni realized that hanging out a hotel window with tourists snapping pictures of him engaged in the quaint Italian custom of hanging out of a window was unwise. He told Signor Dolfin to stay where he was. He'd be right down.

Signor Dolfin, Antonio to everyone on the island, was a throwback to another time, when men fished the lagoon for their livelihood and relied for extras on the occasional tourist buying their wives' handmade lace. He was eighty-one years old, healthy as an ox, and renowned for drinking younger men under the table. Certainly, he'd drunk Alessandro Cenni under the table and later, at three o'clock in the morning, put him to bed.

Cenni dragged Antonio to the nearest café where he could get a coffee or, to be perfectly honest, a *caffè corretto*, to get him started.

"What did you mean you've found my *signorina*?" Cenni

asked, afraid to learn how much 120-proof grappa had loosened his tongue.

"The beautiful Chiara, the love of your life, the woman you've been seeking for twenty years, the woman with four fingers on her right hand, the woman who was kidnapped by *Le Brigate Rosse,* the woman whose hem you are not worthy to kiss, Signor *Poliziotto.* This is the signorina that I've found." Antonio was piqued, but he was a man of experience and knew that drinking buddies part company after a night's sleep, and he also felt compassion for the Umbrian, who needed two hands to raise his coffee to his lips and whose complexion was that of a man who's eaten a bad egg, so he told Cenni what he had come to say.

"The signorina came here to see her mother-in-law, but the old lady is dead and cremated, three days already. Another old lady from Burano owns the house in which Signora Tartare lived. Her sons are there right now stealing from the dead." He twisted his clawed hands in a circular motion that said more clearly than words that the sons of the old lady from Burano were thieves and couldn't be trusted.

"Her mother-in-law," Cenni exclaimed. "I don't understand."

"There's nothing to understand, dottore; the signorina married the dead woman's son."

Cenni's surprise amused the old man, and he asked rhetorically, "Did you think you're the only fish in the sea? A beautiful woman has many opportunities for love, although not with Stefano Tartare. Not any more! He *is* also dead. Your beautiful Chiara comes to visit Stefano's

mamma once a year on his birthday, for ten years now, but
she never stays more than a day. Stefano was Martina's only
child, and very smart, the smartest boy on Murano, until
he left for Bologna and became a *fanatico!* He broke his
mamma's heart," he added, shaking his head at the perfidy
of stupid, ungrateful children.

"Why didn't you tell me all this last night?" Cenni asked.

The fisherman shrugged his shoulders. "Dottore, you
were drunk. Besides, I didn't know the beautiful Chiara
was Martina's daughter-in-law until I told my wife your
story. She reminded me that Martina's daughter-in-law
also has four fingers. Do you want to see the house?" he
asked changing the subject.

"And Chiara? Is she at the house?"

The old man looked at Cenni boldly.

"No, dottore. She left early this morning at seven
o'clock with Luca Loredan. He dropped her off at the *Ferrovia.* She had an eight o'clock train to catch."

CENNI UNDERSTOOD IT all now. Reason and memory had
returned with a vengeance. Chiara had married a local,
whereas he, Alessandro Cenni, was a *straniero* and, worse,
a policeman. The old man lied. He knew last night when
he was drowning his *paesano* in grappas that Chiara was the
old lady's daughter-in-law. At some time after midnight,
Cenni remembered, Antonio had left the bar for ten minutes. Shortly after he returned, Cenni had retired to the
toilet, and when he got back, four drinks were lined up
waiting for him. "From our friends over there, and me,"
Antonio said, pointing to three men sitting next to the slot

machine in the corner. In the glaring light of morning, Cenni realized that he didn't even own his own hangover.

The house of the dead woman was down a narrow cobbled street behind Campo San Bernardo. They arrived in the middle of a firestorm. Some men, but mainly women, were joined at the front door, talking and yelling at the same time. One woman, of a particularly agitated disposition, kept repeating "robbers" while pointing to someone inside the house. A young carabiniere, one of those who'd worked with Cenni yesterday, was outside the house trying to keep the peace. He finally ordered the agitated woman, who'd stopped yelling at the person in the house and was now yelling at him, to go home and feed her children their lunch. He then went inside and slammed the door.

When the women saw Antonio, they moved aside to let him and his friend pass. One of the women said something to the others and they all laughed. It might have been "He's one of us," but since they were speaking Veneziano, for all Cenni knew it might also have been "Let's kill the cop." Inside was no better. Three women and two men were arguing in Veneziano, and the young officer was shouting over them in Italian trying to be heard. Antonio, who had the makings of a dictator, said two words to the senior woman, and she immediately stopped talking, as did the others. The young officer, still under the impression that Cenni was in Murano looking for terrorists, immediately deferred to him. "Please, commissario, see what you can do here."

They started up again and it took Cenni five minutes to get them to agree to speak in Italian and to explain their argument for his and the carabiniere's benefit. In Italy, after a funeral, with property to be divided, it was, of course, about money. The two men, the robbers from Burano, claimed that the signora had owed their mother three months in back rent and they were taking possession of her furniture. The senior woman, who turned out to be Antonio's wife, called it a damned lie.

"Martina never missed paying the rent in twenty years. Her daughter-in-law told us—the three of us who nursed Martina at the end—to take what we want. And what we don't want, to give to the other neighbors."

Cenni asked if there was a will, and they all turned and looked at him in amazement. Even the carabiniere, from a rural village in Sicily, knew not to ask anything so foolish. Antonio, who'd kept quiet until now, suggested they look in Martina's tin box.

"She kept all her official papers in that box. The rent receipts must be there somewhere."

Antonio's wife found the box under the woman's bed, and the carabiniere agreed to force it open since none of them could find a key. Cenni and the young officer started looking through the yellowing papers, a lifetime's collection of official documents, including her son's birth and baptismal certificates, a certificate of excellence from his high school, and a cache of rent receipts that went back a full year. Signora Tartare's rent was paid up until the end of June, which gave her another month of occupancy. Cenni showed the two men his identification and the carabiniere showed them the door, which was followed by a loud shout from the street.

There was nothing left for him to do on Murano. He wasn't even sure why he had accompanied the old man to Signora Tartare's house. Perhaps to see the kind of life that Chiara had chosen in preference to marrying him. In a matter of hours, he had gone from being a man obsessed with finding the killers of a woman he'd loved twenty years ago to a man scorched by jealousy. In the tin box, in addition to the signora's official papers, there was a small packet of letters from Stefano to his mother, a few family pictures, including one of Stefano when he'd graduated from the *liceo classico,* and a postcard from Bari, dated 1989, signed by Stefano and Ceclia. And one other picture. It was a Polaroid of a man and a woman on a beach, standing in front of a gelato stand. It was Chiara as he remembered her, her hair still blonde. She was leaning back against the man and he had his arm around her waist. When he turned it over, he found that someone had scribbled a date, 1989, and the notation: honeymoon, Stefano and Ceclia.

4

HE WAS THE same man, returning to Venice on the same boat that he had boarded less than twenty-four hours earlier. Nothing was broken that you would see on an x-ray; no one had died, other than an old woman in her time. Even with Chiara, nothing had really changed. She had been alive twenty years ago; she was still alive today. He had been twenty-two when he'd put his life on hold, renouncing the profession that he had chosen for himself and embracing a profession that he had always fought against. He had convinced himself that searching for Chiara's kidnappers was the only way to memorialize her life and give dignity to her death. He had turned forty-two three weeks ago, had no wife, no child, and no one to care if he returned home. He stood at the rail of the *vaporetto* looking out at the rough seas of the lagoon. A storm was predicted for evening; the skies had darkened and a light rain was falling. To the north was sky and water and desolation, to the south lay the dying city of Venice. The Queen of the Adriatic was sinking into the salt flats from which it had begun its ascent more than a thousand years earlier. Nothing lasts, and this was now his dilemma.

His reason for being a policeman had ended. The search for Chiara's killers was no longer the sole purpose in his life or the altar upon which he could lay his sacrifices. More than once, Renato had accused him of being a religious fanatic, "just a different religion from the rest of us," he'd said. "Yours is more vengeful and destructive. I have no wife or child, but at least I know why." If he stopped being a policeman, what would he do: sell chocolates, coach football, become a defense lawyer and use what he knew to thwart prosecutors? The last he could do easily enough. He knew the many games that the police play to ensure convictions.

His current case was an example of the futility of his job. What good was he doing anyone, particularly himself, in seeking Jarvinia Baudler's killer? From what he'd surmised so far, the German had been a small-time blackmailer, a bully, and an egotist unbounded. Who would care if her killer was found and brought to justice? No one who had cared about her personally; but the German's murder, particularly its brutality, was viewed as an insult by her government. As Dieter had indicated, his government wanted the murderer found, and now. Rome was very anxious to cooperate with the Germans. The new politics were not so different from the old, and if the Germans needed a sacrificial victim, Rome would be pleased to find them one. Baudler's last lover had been a black woman, an African, the ideal scapegoat. In his last case involving Rome, Carlo had insisted that he arrest a Croatian, not much caring if she were guilty or innocent. If he quit now, the same would happen to Baudler's black lover.

The nearly twenty years that he'd invested in police work did have meaning, profound meaning for those like Sophie Orlic, whom he had saved from prison. It was not the convictions that counted so much, but the men and women who were out in the world today, free because of his efforts. He'd wait to make a decision about his future until after he'd found Jarvinia Baudler's killer. And for that reason alone, he had come to Venice.

BEFORE LEAVING PERUGIA, he had done his homework on both Marcella Molin and Palazzo Molin, the family palace built by Grazia Molin in 1680 along the Canale di Cannaregio with money from her fabulously rich Spanish father. The Molin family, one of the oldest in Venice, had lost all its money by 1680, when the half-witted twenty-year-old heir to the title married Grazia, the thirty-year-old daughter of Don Miguel Peraza. The guidebook that

Cenni consulted described Palazzo Molin as the last great palazzo built in the Byzantine–style architecture that had been popular three hundred years earlier. The Spaniard's daughter, who had purchased her way into the Venetian nobility, had set out to impress Venice by overwhelming it. According to the guidebook, the result was an excessively florid imitation of earlier Renaissance palaces, redeemed only by the addition of frescoes executed some fifty years later on the first *piano nobile*. Sightless and already in her eighties, Grazia, the Spanish upstart, hired Giambattista Tiepolo to decorate the ceilings of the four public rooms with allegorical interpretations of the four continents. Some critics believe that the Molin frescoes predate the frescoes created by Tiepolo for the Würzburger Residenz in Germany.

Information on Marcella Molin, the last direct descendant of Grazia, was easily obtained. She was one of the wealthiest women in Italy. From all accounts, she had built a second and even greater family fortune after the war, some said by profiting from the miseries of postwar Italy. It was rumored that she'd purchased land and buildings from many of Venice's oldest families, initially by making generous loans and then later foreclosing on the properties when the owners couldn't pay the escalating interest rates, the existence of which were in the fine print. Some of the people she destroyed had been close friends of her father. Her vineyards and rice plantations were the most profitable in Italy, and she was also reputed to be the largest slum landlord in the Veneto, owning buildings that were falling down but still providing her with a healthy income. All the migrant workers in Venice were said to live in one of her many apartments, as many as ten to a single room, and it was said that she paid off the police and the judiciary to protect her investments.

Her father, Count Molin, now something of a hero in Venice, had died during the war; his body was found lodged between the pilings that support the *Fondamente Nove vaporetto* stop. No autopsy was performed. Some said he had committed suicide, citing as a reason his wife's madness and his daughter's sexual deviance. But this rumor didn't start until more than five years after his death. The only real clue was information from the family that he'd been picked up by a police launch on the evening before his body was found, and that two Germans in uniform had accompanied the plainclothes police who had taken him away. It was also after his death that the rumor began that the count had been a member of *La Resistenza*. An investigation had been proposed at the end of the war, but the daughter, who was now head of the family, objected. She and her mother wanted to forget the horrors of the war and her father's death, she'd said when approached by the authorities.

THE SOFT RAIN had turned into a downpour by the time the *vaporetto* docked at Ponte delle Guglie. Cenni had no umbrella, so when he arrived at Palazzo Molin, less than a five-minute walk from the ferry stop, he was soaked through. Perhaps it was the misery of the day that affected his first view of the palazzo, but when he peered through the iron gates that shut out the world, he imagined that the original Grazia would be horrified to see the outside of the home that she'd built to impress Venice. The extravagant splendors of plaster and stuccowork described in the guidebook, written fifty years earlier, were gone. The peeling façade would have been appropriate for a gothic B movie, something to scare little children. Marcella Molin could easily afford to repair her ancestral home, yet she'd let it lapse into dissolution. Cenni wondered why.

He waited five full minutes after he rang and was beginning to fear that she had left the city before his arrival. The woman he had spoken to two days earlier when he telephoned to make an appointment had indicated that *la contessa* would only see him if she were up to it, and if she wanted to. No lights or movement were evident behind the *loggia* of the *piano nobile*. He was considering leaving, when he saw a very old woman shuffling toward the gate. Despite the rain, to which they were both exposed, she refused to admit him until she scrutinized his identification. Finally she unlocked the gate, and, as he stepped inside the front garden, she remarked that he was a day late. The countess, who valued punctuality, might not see him. Cenni reflected that the countess had no choice in the matter, but he had no wish to argue with a servant and he nodded.

The servant escorted him into the entrance hall and then up the main stairway to the principal salon, where she left him while she went to inquire if *la contessa* were up to a visit by the police. Cenni noted the stained walls of the long hallway that ran from back to front, but the room's former opulence was still apparent in the row of sixteen matching carved chairs that lined the right side of the room and a series of portraits that hung on the left. He walked slowly down the room, stopping at each briefly to examine the signature of the artist and the name of the sitter. Only one interested him, that of Grazia, the Spanish bride. Her late age at marriage and her choice, or her father's, of a half-wit suitor ten years younger suggested to Cenni, unfairly as it turned out, that she would resemble the Spanish royal family that Vélazquez had painted.

She had black hair, bound in tight curls pulled to the back of her head, and her skin was liquid gold. Her dress was modestly cut, displaying just a hint of cleavage, but elaborate in design, of jade-green velvet with a sheer cape of tulle covering her magnificent shoulders. She wore a single strand of pearls around her neck. It was, however, the beauty of the face and figure that captured his attention. He was sure the painter had added to it with a few deft touches, but the woman behind the painter's artifice shone through. Her pencil-thin eyebrows emphasized large intelligent brown eyes that looked straight out at the viewer. She had a full, generous mouth, and her figure was ample, which would have appealed in the seventeenth century. Yet behind the brush strokes of the portrait painter, he detected a woman of steel. Perhaps he was imputing a personality to Grazia that hadn't existed, but surely a woman, blind and close to death, who'd hired and supervised the most famous artist of the day in the decoration of her ceilings, had something of the tartar in her.

"It's painted by Sebastiano Bombelli. The pearls around her neck are magnificent."

Cenni turned to find a tall black woman standing behind him. She was the woman Orlando had described as the German's lover. She was quite tall, his height, and, as Orlando had said, a beauty.

She held out her hand. "My name is Juliet Mudarikwa. I look for you yesterday. I am wrong?" she asked. Charming accent, Cenni thought, and asked if she spoke English or German.

"Police business detained me," he said, after they had settled on English.

She invited him to sit on one of the very uncomfortable wooden chairs that lined the side of the room, while she explained about *la contessa*.

"She's dying of lung cancer, and her doctor thinks she has a few weeks left, perhaps not even that. Talking exhausts her, so you should keep your questions short." And then, she added, "You know, of course, that I met her through Jarvinia Baudler. We were in Venice on a visit and ran into Marcella at the Caffè Inglese. You'll probably want to talk to me when you finish with her."

Very collected, Cenni thought, and very rehearsed.

The countess had agreed to receive him in her bedroom, the America room, Juliet said, assuming that Cenni knew what that meant. Cenni wasn't sure what Marcella Molin would look like, but he had pictured an older version of Grazia, her Spanish ancestor. She was propped up, on oversized pillows, with legal papers, folders, a wooden casket, and some large leather-bound books, taking up most of the space along the sides of the canopied bed, its immense size dwarfing its inhabitant. He guessed that she was not above five feet in height and probably weighed less than a hundred pounds. Age and disease had been unkind, but Cenni doubted that she had ever been anything but homely. Her nose resembled a bird's beak, her skin was sallow, and her dark eyes were small and exophthalmic; she reminded him of a sparrow. She was wearing a bouffant wig in a brownish color that was far too large for her small head, and it was askew. Underneath it, she was bald. Juliet walked over to her immediately and righted the wig on her head, and, when she'd finished, said "there, now" and kissed the bedridden woman on the forehead.

The countess smiled in thanks. She has one nice feature, Cenni thought. The smile she had given Juliet exuded genuine warmth.

"Sit down, dottore," she said in a rasping voice, pointing to a chair that had been pulled up alongside the bed. "Or, if you wish, you can sit on the bed, the better to see you, my dear," she added with a wolfish grin. Cenni sat on the chair.

"So, dottore. You're looking into the death of my old friend Jarvinia. Murdered! Not surprising, considering the things she got up to. Jarvinia never played it safe, more power to her. Am I one of your suspects?"

Before Cenni had time to answer, she continued, "Before you have time to swear out a warrant, I'll be dead.

I don't mind the notoriety. It's the evil that lives after us; the good is always interred with our bones," she said—and laughed, which set off a paroxysm of coughing.

JULIET PULLED THE drapes across the floor-to-ceiling windows in the America room, lighted the candles in the five candelabra that were placed strategically around the room, and sat on the edge of the bed after moving the wooden casket out of the way. "Take that horrid thing off," she said, removing the countess's wig. A few longish strands of gray hair, the lone survivors of ten rounds of chemotherapy, were sticking up, and Juliet smoothed them down and put her arm around the dying woman's shoulders.

"Are you hungry? Would you like a coffee, or a tea? English breakfast tea with milk and a nice soft cream puff? Or some beef bouillon?"

The countess patted Juliet's hand. "I'm not hungry, not even for a cream puff."

"Do you think he believed us?" Juliet asked anxiously.

"It doesn't matter! I've written out a statement just in case. My lawyer knows the combination of the safe, so it won't be necessary for you to hand it to the police. Better that way. But there's no reason for them to come after you. You didn't need Jarvinia, or her promises of a passport or residency, not after I got your residency approved in Venice. You had no motive for killing her, and neither did I. Let me alone now. We'll talk in the morning. But before you go, put some wood on the fire and blow out those candles. There's no point in burning the house down at this stage of my life. And turn on the lamp. I want to do some reading before I sleep."

Marcella watched Juliet as she moved noiselessly around the room, blowing out the candles. She was six feet tall without shoes, yet she moved with the grace of a cat. "Hand me the wooden casket," she said, observing Juliet as she turned on the lamp. "And stay for a minute; I have something for you." She felt for the long chain around her neck and found the delicate gold key that opened the box. "Here," she said, and pulled out the string of pearls that Juliet had so often admired. "It's the strand of pearls that Grazia wore in her wedding portrait. I reported it stolen, for the insurance, fifteen years ago. I want you to have it, but don't sell it in Italy, and not until I've been dead at least six months. It's worth two hundred thousand, probably a good bit more. Don't sell it for less than a hundred."

Juliet gasped in delight. "I'll never sell it," she said, holding the strand against her copper-colored skin and turning to admire herself in the mirror. "Look, Marcella! Isn't it beautiful?"

"You'll sell it. You'll need something to live on after I die. I'm not leaving you anything else; it's all tied up in my foundation. And if I did, my cousin would make sure you never saw a penny. Now take them away and hide them from that old crone downstairs. And bring me my coffee in the morning. I'm tired of listening to Nannetta's complaints."

5

THERE'S AT LEAST one positive about death: no more
bifocals. Someone had moved them again. She'd been
reading Jarvinia's letters right before the policeman
arrived. She should have refused to see him, arriving a day
late like that. There's no courtesy any more. He hadn't
once addressed her as *contessa*. They must be with the letters, she decided, opening the casket she'd just closed.
Most of the letters, the early ones, were written on the thin
tissue paper that they'd used right after the war. Postage
had cost a fortune back then, probably Jarvinia's excuse
for writing so seldom. She had filed them in chronological
order, earliest to latest, an expression of what her father
had once called her accountant's soul. She pulled out the
first. The writing was tiny and her lenses needed to be
changed, but she could recite most of it off by heart:

SEPTEMBER 14, 1945—*Darling dearest Queenie,*
You're an angel for sending the biscotti. I finished the entire box myself, not a single crumb for
the peasants! Please, please send more or your darling Jarvinia will starve to death. I keep it under my
mattress and eat one every day before presenting
myself abjectly before the oatmeal that everyone
here calls breakfast. I nibble around the edges and
belch when the nuns fuss that I don't eat enough. It's
darkish brown in color with lumps the size of sea
urchins, without the sticky things on the end. And
the coffee is worse than the oatmeal. Jarvinia, you

bad thing, don't exaggerate! Nothing is worse than the oatmeal. I survive by imagining us back at the Caffè Inglese, feeding each other those wonderful pastries. Do you remember the morning we ordered three each, all of them with cream inside! Your father called us little pigs—well, not so little, after eating three.

I'm something of a star here—nobody knows what to make of me. Fritz paid in advance for my keep—three years, so they can't kick me out, but they'd like to. "That Nazi," I heard Sister Ursula refer to me yesterday. Like she wasn't one herself when the German army went marching across Europe. For sure the silly Schweizerin was beaming ear-to-ear when we entered Poland. Last month they discontinued German classes, and now when I speak German to Ursie, she replies in French. My French improves daily.

Have you seen anything of my mother? She wrote to me just the once since I arrived in May and then only to tell me "to remember." Remember what, she didn't say, but I'm sure she meant *keep your mouth shut, you silly girl*. She writes around the edges, like I eat my oatmeal. Hints here and there, but nothing in the open. She's deathly afraid she'll be rounded up with the Germans and sent to an internment camp, but even more terrified of *La Resistenza*. *La Resistenza* would love to get hold of Fritz and those twenty-pound notes, and mutter is no Clara Petacci!

She'd sell her first-born (oops, that's me!) for a pair
of silk hose, and Fritz for probably less. She's applied
for a Polish passport. Yes, indeed, she's finally come
clean. Pure-bred Aryan mutter is Polish—part,
anyway—and me too, although how many parts is yet
to be determined: one part German, one part Polish,
and two parts bastard, and all belonging to you,
Queenie. As soon as the passport comes, she plans to
leave Venice, but no word of where she'll go. Certainly not to Poland!

Fritz left, by the way, the same week as me, with no
mention of where he was going, but I know he left
her with plenty of lovely English pounds, which is
how she pays the bills here. If they only knew, I'd be
out on my ear. If that happens, can I come back to
you, darling Queenie? Your mother would never
notice, she wanders around in twilight land. We can
rattle around in that grand old palazzo, drinking
coffee and eating pastries all day, and sink licen-
tiously into the mattresses in a different bedroom
every night. Glorious sensual pleasures!

I'm writing this very small on both sides of the
sheet—don't go blind—as I have only one stamp.
Annemarie, maid of all things—All Things!—has a
huge crush and posts my letters from town. Ursie
reads everything I write, so read between the lines if
you receive a letter from me with the school's name
at the top.

Write, write, write, dearest Queenie. I'm desperate

for news, and don't forget the bonbons. Kiss yourself for me.

Jarvinia

DECEMBER 15, 1945—*Dear Queenie,*

A fine Venetian kettle of fish you've landed me in! Ursie reads all my letters, coming and going. Did you forget that my school is in the Confederazione Svizzera? Ursie speaks German, French—and Italian! First off, silly, leave your conscience alone, and it'll leave you alone. The most important thing we learned in second term—*Thus conscience does make cowards of us all.*

I had a time of it explaining that remark about your father, but in the end I convinced Ursie of its innocence. I wasn't so lucky over Annemarie, who's been sent down to the scullery. Her replacement is too greedy—and ugly—to be bowled over by my charms or for me to exercise them. Her charge for posting a letter is outrageous, my pocket money for two weeks, so this may be the last letter for a while.

Jealous of Annemarie! Stupid! She's a fling, not a replacement. Do some flinging yourself, I've got three more years here.

Ursie confiscated the biscotti in retaliation— gorging herself, and her *amore*, in the refectory. Don't send any more, as it's not my intention to feed the peasants on Venetian goodies. They wouldn't appreciate them!

Thanks for visiting my mother. She wrote me last

week that she's off to South Africa. She didn't mention Fritz, but that's where he must be. Not a word of
me going with her and escaping this prison. My
cough is much better and the doctor says my lungs
are healing nicely, so I could have joined them. He
even said that the sun would be so, so good for me.
I wrote mamma and quoted him, but she just ignored
it. She's a selfish pig, but why would I expect anything different! A daughter almost seventeen, with
an ugly limp, won't help her cachet. And who'd
believe she's twenty-nine when I tower over her?
Ciao Amore,

Jarvinia

APRIL 1, 1946—*Dear Queenie,*

Of course I received your letters, all ten of them.
It was your original letter that got Annemarie sent
down to the scullery, so blame yourself if I don't
write that often. Besides, I'm sick again. I was in the
infirmary for two weeks—my cough is worse. Last
night I had blood all down my gown, and writing is
so fatiguing.

Your mother could sit on the right side of the
Almighty compared to mine. So what if she walks
around all day talking to herself and wringing her
hands like Lady Macbeth? Mine couldn't care less if
I live or die, so please don't ask me to send pity. If
she's so annoying, send her away.

Can you really come to visit? Are the borders
open again for regular people to travel? I would like

that so much, dear Queenie. Sorry for my sulks before, but I need love and comfort, and delicious, delicious Venetian goodies: bonbons, marzapani, petit-fours, cannoli, truffles, and lovely, lovely cream puffs! You know what I like. Please, please come, Queenie, and bring a basketful of wonderful things to eat. I need fattening up, I look like a maypole only not so festive.

Queenie, I'm afraid I'm going to die. Please come.

Jarvinia

DECEMBER 9, 1946—*Dear Queenie,*

It's been forever, I know. We had such a wonderful time when you visited in the spring, and I never wrote to thank you. Bad Jarvinia! But when I'm feeling good, I don't want to spend my days indoors writing letters and then trying to bribe someone to mail them. Yes, I remember what you said in April, but I don't want to write letters that Ursie reads even if it makes you happy. It's my happiness that counts. I'm the one who's sick!

No, I'm not better and that's why I'm writing. I'm leaving for England right after the New Year. Fritz is in England, but without my mother. She's still in Johannesburg and even sicker than I am, coughing and spitting up blood all the time. He says her skin is white like parchment with her bones shining through, and that she's more beautiful than ever. That should make her happy, she's always wanted to play Camille. She never let up on me about my weight. Remember the time I brought cream puffs for our tea and she tossed them into the canal? Speaking of which, I'd beg you to post me some if they weren't perishable. Fritz read about a new treatment, a miracle drug, and traveled to England to see if it can cure her, but the doctors tell him it's too late. It's in her spine and she can't sit up for more than fifteen minutes, and she certainly can't travel to England.

Dr. Rossi says my TB—there, I finally said it—is still in my lungs and the doctors in England have agreed to treat me: those lovely twenty-pound notes. Fritz is going back to Johannesburg to be with my mother, but he's arranged for a cousin of his to look after me and settle me into the hospital when I arrive in London. I should have told him to tell my mother that Dr. Rossi is very pleased with my bovine peasant's body. It's probably what's kept me alive so long, but I know Fritz won't tell her. He cares more about her than me, although that's never stopped him from fondling my breasts and other naughty parts. Mother without breasts daughter obliges.

I don't have an address where you can reach me, but I'll write you when I'm settled. I don't know what will happen to me. Fritz's mother was English and his grandfather was a Lord Chamberlain, or did he empty chamberpots for a lord? Can't remember. So perhaps he'll return to England and pay for my university. I'm thinking Oxford. He owes me at least Oxford for all those free squeezes. *Ciao Amore,*

Jarvinia

AUGUST 1, 1947—*Dear Queenie,*

Your letter finally found me. Amazing things, post offices. I know I promised to send my address, but I was so busy with my treatment and London, which is very exciting, although the English are pigs. And now Fritz has returned. My mother died in February and Fritz says she called out for me at the end. Probably wanted someone to light her cigarette. Fritz says I'm a bitch and I should stop saying such things. Am I a bitch, Queenie? You know me better than anyone, certainly better than my mother did.

She didn't leave me any money. Fritz says she didn't have any! He's agreed to put me through Oxford with a living allowance, but after that he says I'm on my own. Catch that happening! He made this promise while we were lying naked in bed smoking cigarettes after coitus interruptus. No more bastards in this family, thank you very much. Fritz does love his little Jarvinia, although she's not so little any more. Which is my good news.

I'm cured! No cough, no blood, no fatigue. No anything. Oh wonderful, wonderful streptomycin! Six months of doctors touching and poking and prodding and never a by-your-leave when asking me to remove my clothes. "Let's just take a look, Jarvinia." The next time someone says "Let's just take a look," I'll strike a blow for all women and give him a black eye.

Do you hear me, Queenie? Cured! It's my favorite word, and I plan to use it twice a day for the rest of my life. But with the blessings of Our Eternal Savior (do record that those early morning hours in chapel weren't wasted), I infected Fritz before the magical cure date and he'll experience a little of what I've suffered in the last five years. I've had to promise to spend the long vacations with him, and you know what that means!

I'm accepted into Somerville College and will go there in October. I plan to finish my course of study in three years. And then? Perhaps Venice, perhaps Germany. The English don't like me. *Bloody Kraut spy* someone called me yesterday, and I returned the favor. Cultural morons! It's going to be difficult to stick it out for three years. It rains and rains and rains and the food is bloody awful and absolutely no beautiful pictures. They talk of Gainsborough and Reynolds with the same awe that we speak of Titian and Tintoretto. And no America room. Can you imagine?

Queenie, if you miss me so much, why don't you join me at Somerville? It's full of sexually repressed women. Read *Gaudy Night* by Dorothy Sayers if you don't believe me. I know you won't, though, too busy making pots of money—you greedy little Venetian. Write me care of Somerville College. *Ciao Amore,*

Jarvinia

OCTOBER 10, 1949—*Dear Queenie,*

I can't believe it's three years since we were together, in that little hotel in Ascona. I coughed all day and we made love all night. You must have the lungs of a horse not to have contracted TB! Remember the cream puffs? They were sour, but I ate them anyway. And the nosy little man who came to our door three times: *Ladies, you make too much noise. The other guests can't sleep.* I almost smothered you with a pillow to keep you from laughing so hard.

Today the college handed me a cache of letters from you, two years' worth. I forgot to write that I changed my name to Baudler. Fritz adopted me, with a little persuasion, and I'm now using his last name. After the papers were official, he said, cryptically, "I should have done this before your mother died." I asked him directly if he's my biological father and he said "No," but he's lying, the incestuous old bugger! But I suppose you could say the same of me, as we're still fucking on the long vacations, and I'm actually enjoying it. Not quite like Christmas dinner together, but it does have a family feel. I noticed for the first time that we have the same feet. My mother called them peasant feet, but since he's actually the grandson of a Lord Chamberlain, I'm now your equal, *contessa*, although I suppose in the First Republic you now have to settle for Queenie. Your father must be turning in his grave.

I can't write any more, as I'm flying out to a party with a junior officer in the Foreign Service. He's wild about my golden tresses, so you two have something in common. *Ciao, ciao,*

Jarvinia

December 27, 1949—*Dear Queenie,*

Take a seat first, and then guess who's married. Me! My junior officer—not so junior with his last promotion—and I got married on Christmas Day. I looked wonderfully bridal, dressed in white lace and pearls. I carried a white prayer book and a spray of white roses, and Fritz gave me away. The dear sisters would be horrified if they knew. We're married in the Church of England. Don't you look horrified either! You know I don't believe in all that heaven-and-earth stuff.

We're leaving for Germany right after the New Year. Jerry—sorry forgot! Gerald St. Clair, or Jerry to every-one except his mother. *Gerald, dear, give me your arm. Gerald, dear, I hate your wife.* She does, you know. She told me two days before we married that she could see right through me, which I thought rather amusing, as I've gained two stone in the last year.

I missed you, Queenie dear. In my mind you were my maid of honor, although in reality it was Jerry's sister. Also a prig like the mother! Anyway, as my maid of honor you're supposed to give me some-thing for my hope chest. I'm thinking Murano glass, red goblets with just the slightest touch of gold on the stems—like the ones your father used at our last Christmas dinner. I'm not sure what our address will be, so I'll have to write in a few weeks when we get to Germany. Germany is Jerry's posting for the next few years. I wish it were Venice.

Even better than sending them by post, why don't
you come and visit. It's been so long and I miss you.
Ciao amore.

Jarvinia

I'LL FINISH READING them later, she thought, closing her
eyes. She had visited Jarvinia six months later with a dozen
Murano goblets carried tenderly by hand. Jerry had been
delighted with them and with her. "I want to know Jarvinia
better. You're her oldest friend. You can help me understand her," he'd whispered when Jarvinia was in the kitchen
mixing drinks. He had been awkward and looked everywhere but at her when he asked if Jarvinia had had any love
interests when she and Queenie were girls together in
Venice. Queenie had answered "Absolutely not," reminding him that they had been schooled in a convent.

In the days when Jerry was at work and Jarvinia didn't
have a lunch date, they made love, but Queenie knew that
she was just a side interest, that Jarvinia had someone else
in addition to Jerry and her, and she wasn't sure whether
that someone else was a man or a woman. Jerry and Jarvinia
had taken her to all the embassy parties, where Jarvinia
flirted indiscriminately. To anyone who viewed sex as a
strictly heterosexual affair, it would appear that Jarvinia was
only interested in men, but Queenie knew differently.
There were a number of women with whom Jarvinia flirted,
one in particular who she spoke to at the beginning and at
the end of every party, a White Russian with dramatic brows
and flaming red hair. Queenie realized that the peacock
had moved beyond the sparrow.

She opened her eyes and collected the letters, in precise order, tied them with parcel string, and returned them to the casket. Tomorrow or the next day, after she'd finished rereading them all, she would burn them; they served no purpose any longer, not with Jarvinia dead and her own death imminent. It was better, as Jarvinia might say, that the peasants should not read them. Whenever Jarvinia was angry—and it didn't matter at whom—she'd call the person a peasant. For that reason alone, Nannetta, who was a peasant, had hated Jarvinia, although she'd had other reasons to hate her as well. Nannetta had been completely delighted when Queenie told her, after her return from Germany, that Jarvinia's mother was Polish, probably the daughter of peasants, and that Jarvinia herself was a bastard.

"*But the peasants—how do the peasants die?*" Jarvinia had asked her one day when they were still at school, as they walked back to their classrooms from chapel. Jarvinia had the oddest habit of reeling off obscure quotations at inopportune moments. "Do you think Tolstoy meant that we are all peasants at the time of death, and that we'll all sit in the same heaven? I don't want to sit in the same heaven with Nannetta," she'd declared spitefully. Queenie was quite sure that Jarvinia need have no fear of that happening.

6

JULIET HAD SETTLED Marcella in for the night, given Nannetta her instructions for the morning, and now had time for herself. When that odd moment of peace arrived and she was alone, she would go into the visitors' salon, select one of the hard chairs from against the wall, and place it directly in front of Grazia's portrait. She'd spent her young life sitting on hard chairs at home or on wooden benches in the missionary school, so sitting on a hard chair was never a punishment, and it kept her back straight. The first time they'd met, Jarvinia had remarked on Juliet's beautiful back: a dancer's back, she had said.

Juliet had wanted to be a dancer and, until the age of thirteen, she'd danced everywhere. On her way to school, while the other children walked or skipped across the fields, she jumped, and leaped, and sprang into the air like a young gazelle. Her mother, who was easily irritated, would yell at her: "Juliet Mudarikwa, you stop showing off." Her mother was the cook on a tobacco farm in the southeast of Zimbabwe, and she was teaching Juliet to cook and to forget all that nonsense about being a dancer. None of the workers on the farm admitted to being Juliet's father, and that was probably true, as everyone supposed he must have been a white man, or at the very least some-one of mixed race. The last white man on the farm, other than Luke McDougal, the farm's owner, was the foreman who'd hailed from Australia and who'd returned home after his African adventure, and that had happened before Juliet was born.

Juliet's skin was luminescent, the color of the copper bowl that her mother used to whip egg whites into shape. Other than the two pink-and-white children of Luke McDougal, Juliet was the only child on the farm with skin lighter than her mother's and that of the other farm workers. In the missionary school, when no adults were around to overhear, the other children tortured Juliet for being different, and while she was still quite young, not even seven, she decided that she would become a great dancer and live among people who looked exactly like her. But that wasn't possible, as Juliet, who was quite beautiful, looked like no one else in the world. Her beauty caused her undoing. When she was thirteen, on her way home from school, walking alone, she was raped by a worker from a neighboring tobacco farm. She didn't tell her mother, who had beaten her too many times for walking alone, and there was no one else to tell. She miscarried at four months and nearly died. When she was finally permitted out of bed, she was beaten by her mother to within an inch of her life. Her mother had been baptized a Christian, and she took the fourth and sixth commandments very seriously.

At seventeen, Juliet was a far better cook than her mother, and she was offered work at a neighboring farm—which she might have taken just to get away from home, but a better opportunity arose. She was asked to accompany the youngest McDougal daughter to her school in Johannesburg, and, instead of returning to the farm, Juliet cashed in her return ticket and found a job in Jo'burg as a cook. A stunningly beautiful woman in a large international city has many opportunities; yet Juliet, who had a great reservoir of patience, turned them all down, saved her money, and waited. Three years passed, and she spent her evenings in her bed-sitter reading *Vanity Fair*, the complete works of Charles Dickens, and the *Oxford English*

Dictionary, and watching *Lifestyles of the Rich and Famous.*
And every night after she'd settled into bed, she would listen to tapes of BBC English to improve her pronunciation.

It was during a performance of *Giselle* by the South
African Ballet Theatre that the wait ended. She was seated
next to a large, elderly woman in the orchestra when
Lorna Maseko danced in the peasant pas de deux. Even
through rape and her mother's beatings, Juliet's tears
hadn't fallen; yet as she watched Lorna Maseko whirl
across the stage of the Civic Theatre, her black skin
translucent under the stage lights, a decade of tears
gushed forth. The packet of tissues that her neighbor
pressed into her hands couldn't contain them. They rolled
down her cheeks, covered her hands, and soaked her little black dress.

The woman was a diplomat, a cultural attaché in Rome,
and someone of importance, which is what Juliet wanted
for herself, to be important. She visited Juliet's restaurant
the next evening, and the evening after that, and compli-
mented her on her cooking. She understood perfectly
Juliet's great desire to live in Europe, to achieve something
in life. "We all need to be recognized for our talents,"
Jarvinia had said, taking Juliet's hands into her own.

Sex was not important to Juliet, although she certainly
understood its importance to others. Once a month, she
slept with the owner of the restaurant (an act of forti-
tude), and once she had accepted an invitation from a
man who'd spoken to her in the bank line. He spoke BBC
English, wore an Armani suit, had white hair, and looked
rich. He was rich: an Englishman, the president of a large

electronics firm doing business in South Africa. He suggested a discreet arrangement: an apartment in the best part of Johannesburg, a generous allowance, and visits twice a week. Juliet refused. Perhaps if he'd asked her to go to London, she might have agreed. Sex in Jo'burg was a dead end for a woman of mixed race, not a beginning.

Rome was just as good as London, and an elderly woman was no more of a burden than an elderly man. For a European passport and the promise of entrée into the first circles in Rome, Juliet could endure a great deal, even the sexual attentions of Jarvinia Baudler. But Jarvinia Baudler had lied. There was no passport, just a visitor's visa to enter Germany, and from Germany a trip by car to Italy. And not to Rome, as Jarvinia had promised, but to a small, obscure village in Umbria.

Jarvinia was more than a liar, she was a bully. She hid Juliet's entry visa, refusing to return it, but Juliet had no intention of returning to Zimbabwe. Her mother would crow in triumph if her ambitious daughter came home in disgrace, so she bided her time once again.

Marcella had told her to hide the pearls, and Juliet knew it was good advice. Nannetta would call Juliet a thief if she saw her with anything that belonged to Palazzo Molin, and after Marcella was dead, there would be no one to say otherwise. Nannetta was very like Juliet's own mother, a servant in someone else's house, yet full of self-importance and jealous of anyone who desired to rise in the world. Juliet held the pearls up to catch the light and admired their luminous glow. The story of Grazia, the Spanish upstart who had commissioned the most famous

artist in Europe to decorate her ceilings, fascinated Juliet,
and sometimes, if she stared long enough at the portrait,
she imagined herself sitting where Grazia had sat. And why
not? Unbeknownst to the countess, she had dined out
four times with Marcella's cousin, Count Volpe. Juliet's
mother had once accused her daughter of being a witch,
and perhaps it was true. She had certainly bewitched Saverio Volpe. After their marriage, she would sit for her portrait wearing Grazia's pearls.

7

"WHERE THE HELL have you been for the last two days?"
Carlo had screamed at him earlier in the day when Cenni
had finally turned on his cell phone. "And don't hand me
that crap about doing interviews. I had my secretary call
around Venice this morning to the people on your list, and
none of them had seen you."

He'd taken three more calls since then, all from Carlo,
and all of them demanding that he arrest someone soon.
"That German fellow's on my back, which means that
somebody's on his back, and you know what that means.
My promotion is twisting in the wind. And, by the way, so
is yours."

Carlo's single concern in life after choosing his shirt and
tie in the morning was his career, and he seemed incapable
of believing that his concerns were not everyone else's. Alex
amused himself with the idea of handing over Baudler's
murderer and his resignation at the same time. Carlo's
expression would be a joy to see. Alex's visit to Venice had

been a success of sorts. He had discovered at least one reason for Baudler's murder, but as yet no way to prove it. Marcella Molin had freely admitted giving money to Baudler.
"Why not, we were great friends once, even lovers. She
needed money. I have money. And who else's business is it
but mine?" she'd asked, challenging him. When he'd
brought up the possibility of blackmail, she'd laughed.

"And what exactly, dottore, was she blackmailing me
about?"

She also insisted that she'd stopped the monthly
deposits when Nannetta, who glued herself to the TV,
told her of Jarvinia's death. Cenni had the fleeting impression that she would have enjoyed the sensation of being
arrested, that she had accepted her imminent death and
would have liked to go out in style. He was tempted to do
just that, arrest her, and give Carlo apoplexy. Carlo wanted
him to arrest somebody, but not somebody who could
fight back with a phalanx of lawyers and put his job at risk.
When Cenni had asked about her recent visits to Paradiso, she responded that they were strictly friendship
calls, adding: "I expect that old cow across the square
gave you an exact accounting."

He had interviewed Juliet Mudarikwa in the visitors'
salon, both of them sitting on hard chairs. Alone, and
without the countess to challenge every question, she was
less collected with her answers. She was noticeably ill at
ease when he'd asked to see her residency permit, and
then her passport. Her permit to stay in Venice had been
issued just two weeks earlier, for a term of ten years. This
was at least five years longer than most EU residents

received on their first try, and Mudarikwa was not an EU resident. Her passport had been issued in Zimbabwe and seemed to be in order, but she couldn't produce an accompanying travel visa, without which she could never have entered Germany legally. She claimed it had been stolen from a hotel in Rome, but when Cenni asked for the police report, she couldn't produce it. Cenni was sure that Molin had used her position and her money to get Mudarikwa her residency permit; at the very least, she must have sponsored the African to the tune of several hundred thousand euros.

Mudarikwa was particularly evasive in her response to how and why she'd left Jarvinia Baudler for Marcella Molin.

"I was hired by the countess as her cook. Nannetta has no idea what foods to cook for a cancer patient. Everything she makes is heavy and unhealthful."

When he mentioned that she'd been seen arguing with the German in Paradiso, she made light of it.

"Jarvinia was angry that I'd left her to join the countess's household. She resented my bettering myself. She hired me in Jo'burg to be her cook, and now I'm the countess's cook."

When he asked if there had been a personal relationship between her and the German, or between her and the countess, her reply was equivocal.

"I trained as a cook for five years in Zimbabwe, and for three years in Jo'burg. Jarvinia came to the restaurant twice, liked my cooking, and offered me a job. She was my employer; I was her employee."

Both women denied having been in Paradiso on the Wednesday that Baudler was killed, and Cenni had no way, yet, of challenging their assertions. So far, the carabinieri and the civil police had found no witnesses who'd seen either woman or the Mercedes in Paradiso on the day of the murder. But it was early in the investigation, and Cenni knew that Juliet Mudarikwa had lied at least twice during her interview. She had been unusually still when answering his questions: her back straight, her hands clasped tightly in her lap, and her feet planted firmly on the floor. Throughout the interview, she'd maintained eye contact, with two notable exceptions: when he asked about the stolen visa, and later when he asked if she'd been in Paradiso on Wednesday. She hesitated both times, looking sideways to the right before answering. He realized afterward that she had been looking at the portrait of Grazia Molin, perhaps for guidance.

8

As Cenni walked across the Piazza San Marco on his way to his third interview of the day, the pigeons took momentary flight, and a vendor tried to sell him a packet of maize. "They'll eat out of your hand, signore, if you're perfectly still."

"*No, grazie,*" Cenni replied politely, and watched as two priests dressed in cassocks accepted the woman's offer. One of them made a half-hearted gesture at looking for some change, but she refused payment. Cenni couldn't hear what the vendor said, but he did hear a "God bless you" from one of the priests. Renato would have paid, he thought, and for one intense moment he had a vision of his younger brother joyfully chasing pigeons across the square and whooping like an Indian. Renato will know what to do, Alex thought, thinking of Chiara. He'll advise me.

Signor Volpe—or Count Volpe, as his secretary addressed him—was a senior director of Banca Centrale Venezia. He had agreed to see the commissario late in the day, at seven, in his office in the Piazza San Marco. Cenni found it interesting that he was a director of the same bank mentioned in Jacob Lagerskjöld's letter. They must hand these positions down with the family silver, he reflected, as he waited for Volpe to appear. The walls of the outer office were covered in plaques, all very fulsome in praising the recipient, and just about every one of them describing Count Volpe as the savior of Venice. When Cenni had asked Marcella Molin about her cousin, she had advised him to "stay away from that 'do-gooder' hypocrite." The walls gave testament to the 'do-gooder' part. He was withholding judgment about the rest.

"Dottor Cenni, my apologies for keeping you waiting," a voice behind him said. Cenni looked around to find a small, very dapper man with a large smile looking up at him.

"Let's go into my office where we can be private," he said. "My secretary told me that you want to discuss my financial dealings with Jarvinia Baudler."

Good, no skirting the issue. Cenni preferred to begin in the middle and not waste time. It turned out to be an easy interview after Volpe acknowledged paying five thousand euros into Baudler's bank account. "For information," he said, and he was quite direct, and unashamed about why. His cousin was trying to deprive him of what was rightfully his—Palazzo Molin—by creating a foundation to honor her father.

"Under Italian law, my uncle had to leave the palazzo to his daughter, or he would have left it to me. He preferred me to her," he said smugly. "And if you've been visiting her, you'll know why. He loved the palazzo, and she's let it fall apart. I'm surprised she hasn't had the Tiepolo frescoes painted over. His will is very specific: at her death, if she dies without heirs, it comes to me. There's nothing I can do about her money, she can leave it to whomever she wants, but not the Palazzo Molin."

Cenni interrupted before Volpe got too wound up defending his rights. "How do you know she's planning to set up a foundation? I gather that you two are not that fond of each other, so I assume she wasn't the one who told you?"

"That African she's living with, Juliet Mudarikwa, she told me. I've wined and dined her a few times," he said. "And a bit more," he added with a sly grin. "My cousin is planning to circumvent her father's will by setting up a foundation to honor him for his bravery during the war. He gave his life to save other members of *La Resistenza,* is what she's claiming in the foundation's by-laws," he said and laughed.

"Why is that funny?"

"He was never in the Resistance. If he were alive today, he'd be Umberto Bossi's biggest supporter. Jarvinia Baudler has a document that proves my uncle was a collaborator during the occupation. My lawyer insists that even without that document, the courts would rule in my favor, but I'm not taking any chances. Five thousand euros is a small price to pay for a building worth millions."

"So, out of the blue, Jarvinia Baudler shows up with a document to save your inheritance!" Cenni responded, beginning to get irritated, not entirely sure why. "How did she know about the foundation, and how did she know about your interest?"

"Juliet," he said with confidence, not picking up on Cenni's changing mood. "She's a good little spy."

"And what's in it for the good little spy?" Cenni asked.

Volpe laughed. "Not what she thinks! She sees herself as the mistress of Palazzo Molin. Can you imagine—an African of no family or education, mistress of one of the great palaces in Venice!" He grew serious. "The Volpe family traces its roots back to the founding of Venice. The Molins are parvenus, as far as we're concerned."

But you'll take their palazzo!

Cenni suggested that there might be another reason for Volpe's payment to the German. Blackmail! For the miserly sum of five thousand euros, she promised not to reveal that the bank, or one of its directors, had hidden the counterfeit pounds and used them after the war?

Volpe denied the charge. "I never heard of a sum that size being shipped to our bank until Baudler showed me a letter, less than a month ago. The money never arrived here. If it had, I would have known about it." As much as he was beginning to dislike this self-satisfied little man, Cenni was inclined to believe him.

At the end of the interview, Saverio Volpe was confident that the commissario was in complete sympathy with his cause. "When you find the letter, you'll provide me with a copy so I can give it to my lawyers," he said in parting. In a final show of male camaraderie, he revealed to Cenni that the count had wanted Marcella to marry him, but that she had refused. "Can you believe it? That homely lesbian refused to marry me!" he said, still licking his wound some sixty years later. Cenni smiled in sympathy.

I hope she screws him out of the palazzo and the other one gives him a good dose of the clap, Cenni thought, as he walked toward the train station.

9

THE TRAIN WAS just pulling into the Santa Lucia station, forty minutes late. A half-day strike in the morning had played havoc with train schedules, and Cenni should have been grateful that his train wasn't four hours late instead of a mere forty minutes. But he wasn't, although he'd never admit it to the questore, who religiously blamed everything that went wrong in Italy on the Left, even during the five years that *Forza Italia* was in power. Cenni had concluded years ago that Carlo's affinity for the Right had little if anything to do with politics and almost everything to do with his resemblance to Silvio Berlusconi: short and stocky, with a large head, a mouth full of teeth, and an overriding physical vanity. Someone who didn't know Carlo, or his wife, might have concluded otherwise, and assumed it had something to do with their economic status, which was filthy rich, except that the money was Romina's, and in the last election, Romina had stood as a delegate for Prodi. The questore was demanding a meeting in the morning, which meant that Cenni would have to leave Bologna no later than seven to arrive at the Perugia Questura by ten. Damn you, Carlo! I'll get there when I get there, was Cenni's thought as he boarded the last intercity train leaving Venice.

Two hours, eight minutes to Bologna. It was early in the tourist season, and the train was almost empty, at least in first class. Just a few English-speaking students sitting at the other end of the carriage, text-messaging one another. Peace and quiet, and a bit more than two hours to solve the puzzle of who had killed Jarvinia Baudler. What he found unsettling was that the case had two distinct lines of investigation. The Swedish letter offered the most possibilities. Baudler had been a blackmailer, promising Marcella to withhold the letter for money and then, doing a neat little pirouette, promising Saverio to release the letter for money, a tricky balancing act that could have easily gotten her killed. And how did Juliet, "the good little spy," fit in? Was she Baudler's assistant, playing the Venetian cousins against one another, or was she running away from Baudler? If the latter, why was she running, and was it a motive for murder? And then there was the Rome connection. Dieter Reimann wanted that letter as much as the Venetian cousins. Was he acting for his government or playing a lone hand? Initially, Cenni had thought the revelations in the letter were innocuous, particularly if viewed through the prism of time; but his grandmother, who had a dead-on political sense, disagreed.

The other aspect of the case, at least on its surface, had nothing to do with Baudler's blackmailing propensities. Anita Tangassi and Lorenzo Vannicelli had both acted strangely when questioned about the 1978 murders. The use of excessive violence in both cases was similar, and it seemed too coincidental that Vannicelli was the one who'd found Baudler's body—and in the house of Anita Tangassi no less! And how did the mutilation of Baudler's body fit into all this? The medical examiner believed the mutilation occurred after the body was moved, suggesting it was a cold deliberate act. Was it meant to be a symbol of some sort, or did the killer conceive of the mutilation as a diversion, a signpost pointing to those who had sent Baudler the poison-pen letters?

This was not one of those cases where he could sit back in an armchair, consult his little gray cells, and arrive at the name of the murderer, and there were no forensic clues— at least not yet—to get him there. The victim had conveniently provided the means for her own murder, a log of firewood; and she had provided motive as well, through her blackmailing schemes. What he needed was opportunity. The postmortem indicated that Baudler had been killed between two and four in the afternoon, but Cenni wanted to determine a more exact time. A narrower time frame would give him a better chance of finding her killer. Paradiso was far too small for anyone, particularly a stranger, to move around freely on a beautiful sunny day without being seen. Signora Cecchetti was not the only close observer in Paradiso.

Lorenzo Vannicelli said that the German was wearing her going-out shoes when he found her body. Her comfortable shoes, the ones that she wore around the house, were found sitting on a shelf just inside the front door, which suggested to Cenni that she changed her footwear right before she left or entered the house. So why was she wearing her good shoes and best dress in the dirty basement? The other open question was the disappearance of her car. He'd been mulling this over for two days now, and he thought he had an answer. She must have driven her car to a local garage for repair, and someone from the garage had driven her home. The person who drove her home would have noticed if other cars were parked in the square; maybe Baudler had mentioned something to the driver. If they could find that person, they'd be a lot closer to knowing the time she was killed.

Perhaps when she entered the house, she realized that someone was inside and, instead of changing her shoes, she went looking for the intruder. Or perhaps she heard the neighbor's cat meowing. He could see her calling down from the top of the stairs, *Is anyone there?* Getting no answer, she would have started down slowly, hesitating on each step, wondering if she should continue, wondering who waited for her below. Too melodramatic, he decided. He had visited the basement, and there was no place where an intruder could hide and not be visible from the middle step, and that included the cave. If a stranger had been lurking down there, she would have immediately

retreated. But she hadn't; she had walked over to where
the firewood was stacked, some ten feet distant from the
last basement step. Wouldn't that indicate that she had
known the intruder?

He liked it! He'd send Elena a list of questions to be
researched, and he'd emphasize again the urgency in
finding that garage. On Thursday, he had been issued
one of those new text-messaging phones, but he was clue-
less about how to use it. Perhaps he should get a coffee first
and attempt to use it later. That's when he noticed one of
the English-speaking students, a good-looking blonde,
walking toward him, headed toward the toilets.

"Excuse me, signorina," he said, displaying his best
Cenni smile. "I wonder if I could impose on you for a
minute?"

Book Four

Speak me fair in death

I

"So, what have you to say for yourself?" the questore asked, mindful that it was unlikely that Cenni would have anything to say that he wanted to hear.

"I'm not sure what you want to know, Carlo," Cenni replied. "I spent two days in Venice, interviewing the two major suspects in this case: Countess Molin and Count Volpe. Baudler was blackmailing them both. I haven't decided to arrest either one of them yet, but I'm certainly thinking about it. That should keep Dieter Reimann off your back—metaphorically, of course," Cenni responded.

"Metaphorically! Good God, Alex, what are you trying to do to me? I bring you back from Foligno, promise to make you vice-questore, and you're off again on one of your ridiculous starts. Molin is one of the richest women in Italy and comes from a very important family. I never heard of this Count Volpe, but I'm sure he's important too. That's not the kind of arrest I meant, and you know it."

"Who is it you're expecting me to arrest, Carlo? Is there something about this case that you're not telling me?"

"Damn it, Alex. Don't play cat-and-mouse with me. You know very well who I want you to arrest. Reimann told me that Baudler was living with a black woman, an illegal from Zimbabwe. Who else do we look to in a domestic quarrel but the husband or the wife—the wife, I guess, in this case? And this murder certainly appears to be a domestic quarrel, particularly if you consider what was done to her afterward."

"Sorry to disappoint you, Carlo. But there's a lot more going on here than a domestic quarrel, and Juliet Mudarikwa, the illegal you speak of, hasn't been living with the German for a number of months now. And she's not an illegal. In fact, she's Molin's cook and general factotum, and she recently acquired legal residence. To add to the mix, she's been dating Volpe, and you're right, he is important, very important."

The questore, who'd been standing by the window trying to determine if one of his people was blowing his horn like that, groaned loudly and sat down again. "Every time you get involved in one of these high-profile cases, Alex, I get screwed. Give me something I can tell Reimann to pacify his government, and ours. If we don't hand them the murderer soon, I can kiss Rome good-bye. You know, Romina was really looking forward to moving to the capital. She's been up there twice this week, looking at apartments. She says hello, by the way."

"I have two additional suspects, aside from the Venetians, so we may get you to Rome yet. Neither of them is so

important that an arrest would incur anyone's wrath."
Cenni paused for a moment, wondering if he dared, and
thought: why not. "Actually, that's not entirely true. One of
them is a very important official in *Rifondazione Comunista*
and may be a good friend of Bertinotti, or at least that's
what I'm hearing."

"Good Lord, Alex, you can't arrest a friend of Bertinotti.
He's the head of Parliament."

"You'll have to make up your mind, Carlo. Apparently,
you want me to arrest someone, but also, apparently, not
the murderer. Is it to be the Right or the Left? You decide!"
Cenni had a strong suspicion that the questore didn't
really want him to put an innocent in jail, and that he
staged these little dramas only because he knew his senior
commissario would never follow through. But it was only
a suspicion and one he hoped never to test.

"Have it your own way, Alex, but don't expect me to
smooth this over with the Germans. From now on, when
Reimann calls, I'm going to have Vittoria transfer his calls
to you. I don't want to know any more about this case until
you have the murderer in custody. And don't turn your
cell phone off again. You work for me, and don't forget it."

He slammed the door of Cenni's office when he was
leaving, rocking it on its hinges, and Cenni didn't know if
he should laugh or start cleaning out his desk. A minute
later, Carlo stuck his head back in the doorway:

"Don't look for me for the rest of the day. I'm going to
Rome with Romina. She says she's found the perfect
apartment."

* * *

THE MEETING WITH the questore had ended pretty much the way Cenni thought it would. Carlo did his dance of death, threatening all kinds of dire happenings if Cenni didn't arrest someone soon, but not, of course, anyone important enough to cause him political heartburn. It happened in every case that had political implications. He always managed to pacify Carlo while still doing exactly what he wanted, but it was getting increasingly tedious, and he was getting increasingly tired and old, too old to continue playing political games. Since Venice, he had been mulling over the possibilities of a career change, should he decide to leave the police, and he'd finally decided to become a defense lawyer. At least he would do some good for someone, and his years of experience in the police wouldn't be totally wasted. As soon as this case was wrapped up, he'd visit his brother and talk it over with him, and in the meantime he had a stack of files on his desk to review, including the photographs of the basement where Baudler had been killed, which had finally arrived from forensics. But first he'd send a text message to Elena, whose office was across from his.

"Lots of goodies for you," Elena announced, putting her head around the door twenty minutes later. "Real coffee as you requested, *capo*."

"Come in and shut the door," Cenni responded. "And be quick about it! Carlo's looking for you."

"Why's he looking for me?" Elena asked a bit surprised. She was convinced he didn't even know her name.

"He wants you to train a new officer."

"A woman?" Elena asked rhetorically, sure already that it was a woman.

"Probably. I told him you're far too busy on this case, but whenever Carlo decides to do something, it's rather difficult to dissuade him. Hide out in my office for a while. He's not too happy with me at the moment, so I doubt he'll check in here. And he's off to Rome later this morning."

Elena nodded in agreement, scowling. She was rather tired of being the token female in her position, the only woman holding the rank of inspector. She was beginning to wonder if, by the time she was ready to retire in thirty years, she'd still be the only female inspector in the department.

"So, you got my text messages last night, I assume," Cenni said, trying to suppress a grin of self-appreciation, but it broke out despite himself. "Pretty good for a rank beginner, wasn't it?"

"Remarkable. I showed it to Piero."

Cenni detected a note of irony in her response and decided to ignore it.

"So, how about the car? Any news there? Finding that car is more important than anything else I asked you to do."

"Then you'll be very happy. We found the man who's repairing Baudler's car. He lives between Paradiso and Spello and works on cars after he finishes his regular job, which is driving a gas-delivery truck. No doubt he charges less than a licensed garage for the same repairs. He's coming in later today to sign a statement, but he told me over the telephone that he drove Baudler back to her house and dropped her off at precisely three thirty, right in front of the house. He remembers the time because Baudler said she was meeting someone at the house at four and she was fussing about the time."

"Did he see anyone, or any cars, in the square?"

"Not a one!" Elena replied blithely.

"Damn! I was hoping he'd provide a lead."

"He did. When they were returning to Paradiso, as they were passing that gas station that's located just before the entrance to town, a black Mercedes was pulling out of the station, headed away from Paradiso. He says that Baudler made a comment about it, so he took particular note of the license plate. He can't remember the exact number, but it was a Veneto plate."

"And the comment," Cenni asked, clearly elated.

"'So the bitches are still together,' is what he says she said. According to him, whatever it was about, she wasn't particularly happy."

"I suppose if he had to identify the car and the plate, he could do it?"

"I think so. He was trying to remember the plate number while on the telephone, but he could remember only two numbers: four and seven, and the VE. And the driver of the Mercedes was a man, by the way. He couldn't see if anyone was in the back. Tinted glass, he said."

"That's Molin's car. She and Juliet Mudarikwa both denied being in or anywhere near Paradiso on the day of the murder. This gives me something with which to squeeze the African. There's something she's not telling us."

"Yeah, but he said the car was headed in the opposite direction. I assume it was returning to Venice."

"Maybe, maybe not. They, or she, could have turned around and come back, maybe even for the four o'clock appointment, although it doesn't sound like it from Baudler's comment to the garage guy. When you take this guy's statement, try to get as many details as possible, including a description of the driver. Anything else?"

"As your text message requested—at least I think it's what you requested—I called our people in Venice for a copy of Mudarikwa's residency application. It should be here this afternoon. By the way, you might want to work on your shorthand if you're going to be texting a lot. I still haven't figured out what CLABTMLNDRVVNC means. And MUSM doesn't mean what you think it means. That one I won't show to Piero," she said. "Still nothing from our door-to-door inquiries in Paradiso, but we've just started. I'll let you know as soon as anything turns up. And now I'm going to find a closet to hide in until after eleven."

"Before you do, call Venice and see if they can find out the name of Molin's driver. She employs only two full-time people at the house: an old crone and the African. She probably uses an agency when she needs a driver or temporary help. Our people in Venice can find out."

As Elena got up to leave, he added, clearly pleased, "Nice job, Elena. If you run into Carlo and he gives you a hard time, tell him to come see me."

After Elena left, Cenni opened the envelope that Fausto Greci, Perugia's senior forensic officer, had delivered that morning. There wasn't anything in the written report that

Cenni didn't already know from the medical examiner, but
he was curious to see the photographs. There was always
something to be learned from the way the body had been
left by the killer. One thing about Greci, Cenni thought:
he's thorough. The envelope contained more than forty
photographs. A good number of them were of the victim
sprawled against the bottom two steps. He found it difficult
to view the body without getting angry; he was relieved
when he reached photos of the area surrounding the
woodpile. He flipped through them absentmindedly,
thinking of what Lorenzo Vannicelli had said about the
killer humiliating and degrading Baudler. Maybe because he agreed with Vannicelli, he'd found himself liking
the man. That was always something to watch out for in a
murder investigation, liking a suspect. You start liking suspects, and then you find yourself believing whatever they
tell you. Another good reason to work with Elena. She
usually took an instant dislike to all of them.

As he was thinking about Vannicelli, he realized that
he had flipped back to one particular photograph of the
stacked firewood. Something's wrong, he thought. The
wood was stacked neatly just as it had been when he was in
the house on Thursday afternoon, but in the photograph
the wood was in a different location, some three to four
feet further to the right. It makes sense, he concluded.
The carabinieri probably restacked the firewood after
searching for the log that had killed Baudler. But just to be
sure, he started to call Elena. Instead, he decided to use his
newly acquired skill for text messaging. He rather liked

communicating this way and considered himself surprisingly good at it for a beginner.

2

"WHAT?" ELENA SAID, blasting into his office a few minutes later holding up her mobile phone. "I haven't a clue what this says."

"It's very simple," Cenni responded. "You drop the vowels when you write, then fill them in when you read. I asked if the carabinieri had searched the woodpile after the body was removed from the cellar."

"Who taught you to text-message, anyway?" Elena asked, thinking she'd like to wring the person's neck.

"A woman I met on the train last night."

One of his blondes, no doubt! "Well, she doesn't know what she's talking about. How am I supposed to know which vowels you dropped? My office is right across the hall. Wouldn't it be easier if you just walked across?"

After they'd agreed that Cenni would stop the texting, Elena admitted that she didn't know if the carabinieri had searched through the woodpile. "But I doubt it. They left everything else in a mess, so why would they neatly stack the wood again?" She promised to call Gianluca in Paradiso to find out. "Immediately!" she said, realizing from the wrinkle between Cenni's brows that he was on to something. And like the questore, when he was on to something he was not easily dissuaded.

While Elena was telephoning Gianluca, Cenni was

reviewing the likelihood that the person who'd entered or exited the back door on Thursday evening or Friday morning had been searching for the papers that Baudler had stolen from the embassy, and that one of the areas searched had been the woodpile. A clever hiding place, Cenni conceded. It would be a dirty job looking through that stack of firewood, and not a place that most people would think to look. Baudler's lover might have known if she usually hid things in the woodpile; so might Reimann, who'd known her for twenty-five years. But if either of them was the murderer, why not search the pile immediately after killing her? Why risk getting caught by coming back?

"Nope!" Elena said, hanging up the telephone. "Gianluca says the log that killed Baudler was found lying a few feet from the stack. Probably it's shown in one of those photographs. They didn't think to search through the firewood, as they already had the weapon. And get this: Anita Tangassi has been to the station house to make a claim for broken dishes. Remember, how she insisted on unwrapping each one of her *periwinkle* dishes to check for damage. She claims that two are broken and that the carabinieri are responsible."

"I suppose if they broke them, they should pay," Cenni responded, always looking at it from the other point of view.

"Gianluca says he was the one who searched through that box, and the dishes were already broken. The broken dishes were wrapped differently from the others, with the broken pieces stacked within the wrapping, so they must have been broken before they were packed. My God, but that woman is cheap! Imagine trying to get a free set of dishes from the carabinieri—good luck to that! Do you want me to go to Paradiso with the photographs just to be sure the firewood, was actually moved?" she asked skeptically.

"It was moved," Cenni responded, "but look again, just to be sure nothing was missed in the search. I'm off to see Giuseppe Landi, my counterpart, who investigated the 1978 murders in Paradiso." He noticed Elena's raised right eyebrow, and added, "Just a hunch."

GIUSEPPE LANDI HAD risen to the position of commissario at a time when being in the "old boy" network was still the only way to get ahead in government circles. Those who rose in the ranks had three things in common: the habit of dotting their *i*'s, the ability to flatter their superiors, and, most important of all, *una raccomandazione*. You didn't aspire to a high rank unless you had a *padrino* in an even higher rank. It hadn't changed a whole lot in thirty years, but it had changed some. Cenni never dotted anything, and he certainly never flattered Carlo, but he had to admit that his mother, a Baglioni before her marriage, knew everyone who was anyone in Umbria, and he had no guarantee that she hadn't used her influence to get him his promotions, although he doubted it, as she cringed any time someone referred to him as a policeman.

Landi, who had agreed to a meeting to review the Paradiso murders, was exactly as Cenni remembered him: portly, garrulous, and a gentleman. Cenni suspected, after sitting with him in his garden for less than ten minutes, that Landi was bored to death with tomatoes and zucchini and his wife's complaints about their children never visiting. He was ripe to talk about anything and anyone.

"Absolutely not!" was Landi's response when Cenni asked if Anita might have committed the murders. "I'm sorry they got rid of all the evidence from the case, or you'd see for yourself that a nine-year-old girl could never lift an ax that size, let alone deliver the ferocious blows that killed that poor woman and her child. You're thinking of those lightweight tools they sell nowadays. The ax used in the Paradiso murders was made for a lumberjack."

Alex nodded his head in agreement, but he was still not totally convinced. "You were on the scene, Giuseppe, so, of course, you'd have a far better sense of what was possible. I was just wondering about some of the child's cryptic answers and the infighting that went on between the mother, the parish priest, and the neighbor. What was that all about?"

"That trio—I had my fill of them, let me tell you." He leaned closer to Cenni. "Some very strange things went on within that circle." He looked up to the heavens as though seeking guidance from a higher power. "Things have changed a lot; did you see that special a few nights ago about the Vatican giving a pass to priests who are sexual predators? Nothing of that nature was aired on public TV thirty years ago. The church is losing its power."

"Are you suggesting that the priest—Monsignor Lacrimosa—had something to do with the murders? Was he preying on the two little girls? Is that why Anita looked over at him during your interview, when you asked if she'd seen any strange men lurking around their play area?"

"I'm not thinking little girls," Landi said. "Did you read the pathology report?"

"No, because it's missing, along with the ax and the crime-scene photographs. The only file left is the interview you conducted with the girl, and one very short police report. I looked through both, and couldn't find the addresses of the father or the brother."

"Don't bother! Believe me, we were very careful to check their whereabouts. They were both in Switzerland at the time of the murders. It would have made things so much easier if either of them had been the killer."

"Why?"

"If you'd read the pathology report, you'd know why. I'm surprised they didn't destroy all the files, but I suppose since the case is still officially open, they couldn't dump everything. The woman was pregnant, four months according to the doctor who did the autopsy, and the husband had been gone for more than a year. So we knew for sure that she'd been having an affair, we just didn't know with whom."

"But wasn't there a reasonable chance that the man who'd gotten her pregnant was also her killer?" Cenni asked.

"Reasonable! Of course it was reasonable. Her only close neighbor, an old man who lived down the road, said he'd seen a man going in and coming out of the house on numerous occasions, and always after dark, so he couldn't give us a description. But on the day before the murder, he saw the priest coming out of her house, and in mid-afternoon—he swore it was the priest. He also claimed to have seen Orazio Vannicelli, Anita Tangassi's uncle, hanging out at the back of the house earlier in the week. But I was instructed to *let it go* when I wanted to bring them both in for questioning. Whatever you do, they said, don't talk to the priest. *He's a saver of souls.* I don't know about the woman who was killed, but in my view there was definitely something going on between the priest and Marta Tangassi, the child's mother. I don't say it was sexual, but it was strange. You've heard of Svengali, I suppose. Well, the priest was Marta Tangassi's Svengali. Whatever he told her to do, she did. The woman was priest-ridden. You see it all the time in small towns."

He stopped abruptly in the middle of his story and got up to chase a ginger cat that was sniffing around his tomato plants. "Every year, that cat destroys at least one of my tomato plants. He'd eat all the leaves if I let him. Now where was I?"

"Svengali!"

"Yes, well this particular Svengali had the right connections in Rome, or someone did. *Tell the press you're looking for a vagrant and shut the investigation down,* was the message we received from Rome. What did you expect me to do?" he asked defensively. "Go against direct orders?"

Cenni hadn't said a word in criticism, but he knew guilt when he heard it. He said, "I know the influence the Church used to have, but I would have thought it drew the line at impeding a murder investigation, particularly one involving the brutal murder of a child."

"As that TV program made clear the other evening, the Church doesn't draw lines when its prerogatives are in jeopardy. It's just another political party as far as I'm concerned. And remember, Alex, the Lanese case made its way onto the world stage a month after Aldo Moro was kidnapped. Imagine the scandal if it turned out that the local priest murdered his pregnant mistress by putting an ax through her head, and then did the same to an innocent child. Bianca Lanese was buried in her First Communion Dress. Prime Ministers snatched in broad daylight; innocent children axed to death by priests. All hell would have broken loose, and Italy's reputation as a nation that loves children would have been shattered."

"So, you think it was the priest?"

"Not at all, although I'm absolutely sure it wasn't a vagrant. I wasn't given the opportunity to investigate properly, so how can I know anything? But it certainly looked suspicious when our investigation was shut down. You were still a child then, but you probably remember the trauma we suffered as a nation. Aldo Moro had just been kidnapped, and Italy was in a state of siege. I suppose in someone's mind, it was a reasonable tradeoff: *We let a killer go free, but we don't stir up any more national scandals.* Was it the priest, the uncle, the butcher, the baker? We'll never know."

"Perhaps one of them will make a deathbed confession. The uncle is dead, but there's still the monsignore," Cenni said.

"A little late in the day for the monsignore. He died in 2000, from eating some bad mushrooms. I thought you knew!"

3

ALEX LOVED ALMOST every month in the year, although January, February, and March were a bit like one's slower children. You loved them equally with the others but wished they were a bit smarter. But if he really had to choose a favorite month, it would have been June. In Umbria, June is the month of perfection. The spring rains are forgotten, the flowers are in bloom, and the fields are green with the shoots of new crops. The crime rate in June is lower than in any other month, and everyone you meet has something good to say about the weather. It's the ideal time for a trip to Urbino.

He had promised himself that he would talk to Renato about Chiara when the Baudler case was wrapped up, but he decided after leaving Giuseppe Landi that he had to see his brother today. Renato was a bishop, so surely he had the connections to find out what had happened in 1978—whether the Church was involved in shutting down the Lanese investigation, and, if so, why? He arrived in Urbino at four in the afternoon, parked his car outside Renato's residence, stuck a police card in the windshield, and rang the front doorbell. The official residence of the Bishop of Urbino is a vast palace with more rooms than can be comfortably viewed in a single visit, and in the new millennium it still lacked central heating. Even his mother, who bragged mercilessly to her friends about her son the bishop and his palazzo, managed to stay away in the winter months. Renato was currently negotiating with his superiors to turn the palace into a museum. As he confessed to Alex, he was not above feigning a painfully arthritic hip to secure a centrally heated residence. After minutes spent listening to the bell echo through the cavernous rooms, Alex was finally greeted by Renato's dour housekeeper, who directed him to the Cathedral, "where His Excellency is hearing confessions."

"Bless me, father, for I have sinned. It's been a while since my last confession," Alex recited when Renato opened the confessional screen.

"And since when is twenty-five years *a while?*" Renato asked.

"I need to talk."

"It's not Hanna, is it?" Renato asked, worried.

"Hanna's fine. It's about me."

"That's a relief. When you say 'talk,' do you mean in here?" Renato asked, without any actual expectation that his brother was in the throes of a religious rebirth.

"No, outside, if you can leave, although I don't see why not. No one else is waiting in line. *His Excellency* isn't very popular," Alex said laughing. He liked to tease his brother, who almost never took offense.

"My parishioners think a bishop will give them longer lectures and extra Our Father's. I use the time to write my Sunday sermon. I'll change and we can walk and talk, perhaps stop for a coffee in the Piazza della Repubblica."

Renato listened to what Alex had to say concerning the Lanese case without interrupting; but when his brother had finished, he launched forth on what Alex knew to be one of his very rare lectures:

"I know the Church has its faults, far better than you, Alex, but Landi has no idea why the investigation was stopped, and to assume it had something to do with the priest and, even if it did, that the Vatican was involved, is ridiculous. I've had access to a good deal of information about what was happening at the time of Aldo Moro's kidnapping, and I can assure you that the Church was far too busy trying to save Moro's life to influence a murder investigation in Paradiso. My gut tells me that the government put a stop to the investigation; it was probably afraid to stir up more ugly feelings and reactions at a time when Italy was in crisis. Easier all around to blame it on a vagrant, *an immigrant vagrant*, than to take a chance that it was the parish priest. Listen, Alex, I'll do some snooping for you, but I'm sure I'm right. And now that we've gotten that out of the way, what's really bugging you? You didn't drive two hours to Urbino to discuss a case that goes back to 1978."

Alex told his brother of his visit to Murano and about Chiara. He'd been prepared for some skepticism on Renato's part, but his brother agreed immediately that it must have been Chiara. He also agreed that she appeared to be running away.

"Covering her hair with a scarf and holding hands with a child as she got off the vaporetto in Murano—definitely Chiara. She was always the brains in the outfit," Renato said smiling. "Obviously, you know Chiara better than I do, Alex. But I doubt that she ran away because of her scarred face. She was the least vain woman I've ever known; I wonder if she even knew she was beautiful. The Chiara I knew twenty years ago was a rare and remarkable woman, and I assume she still is. For Christ's sake, Alex, I never thought you were a wimp. Do you really plan to let her go without making a single effort to find her?"

"She knew it was me, and she ran away. How can I justify going after a woman who's running away from me? Maybe she's married again."

"Sounds a little like wounded vanity to me. *If she doesn't want me, I don't want her.* Possibly she's remarried, but I doubt it. When the glass dealer asked her out, she gave a sick relative as an excuse. From what I remember of Chiara, she would have said directly that she had a husband. And even if she's married, don't you want to see her again? You've been in love with her for twenty-two years; you need to find her, Alex, if only to say good-bye."

"Then you agree that I should quit the police?"

"I do not. Your original reason for joining the police still holds true. You have access to information that a private citizen would never have. You can ask questions, make inquiries, demand answers in true police style. My own guess is that she's still living in Puglia. She may have a child. Twenty years have passed. She may even have grand-children. Maybe she thinks you'd reject her if you knew she had a child. You can be pretty stubborn at times, Alex. Don't forget your reaction when she wanted to get an advanced degree and hold off marrying for two years. You threw a fit!"

"That's what I love about family," Alex responded, with annoyance. "They remember everything you don't want them to remember."

Renato grabbed his twin and wrapped him in a bearhug. "Find her, Alex. If I ever saw two people who belonged together, it's you and Chiara. And like it or not, you are a stubborn bastard." He moved quickly to avoid getting hit. "Just telling it like it is, *figlio mio!*"

They had dinner later that night in the residency, or what Renato referred to as the *icebox*. The food was the worst Alex had ever eaten, and he found himself pushing away most of it after a few bites. "I thought you looked thinner, and now I know why. The pasta was overcooked, the chicken was raw, and I have no clue what this is," Alex said, referring to the dish the housekeeper had just set before him. "Is this supposed to be some type of sweet? It looks like melted ice cream!" He pushed it away.

"Shush! She'll hear you. It is ice cream; it's all she ever serves. We switch off every other night. Vanilla or strawberry."

"You hate vanilla. And speaking of stubborn bastards, the only flavor you'd ever touch at home was chocolate. Here we are, all of us thinking you live in the lap of luxury. *Fratello,* this place is a dump. Considering the state of this ice cream, this room is probably colder than the inside of your refrigerator, and this is June! Hard to believe you took up wearing dresses for this."

"Give it up, Alex. I've accepted the choices you've made in life, and I expect the same of you. I'm a man of God, so stop the dress jokes and stop being an ass!"

"Sorry, Renato. No more dress jokes, I promise. But if this is the way you eat every night, you'll be dead in a year, from starvation or trichinosis. Can't you fire her and hire someone who can cook?"

"The woman does her best. She's mildly retarded and without family, and if she weren't working here, she'd be in a home somewhere."

"So hire yourself a cook and have this one clean the floors, or maybe even dust the furniture. I could write my name on that mirror behind you."

"How do I do that and not hurt her feelings?"

Alex was momentarily speechless in admiration of his brother's innate kindness. Renato was the twin with the soft heart. When they were children, he'd carry home every stray animal he found in the streets. Most of them were sent off to his grandparents' farm in Bevagna. It wasn't until he started bringing home people that his parents finally said *stop*. He's too good for the Church, Alex reflected.

"Give her a new title and tell her that cooking is beneath her. And if your bosses object to paying two salaries, remind them of all the money you'll be coming into when Hanna dies. Or better yet, have Hanna remind them. Even a man of God deserves a decent meal." Alex was the twin with an answer to everything.

IT WAS CLOSE to eleven when Alex put his key into the ignition to begin the return drive. The brothers had talked about everything, just like old times: Hanna's health, Alex's search for Chiara, his current case, Prodi's government. The only thing they didn't talk about was Renato. It wasn't until he was halfway home that Alex acknowledged that it was exactly like old times, mostly about him, with Renato doing the listening. He just assumed that his brother was happy, but decided that the next time he'd at least ask.

At any other time, he would have driven well over the speed limit. He loved to test his car on the open road, and the superstrada was empty of traffic. There was even a three-quarter moon and a sky full of stars to light the way, but tonight he had too much to think about to concentrate on driving. Renato was right; he should continue his search for Chiara. He knew that even before he'd spoken to his brother, but he'd wanted confirmation. Renato was also right that he should stay with the police. He had access to all the national databases. It would be much easier to track Chiara down now, as he had Puglia as a focus. Chiara had always preferred cities with their libraries and museums, so he'd begin with Lecce and work his way up along the heel to Bari. He'd find her.

He had to solve the Baudler case first, and aspects of it were beginning to irritate him. It wasn't a particularly difficult case, as cases go. Access to Baudler's house was limited. He had a clearly identified set of suspects, and he was sure that one of them had murdered the German. The political considerations didn't bother him. In Italy, there were always political considerations, and he'd always worked through them. It was the surrounding set of circumstances that was keeping him awake at nights. Even with an outright confession from one of the suspects, he'd never rest until he tied it all together. Who killed the mother and child in 1978? What happened to Count Molin: was it murder or suicide? What happened to the counterfeit banknotes? And now there was a further twist: the priest and the uncle had both died from eating bad mushrooms. Way too much of a coincidence!

Renato had given him a few ideas, one in particular about the counterfeit notes. "Why is the German government trying to suppress information?" he'd asked. "The world knows Germany produced counterfeit money during the war. I disagree with Hanna that the motive is to stop further talk about the money. It's been the subject of dozens of documentaries, films, even a TV series. A few years back, the English made a tongue-in-cheek series with Ian Richardson playing an evil SS officer. There's no way the Germans can suppress this information. To kill someone to keep quiet what's been known for fifty years! Way too Machiavellian. Hanna is beginning to see spies under her bed."

"What, then?"

"That money went somewhere. I'd start wondering if Germany used the money *after* the war. Now, that *would* cause a scandal. The British would demand restitution, and probably for a lot more than the few paltry pounds involved in this particular case. Nobody talks millions these days. Today, it's always billions."

"Where do you suggest I go looking?"

"Focus on the German's job. She was the cultural attaché in Rome and, from what you tell me, an expert on Renaissance art. I'd start there. One of my former teachers is still complaining that the Germans purchased a number of Leonardo's drawings and papers for the German Institute in Rome, outbidding the Vatican Library, and this was in the decade after the war when everyone was supposed to be broke. He's still wondering where the Germans found that kind of money for culture. You might want to contact him. But if you do, lay off the priest jokes. He's a dear friend."

"It sounds as though we should trade jobs," Alex responded, surprised at how much sense Renato made.

"I might be able to do your job," Renato responded. "You'd definitely screw up mine and instigate the next Reformation, no doubt."

His brother also had some suggestions about finding surviving members of the Resistance in the Veneto. He gave him the name of an elderly priest. "He was with the *partigiani* in Umbria, but these old guys have a wide network. He might have the names of men who were active in the Resistance in Venice."

As he approached Gubbio, the road narrowed and twisted and he had to concentrate on his driving. He could see the lights of an approaching car in the rearview mirror. The driver of the other car flashed his lights six times, warning him to move over. "Aggressive ass," he muttered as he pulled to the right. The car went speeding past—a Citroën 2CV had just thumbed its nose at a 2002 Alpine BMW. "Not in this lifetime," Alex said, pressing down hard on the accelerator.

4

At a surprisingly early hour the next morning, Cenni was at the Foligno station catching the train to Rome. He'd been tempted to text Elena with some instructions before leaving, but decided to honor her request for phone calls only. He had three things he wanted to do in Rome, and two of them had come up during his conversation with Renato the previous evening. The priest who had objected to Germany's purchase of Leonardo's drawings was also up early, thanks to Cenni's phone call. They agreed to meet at the Vatican Library at nine thirty. The partisan priest who might lead Cenni to information about the Resistance in Venice during the war had been luckier. He had a housekeeper, and she refused to wake him at "this ungodly hour." That she was speaking to a future vice-questore made not a particle of difference. "When you're ninety, you'll want a sleep-in too," she'd snapped before hanging up.

His main reason for traveling to Rome, though, was to visit the German Embassy and question some of the people who had worked with Baudler before she retired, and also to see Dieter Reimann. Reimann had been too anxious to keep him away from Rome, so Cenni decided to pay him an unannounced visit at the embassy when he finished at the Vatican Library. His train arrived in Roma Termini exactly on time, so he stopped for a quick coffee before grabbing a taxi outside the station.

Ettore Hyppolito was a priest of the scholarly Jesuit variety and had been a Latin teacher when Renato was training for the priesthood. He was a shy, elderly man in his late seventies, with a thatch of thick white hair that stood straight up from its roots. He had the habit of grabbing at his hair and pulling on it as he talked, which might have accounted for his decidedly youthful hairstyle. His only duty, besides prayer and fasting, was study—and in particular, study of the Vatican Apostolic Library's Renaissance manuscripts. Before Cenni could ask any questions, Ettore, as he insisted on being called—the commissario was, after all, the bishop's brother—gave him a brief description of the Library and its holdings. It seemed he also served as a tour guide for visiting dignitaries.

The Library, he informed Cenni, was built by Pope Nicholas V, *"pro communi doctorum virorum commodo."* Sorry, he said, when he noticed the puzzled look on Alex's face. "Renato was my finest Latin scholar, and you two look so much alike. For the common convenience of the learned," he translated before continuing his talk. "The Library houses a collection of over 1.6 million books, 8,300 incunabile, and 75,000 manuscripts, over 100,000 engravings, and 300,000 coins and medals. The *Codex Vaticanus* is the most famous manuscript in our possession and is generally believed to date from the fourth century. It's the oldest nearly complete copy of the Greek Bible in existence. Of course, it lacks the Book of Genesis, Hebrews 9:14 to the end, the Pastoral Epistles, and the Book of Revelation, but we make do," he said, and smiled shyly at his own witticism. "The architect Domenico Fontana was commissioned by Pope Sixtus V to design this building in 1587, and we've been here ever since." It was at this point that he stopped and grabbed Alex's arm. "You're here just in time to see the building before it's closed to the public. In July, we begin extensive renovations. The Vatican architects say it has to be done, that there are serious structural weaknesses in this part of the building, but I'll confess to you, Alex, I'm very afraid it's all about modernizing, and in the end it will ruin us. Imagine the Vatican Library with air conditioning and elevators. Your generation is very spoiled, Alex."

"Jarvinia Baudler," the priest exclaimed when they finally got around to the reason for the commissario's visit. "I knew Jarvinia very well. She was an excellent scholar of Renaissance art, with a first-rate mind. You say she was murdered. I didn't know that, but then I rarely read the papers and I never watch TV. Very upsetting. I wish I didn't know," he added truthfully. "I prefer not to know about the wickedness in this world."

He informed Cenni that he'd met Jarvinia about twelve years earlier, when she was doing research on certain drawings and writings of Leonardo that were part of the holdings of the German Cultural Institute in Rome. "She was reviewing the Institute's collection with the thought of mounting an exhibit at the embassy and was curious as to how the Institute came to own Leonardo's drawings, which had been held privately for some hundreds of years by a Roman family. The Vatican librarian sent her to see me. She asked why we let the drawings go. 'This is where they rightfully belong,' she said. A very intelligent woman!" the priest repeated.

"Why didn't the Vatican bid on them?" Cenni asked.

"But we did, a very generous offer. Unfortunately, the bidding was closed, but we never had any doubts that we would win. None of the other museums in Rome had that kind of money, and even if they did, it was unlikely that they'd bid against the Vatican. There were only two requirements of bidders, that the drawings remain in Rome and that they be made available to scholars for research. So where else would they go but to the Vatican Library?"

"Where did the German Institute get the money, and how much did they bid?" Cenni asked.

"It was very suspicious to me, which is what I told Jarvinia. We never did learn the exact price, but I know it was well more than a million English pounds higher than our bid. That was another requirement: that payment be made in either English pounds or U.S. dollars. The lire was somewhat unstable back then."

Cenni finished with the priest close to eleven and tactfully refused an invitation to lunch "at a delightful little trattoria in Trastevere. Nothing too good for a brother of the bishop," the Jesuit said in issuing his invitation. "You know, Alex, your brother had the makings of a true scholar, but he preferred the pastoral role. Well, I suppose in the end we'll be glad he did. Your mother will be enormously proud on the day he's invested as Pope. It's where he's headed, Alex, and it will atone for all that wickedness perpetrated by your ancestors."

Cenni decided to walk to the embassy. It would give him time to review what the priest had told him about Jarvinia and her research on Leonardo's drawings. One thing he was sure of: Jarvinia was not doing scholarly research when she'd contacted the Vatican librarian. She'd been on to something, and so was he. He now had ammunition for his talk with Reimann. He also enjoyed a private laugh at his mother's expense: she was a direct descendant of Gianpaolo Baglioni and inordinately proud of her family name, and somehow she managed to ignore its infamous history of torture and rape of friend and foe alike. She would have been dismayed to learn that her favorite son's teacher considered the noble Gianpaolo Baglioni of Perugia the equivalent of Saddam Hussein of Iraq. That the priest was predicting his brother's future as the Bishop of Rome was more than Alex was prepared to consider, and he pushed it to the back of his mind.

"DOTTOR CENNI, THIS is a surprise, and a pleasure. What can I do for you?" Reimann asked when Cenni was shown into his office.

After Cenni described the reason for his visit, Reimann seemed agitated. "We have an important delegation arriving shortly, and I'll be busy seeing to them and their security. Perhaps we can do this at another time, maybe next week."

"I intend to have someone under lock and key by next week, so I'm afraid it will have to be today," Cenni responded, not attempting to hide his annoyance. "Carlo tells me you've been calling him daily for reports, so I assume this means you're as anxious to get Baudler's murderer behind bars as we are. I also want to talk to anyone in the embassy who worked closely with Baudler when she was here: secretaries, clerks, assistants—and the ambassador, of course."

Reimann jumped on Cenni's mention of the ambassador immediately. "That's not possible. He has a full round of meetings today, and throughout this week. Equally important, he had been here for less than a month when Jarvinia retired. In fact, he was the person who insisted that she retire. In a position of that sort, normal retirement age is sixty-five. She had received waivers for ten years from the former ambassador. The incoming ambassador refused to grant her another."

"I assume, then, there were some bad feelings there," Cenni countered.

"On Jarvinia's part, lots of bad feelings. Certainly none on the ambassador's part. He was just doing his job."

"In Italy, we think of Germany as a country that never bends the rules, yet Baudler managed to *break* them, and for ten years. How did she bring that off?"

Reimann looked up at the frescoed ceiling before answering. "She was very good at her job, so exceptions were made by the former ambassador. When he left, things changed. And rightly so, she was seventy-five; her health was deteriorating. It was time for her to leave."

"So she didn't blackmail someone to keep her job?" Cenni said and watched for Reimann's reaction.

He didn't blink. "You mean the papers that she stole from the embassy. No, she just took them for spite. Who was she going to blackmail? The German government?"

Cenni decided to go a bit further with this line of questioning before revealing that the police had found the letter concerning the counterfeit pounds. He wanted to see how long Reimann would continue with the story that the papers Baudler had removed from the embassy were embarrassing to his government but nothing else.

"Why not?" Cenni responded. "If she had information your government didn't want publicized, letting her stay in her job, a job that you say she was very good at, was a small price to pay. Let's say the new ambassador decides to call her bluff; only Baudler's not bluffing."

"I think, Dottor Cenni, that perhaps you've found the letter we're looking for."

Cenni responded, "Letter, a single letter. When we spoke on Wednesday, you said 'papers'."

"Force of habit, I suppose. I should have said letter."

"You also told me that you didn't know what was in the papers. Do you know what's in this letter?" Cenni asked, confident now that Reimann was lying.

"I do. The ambassador informed me just yesterday of its contents. He also gave me permission to tell the Italian police, on the assumption that you'd get the letter translated if you ever found it."

"Nice of your ambassador," Cenni said sarcastically. "Letting me run myself ragged looking for the murderer while you're sitting on information that could have helped. So what was in this letter?" he asked.

"I think you already know, Dottor Cenni," Reimann responded.

Cenni noticed that their agreement to address each other by first names had gone by the boards, at least as far as Reimann was concerned.

"As a matter of fact, I do," Cenni said, taking his billfold out of his jacket. "One very small piece of paper. Certainly not the cache of documents we were looking for. And I take it you're now telling me there is no cache, just this piece of paper."

"That's correct," Reimann responded, reaching out for the letter.

"Sorry, Dieter. This is evidence in a murder case. But I have no problem discussing its contents. So tell me. If this letter is just an innocent piece of paper, why is the German government so anxious to get it back?"

"You obviously know what it says, so you must know why we don't want this letter published in the papers. It's an embarrassment. It brings back memories of the war, which we're all trying to forget, Italians included. Don't forget, Italy was our ally, until it switched to the winning side."

Getting personal!

"True, but this letter doesn't reveal anything new. It might embarrass the Swedish government, but embarrass Germany? I doubt it. There've been half a dozen documentaries made on the counterfeit pounds. My brother even tells me the English made a TV series—"

"Private Schulz," Reimann interrupted. "Very funny, although as a German I shouldn't admit it."

"There's something else involved beyond the fact that Hitler counterfeited money during the war. How come Baudler found this paper in the embassy? It's addressed to Count Molin at the Banca Centrale Venezia, and it was sent from a Swedish bank."

"Obviously, I wasn't here during the war, but as you've

already implied, we're an efficient people. I assume a copy was sent to someone in the embassy and it was filed, as everything gets filed. And Jarvinia found it. She snooped a lot."

"And the money. Where did that wind up?"

"With Count Molin at Banca Centrale, where else? You should check with the bank in Venice, but I suppose they're embarrassed to admit accepting counterfeit money," he added, snidely, Cenni thought.

"I've already checked with the bank. It denies receiving the money. And just to be sure, the Finance Police are going through their books while we're speaking. Our Finance Police can sniff out a single euro of unpaid taxes. If the bank received ten million pounds from Sweden, we'll know about it soon enough. My own suspicion right now is that the money was diverted to Rome after Count Molin was killed—perhaps to the German Institute, which continued to function throughout the war. Baudler was a well-known expert on Renaissance art, and very quick-witted. Perhaps she discovered that the money was used to make questionable purchases of art for the German government *after the war.* That would be more than an embarrassment. And as we both know, she wasn't above blackmail."

"What do you mean? Who else was she blackmailing—" He stopped in confusion.

"Besides the German government, you were going to say. Frau Baudler had quite a few scams going. She was blackmailing Molin's daughter, promising *not* to reveal to the world that the count had worked with the German occupation. And in a complete turnabout, she was paid by

Count Volpe, a cousin of Molin's, to publish the letter. Two for the price of one, three if you include the German government. And let's not forget the girlfriend from South Africa. I think she had something on her, which is where you can help."

Reimann was relieved that Cenni, at least for the moment, had dropped his insistence on tying the German government to Baudler's murder and was only too ready to help indict the Venetians or the African, when Cenni's cell phone rang.

Cenni looked at the number. It was Elena, and he excused himself to take the call outside. Elena never called him on his cell phone unless it was important.

When he returned, he was smiling broadly.

"Something good?" Reimann asked, hoping that whatever it was, it would let him off the hook.

"Very good. We've traced the license plate of the man who's been visiting Baudler. You," he added.

"Is that all?" Reimann sounded relieved. "I often visited Jarvinia. We were friends for nearly twenty-five years. You could have saved yourself the trouble and just asked me."

"You could have saved me the trouble and just told me," Cenni responded. "You were such great friends, apparently, that you visited the house the day after she was killed. Holding a séance?"

"I don't know what you're talking about."

"One of our local farmers—thanks to the EU, we still have local farmers—saw your car parked Thursday evening on the unused road that runs behind the pink house. He also identified the man he saw climbing over the hedge and going into the garden. Described you down to your galoshes, Dieter. We knew someone had gone through the back door; it was left unlatched. Where did you get the key? The landlord told us it's been lost for years."

"Jarvinia asked me to take an impression on one of my visits. It's an old lock but a very common one. I had two keys made in Rome. I kept one."

"Why didn't you lock it afterward? It was a dead give-away that someone had been inside."

"It opened the door but wouldn't lock it again. Believe me, I tried!"

"We also knew that someone searched through the woodpile. It was restacked so neatly, I thought it might have been you. Did you find what you were looking for?"

"Obviously not. You have it in your billfold."

"So you're planning to stick to the story that the letter from the Swedish bank comprises the full extent of the papers you say were stolen from the Embassy?" Cenni asked, wanting Reimann's denial on record.

"Yes, I am. Now I'm going to offer my apologies. It's noon and I have a meeting. About your request to talk to staff, I don't see how that's possible. I shouldn't have to remind you, Dottor Cenni, that this embassy does not fall within the jurisdiction of the Italian police."

"Cut the crap, Dieter! We're talking murder here, and of one of your own people too. I'll walk out the front door and make my first stop *Il Corriere della Sera*. How's this for a headline? *Murdered German diplomat involved in counterfeiting scheme for millions!* Let's change that to billions; it'll sell more papers. Or would you prefer: *German diplomat tortured for war secrets!* And then, of course, there's the headline about *how* she was tortured. You'd be out of this job so fast, your head would still be spinning when you begin your new job, cleaning toilets in Roma Termini."

"You wouldn't dare!" Reimann gasped. "I'm not the only one here with a job to hold on to," he said, returning the threat.

Cenni laughed. "But you're the only one here who wants to keep his job. Believe me, Dieter, I dare. I can also wait at the embassy gates and invite any staff member not holding a diplomatic passport to headquarters for questioning. You have a number of Italians working in clerical positions. Let's start with them and work our way up to the Germans. And before I forget. Let's have that key you say doesn't work. You're still not in the clear for this murder."

REIMANN CAPITULATED, AS Cenni knew he would. The rest of the afternoon was spent interviewing various members of the staff who'd worked with Jarvinia Baudler. She'd been something of a chameleon, he discovered.

Signora Angelli, her former secretary, gave him a dispassionate rendering of her character: "She was an egoist. If you didn't get in her way, she was charming and generous—and extremely intelligent. Of course, her generosity never extended to giving anything of her own away or interfering with her own pleasures. If I wanted to leave early, and she had nothing for me to do, she'd always agree. Even if it were five days in a row. She cared nothing about protocol or rules. But when my mother was in the hospital and she had some letters for me to type, and I asked to leave early, she refused. That's the way she was; but we rubbed along fine together once I accepted her limitations as a human being. She had plenty of those."

Signora Galassi hated her. She'd been Baudler's secretary for a brief two weeks when the German had first arrived at the embassy in 1980, until Baudler had her demoted for incompetence: "She said I couldn't type and I couldn't spell. My mother was German, so I speak it fine, but my spelling is not so good. Nobody else ever complained until she came along. I'm not surprised someone murdered her. She was a bitch! Herr Reimann's wife died because of her. She had a stroke of some kind after she found out about their affair."

"How did his wife know they had an affair?" Cenni asked.

"It was disgraceful. She was ten years older than Herr Reimann. Not only that, she preferred women to men, yet he still couldn't take his eyes off her. She made passes at every good-looking woman who worked in the embassy. Most of them hated it, but they were afraid to complain, afraid of losing their jobs. She should have been fired years ago, and instead she stayed on when anyone else would have been made to leave. Catch them letting me stay on after I'm sixty-five."

"How do you know Herr Reimann's wife knew they were having an affair?" Cenni asked again.

"Because Jarvinia told her," she replied.

"But how do you know this, Signora?" Cenni asked for the third time.

"Will you tell?"

"Not unless I have to," Cenni responded conscientiously.

"I was filling in for his secretary, who was on vacation. Ever since the time *she* complained about me, that's how they use me, to fill in for other people."

"The wife," Cenni reminded her.

"Herr Reimann's wife called while he was on his other line. I could tell she was crying. She didn't want him to call her back—'I'll wait,' she said. I listened in . . ." She stopped in mid-sentence. "You know I could lose my job over this!"

"Signora, you have my assurance."

"It was difficult, at first, understanding her because she couldn't stop crying. But she said it over and over again: *'How could you do this to me, Dieter? She's a lesbian!'*"

"Did she say how she found out, Signora?"

"That was the worst part. Jarvinia told her. She called her on the telephone. Four days later, Frau Reimann was dead, of a stroke or a heart attack. I'm not sure which."

Once she'd started talking, Cenni had a difficult time getting her to stop. Every rumor that had ever circulated about Jarvinia Baudler—there had been plenty!—was tucked away in Signora Galassi's memory for future use.

She stole office supplies!

She stole from petty cash!

She stole umbrellas from the cloakroom on rainy days!

She stole other people's lunches from the common refrigerator!

She had an affair with the former ambassador's wife! (Cenni pursued that one briefly, but it went nowhere. Just a rumor, he decided.)

She was forced to retire because she stole confidential papers from the embassy files!

The last rumor was of definite interest.

Herr Bauer, Baudler's replacement as cultural attaché, had adored her. "There was absolutely no one like Jarvinia. The Da Vinci show she mounted in the embassy is still being talked about. The German Institute would never show the papers or drawings publicly, not even in its own exhibit room, and they absolutely refused to lend them to any museum, not even to the Metropolitan in New York. Too fragile and too valuable, they always said. Yet Jarvinia wrapped them around her little finger. I'll never be able to follow in her footsteps."

Not unless you're into blackmail!

He had better luck with the embassy's office manager. Herr Greenwald was discreet and proper, but also curious, a bit too curious to stonewall effectively. "I always wondered how Jarvinia managed to stay on so long," he said in reply to one of Cenni's insinuations. "National self-interest is the only reason to permit someone of retirement age to stay beyond the age of sixty-five, but not for ten years! Was that it, do you think, that she was blackmailing someone? I knew there was something—"

Cenni jumped in, ready with his little white lie. "We know, of course, that she was blackmailing your government over those counterfeit pound notes that were shipped to the embassy in 1945. What I need from you are copies of the receipts."

"But I don't have them. I never did!" Herr Greenwald responded, flustered. "You'll have to get them from Herr

Reimann," and he immediately picked up the telephone receiver.

"Don't bother calling Herr Reimann," Cenni said. "I'll stop by to see him on my way out."

BUT ON HIS way out, Cenni breezed past Herr Reimann's office without so much as a glance inside. He'd heard enough for the day about Jarvinia Baudler. She had been an amazing woman, and he tended to agree with Signora Galassi that the only real surprise with respect to her murder was that it was so long in coming. He was beginning to feel a bit too cocky, and he decided to talk himself down by tallying what he actually knew versus what he thought he knew. A disgruntled clerk was not totally reliable. Even if Baudler had eaten other people's lunches, so what. But the story about Baudler's affair with Dieter Reimann was important, and it rang true; so just to be sure, he decided to visit Baudler's former secretary a second time before he left the building. He asked her point-blank about the affair, but she evaded his question:

"I don't get paid to check on people's personal lives."

"That's true," Cenni responded. "And nobody likes a gossip. But if they did have an affair, I want to know. This is a police matter, so I suggest you respond truthfully, Signora."

"In that case, the answer is *yes,* they had an affair."

"How did you know?"

"Anyone who was around at the time was aware of it, but that was ages ago. He acted the fool, if you must know. I don't think Jarvinia cared one way or the other, although I think she used him to get things."

Cenni pounced on her last statement. "What do you mean, used him?"

Signora Angelli's desk was in the hallway outside Herr Bauer's office, and she looked around before answering.

"Favors, that kind of thing."

"What kind of favors?"

"Herr Reimann can approve passports, have visas issued: the types of thing a senior security officer can do."

"Do you have any specifics?" Cenni asked.

"I can't even remember the year. It was a long time ago. I heard her asking him to reissue a friend's passport. She said it had been stolen."

"Did he?"

"I don't know. He noticed the door was open and shut it. I never heard any more about it."

"And the visas?"

"That one is easy, and probably most people around here know about it. Right before she retired, she asked for a visa for a friend, a woman who lived in South Africa."

"Did she get it?"

"For sure, or she would have been in one of her foul moods on the day she retired."

"And she wasn't?"

"Just the opposite: on the day of her retirement lunch, when she stood up to thank everyone, she referred to it openly. Too openly, I thought."

"What did she say?"

"She thanked him for all the goodies he'd given her over the years. I had to suppress a laugh when she said that. Then she added *And for this one in particular,* and she held up one of our passport envelopes. I assume the visa was inside, attached to the passport."

"What was his reaction?"

"Not comfortable. He was sitting across from me, and he definitely squirmed. He and the ambassador, who was sitting next to him, exchanged what I'd call *knowing looks*."

"Did Herr Reimann's wife know about the affair?" Cenni asked, hoping for a second strike.

She looked at him blankly. "I honestly don't know. They always seemed friendly enough when they met at a function. If I had to go by her demeanor, I'd say *no*."

Cenni thought for a moment, and spoke again:

"Signora Galassi says—"

"Melina! I wouldn't put too much stock in what she says. She hated Jarvinia for twenty-five years, if it's possible to hold a grudge that long. Did she tell you about her umbrella, and the missing veal cutlet sandwich?"

5

ELENA WAS IN a bad mood, and Cenni got the brunt of it when he called her from Rome. "Now Carlo wants me to take this new officer around, introduce her to the *boys* and help her get settled in. At least ten men in this building are sitting on their backsides doing absolutely nothing. 'Introduce her to the *boys*.' Luckily for him, he didn't ask me to introduce her to the *girls* or, so help me God, Alex, I'd have punched him."

"I can't leave that man alone for half a day," Cenni

responded. "Don't do any more training, and I'll talk to Carlo when I get back."

"So what do you propose I do with her?" Elena asked, not ready yet to be pacified.

"Have you tracked down the driver of Molin's car?"

"I just told you that Carlo has me training this new officer."

"Elena, you need to think out of the box. Sit her down at a desk with a telephone, a pad, and the Venice phone book. If she can't figure out how to get started on a simple job like that, no amount of training is going to help. I need you to do something else for me."

"All right, then, tell me," Elena said.

"Take these two names down: Alberto Lacrimosa and Orazio Vannicelli. The first was a priest in Paradiso and the second was Anita Tangassi's uncle. Both of them died of mushroom poisoning some time around 2000. Find out everything you can about what happened, including police reports, pathology reports, the works. Also, see if you can find out where Anita Tangassi was at the time they died. Lorenzo Vannicelli told me she was out of town. And what's happening between you and your pillar of salt?"

"Signora Cecchetti? What do you mean?"

"Lorenzo Vannicelli and Anita Tangassi are more than distant cousins. What's the relationship there? I thought I asked you to do this before," he added, before hanging up.

Cenni still had one more thing to do before leaving Rome, but he'd put it off most of the day to avoid the avenging housekeeper. When he finally got the Partisan priest on the line ("Out of bed since dawn," he told Cenni), he provided a name.

"Serge Cattelan is the man you want. Headed up a unit of Resistance fighters when he was just a lad. He's a fisherman out of Murano. If anyone can tell you what happened in '45, Serge can."

When Cenni asked for his telephone number, he was hard put to believe the answer. "You're serious! He doesn't have a telephone! How do you communicate with him? Oh, I see, by post."

Cenni had no intention in this lifetime of ever spending another night at the Hotel Da Mula, and he asked himself why he was even trying to solve the mystery of Molin's death some sixty years after the fact. The connection to Baudler's murder was a slight thread. Even worse, he might be turning into one of those cops who sticks his nose into places where it's not needed, a trait he distinctly disliked in some of his colleagues. If Serge Cattelan doesn't have a telephone because he likes his privacy, he's safe from me.

That's when his cell phone rang.

"*Pronto!*"

"Nice, very nice!" Cenni said when Elena had finished speaking. "Make sure you keep her on our team, and say thanks from me. And Elena, reserve rooms for the two of us tomorrow night in Venice, and don't book into a cheap hotel. Find us something along the Grand Canal. Maybe the Hotel Danielli!" That'll set Carlo off into apoplexy, Cenni thought.

6

ELENA'S NEWS HAD been the push he needed to get him back to Venice. Her recruit had found the driver of Molin's Mercedes by calling the car services listed in the Venice directory. It took only five calls to find him. Molin always used the same driver and, when first asked, he'd responded that he'd been up and back to Umbria a number of times in the last two months, including last Wednesday. Sergeant Giachini was a new recruit, so Cenni could forgive her slip, and no doubt Elena would instruct her in the future to *never* mention the reason for the call unless asked, and not even then. When Molin's driver realized that the police were calling about a murder investigation, he got cagey and stopped talking. He couldn't remember if they'd actually gone to the house that day and, if they had gone to the house, he couldn't remember the time.

Cenni decided immediately to handle the questioning himself. He also had unfinished business with the African. Her residency application was just about in order, but not quite, and *not quite* is sufficient reason in Italy to have an approval overturned. She had lied to him on his last visit. This time he expected she wouldn't lie. And since he was planning to be in Venice, he might as well visit Serge Cattelan in Murano while he was there.

This time he arrived in Venice by car, with Elena doing the driving. She was an excellent driver, and Cenni wondered if it caused any problems in her marriage. Good drivers hate being driven by bad drivers, and men hate being driven by their wives. Cenni was convinced that bad driving must be at least one of the reasons for the recent increase in divorce rates.

Elena, who had a parsimonious nature, was horrified at the 24-euro charge to park the car, and couldn't stop talking about it, until Cenni ordered her to cease and desist, at which point she confessed that they were not staying at the Hotel Danielli.

"No rooms?" Cenni asked.

"Not exactly," Elena responded.

"Not exactly, what? Do they have a problem with the police?" Cenni asked.

"Alex, we can't stay there. A single room is more than 500 euros a night."

"Don't you think you deserve a good night's sleep, and a good shower?" Cenni asked.

"More than 50 euros an hour to sleep! I'd be awake all night thinking about it."

They were walking toward the *vaporetto* landings, and Elena steered him away from the No. 3. "We're supposed to take the 42."

Cenni groaned. "Tell me the worst!"

"It's in Cannaregio. The woman on the telephone said it's just a five-minute walk from Fondamente Nove, and there's a view of the canal."

"But of which canal?" Cenni asked, rhetorically.

THE CAR SERVICE office was in Cannaregio, just a short distance from their hotel, so Elena hadn't chosen so badly after all. Cenni tested the mattress—firm—and the shower—hot and strong—and decided to forgive her this

time. He couldn't see the canal but assumed from the
salt-scented air and the splashing sounds emanating from
below his window that it was out there somewhere. On
previous trips, he'd never visited the back streets of Venice
and was surprised to find them empty in the middle of the
day. When you get away from the tourists and the boats, it
isn't much different from the hill towns in Umbria, he
thought. Wash was hanging out to dry, flowers tumbled
over stone walls, red geraniums bloomed in window boxes
along the back streets, and young girls played a game of
jump rope in the summer sun.

"*Ragazzi, tirate il Pallone,*" Alex called out to two boys
who were kicking a football around a lamp post. He
handed his jacket to Elena, did some kicks and starts, con-
gratulated the boys on their footwork, and finally let them
get back to their game.

"You'd make a good father, Alex. You should think about
getting married," Elena remarked. To herself, she thought,
*I wonder what he'd say if every time I passed some girls jumping
rope I horned in.*

Signor Baldi was waiting for them at the office with a
pout on his face. "I just turned down a call to drive someone to Verona," he complained. Cenni didn't believe him,
but he handed him his card and told him to submit a
voucher, eliciting a faint smile. "Be sure to attach the customer's affidavit," he said and watched the pout return.

Cenni was a reasonable man, and he understood perfectly that no one wants to lose business by talking to the
police, so he assured and reassured Signor Baldi before
they began that whatever he told the police would be kept

confidential, and his name, as the source of the information, would only be given to the investigating judge, and
then only if he, Cenni, thought it absolutely necessary. But
nobody ever believes the police.

"I really can't remember," Baldi protested for the third
time. "I probably have the dates wrong and we weren't
even in Umbria on that day."

"Perhaps you can check your records," Cenni suggested
looking around the office. There were some folders
thrown willy-nilly on the top of filing cabinets, and loose
papers stuck out of some of the cabinet drawers.

"I don't keep trip records for regulars," he said. "They
pay me a monthly service fee. The countess is a regular."

"That's too bad," Cenni said, shaking his head sympathetically. "You may not be aware of this, but the tax laws
require you to keep records of where you go, when, and at
what price. I wouldn't want to see you in trouble with the
Finance Police," he added, again in a non-threatening
voice.

"YOU KNOW, ALEX, everyone at the Questura thinks of
you as Mr. Nice Guy. They should only know how you
blackmail witnesses to get what you want," Elena said as
they were walking back to the hotel.

Alex stopped in his tracks to reply. "We're the police
and we have a job to do. I gave Signor Baldi every chance
to assist in a murder investigation. I even promised to
keep his name confidential. Like every other job in the
world, we need results. Hopefully, they're honest results.
If witnesses refuse to honor the law, it's hardly blackmail to

use the law to change their minds. Frankly, Elena, I don't
care if Baldi is cheating on his taxes, particularly when
the richest man in Italy, our former Prime Minister, has
made it into an Olympic sport. But if threatening a visit by
the Finance Police gets me what I want, then I'll threaten
every time." He added, "It also works every time."

7

THE FONDAMENTE NOVE is the point at which the
vaporetti leave Venice for San Michele, Murano, and the
northern lagoon. The long waterfront with its half dozen
waterbus stops and its numerous cafés, tobacconists, pizza
stands, gelaterea, and bank machines is never quiet, and at
rush hour in the mornings and evenings it's a wall of trav-
elers, at least half of whom are busy grabbing a quick bite
and a coffee on their way to work or a quick bite and a
grappa on their way home from work. Cenni, who had a
passion for seafood tramezzini, particularly shrimp-and-
egg, rarely found any worth the cost of indigestion in
landlocked Umbria. But in the small café on the corner of
Strada del Buranelli, which serves hundreds every day, he
found nirvana. He ordered three shrimp-and-egg and a
square of pizza for Elena as they waited for the boat to
Murano to dock.

Elena was anxious to talk about their visit to Signor
Baldi, but first she found it necessary to point out that
"even Piero doesn't eat three sandwiches for lunch."

"You're sure about that, are you!" Cenni said. "How
often do you and he have lunch together?"

"Figures," Elena said, making a face. "So, what about the information we got from the driver? Are we ready to make an arrest? Can we go home tonight?"

"No, to both your questions. The driver says they got to Paradiso early and drove around. At four o'clock he parked in front of the pink house. He also says that Juliet Mudarikwa was the only one to go inside, that Marcella Molin stayed in the car. According to him, Juliet rang the bell a few times before she finally let herself in with a key. She returned to the car less than fifteen minutes later carrying a small suitcase. Less than fifteen minutes to find Baudler, go down to the basement, argue with her, batter her to death, mutilate her, find a suitcase, pack it, and leave? The African is quite tall, but she's also slight, maybe 130 pounds at best. Baudler was a large woman, tall, and weighed over 200 pounds. After killing her, Mudarikwa would have had to drag her over to the steps and then do the rest. And don't forget the blood, Elena. The post-mortem said 'little bleeding.' It didn't say 'no bleeding.'"

He paused when he saw the waiter go by. "*Scusi,* another coffee, *per favore.*"

"We also know," Cenni continued, "that Baudler re-turned home at precisely three thirty, so we know she was inside when Juliet Mudarikwa let herself in with the key. If Baudler was alive when Juliet arrived, why didn't she answer the door? We know from the garage man that she was expecting someone at four. Let's assume it was Juliet. Murdering another human being is hot, messy work. So, again, how could Juliet have done all that and returned to the car, as the driver said, *looking cool as a cucumber?*"

"So why did she lie about not being there?" Elena asked. "If she'd left the house as soon as she found the body, she'd have witnesses to prove she didn't do it."

"You're assuming she saw the body. Unless she went to the top of the cellar steps, she couldn't know that Baudler was lying dead below."

"Yeah," rejoined Elena; "then what was she doing in someone else's house for almost fifteen minutes? I doubt she was sitting on the couch waiting patiently for Baudler to return. She must have checked things out."

"The house," Alex replied, "has four floors. Maybe she was upstairs packing her suitcase? To your question, 'why did she lie about being there,' let's see: she's black, she's African, she's living with another woman in an iffy situation, she can't show a visa for how she got into Italy, and she was Baudler's live-in lover at one time. There's also the possibility that Baudler was blackmailing her or that she and Baudler were blackmailing the Venetians as a joint venture. That's a whole laundry list of reasons for her not to get involved with the police."

"Are you just going to let her go, then?" Elena asked, annoyed that a perfectly good suspect was getting away.

"Juliet Mudarikwa knows a lot more about Baudler and her blackmailing schemes than she let on when I questioned her a few days ago. The evidence suggests that Baudler didn't start blackmailing the Venetians until she ran into Marcella Molin in Venice a few months ago, but she was blackmailing her own people for years, usually for small favors. Maybe she decided to branch out big-time when she had a girlfriend to support. And maybe the girlfriend knew what she was doing. Juliet Mudarikwa may still be our best lead to finding Baudler's killer. Sorry, Elena, but Piero will have to spend the night alone. We're definitely on for tomorrow."

8

UNTIL THEY BOARDED the vaporetto for Murano, it had been the perfect June day—too perfect, in fact, to be grilling witnesses in a murder investigation. But just a few minutes out into the lagoon, dark clouds appeared on the horizon. "A storm is moving this way," Elena remarked casually, unaware that the rapid change in weather had wrought a similar change in her boss's mood.

"I'm going out on the deck to get some fresh air," Cenni said, without inviting Elena to join him.

That was fast, she thought. Most times she could tell when he was in a mood, but this one had come on quickly. She stayed in her seat and unwrapped the tourist book that she'd purchased from a small shop on the waterfront. Two women in their twenties, also carrying guidebooks, were sitting in front of Elena, and they started discussing Cenni after he left the cabin. Elena understood English quite well, so she caught every word:

"It's the same one who was sitting in the café. Shit, but he's gorgeous!"

"Shssh!" the second one said, "The woman from the café is right behind us."

"She can't understand us. They were talking in Italian."

"Are they married, do you think?"

"Definitely not. He wasn't wearing a wedding ring, and she is. I checked when we were leaving the café."

"Do Italian men wear wedding rings?"

"I don't know, but those two don't look married."

"How do you look married?" the second one asked.

"Funny!" the other one said. "He got up and left her abruptly. In the café he seemed to be lecturing her. They probably work together," she concluded.

Astute, particularly about the lecturing.

"Did you notice his eyes? Violet blue."

"Like Elizabeth Taylor."

"The color maybe, but there's nothing feminine about that stud. Did you catch the body! He's like a human version of a panther! Grrrr!"

"Restrain yourself, Joanne. He's Italian; you're from Detroit. No future in it!"

"You never know. Come on, I'm going out on the deck. Maybe we can pick him up, at least for dinner tonight. Italian men are supposed to go wild over American women."

Elena watched the huntress and her friend go out the cabin door. Nice-looking women, but not a blonde hair between them. *Good luck, ladies,* she said to herself before opening her book to the section on Murano glass.

When the boat docked at Murano Colonna, the two women were the first ones off. When Elena met up with Cenni on the deck where he was waiting, she asked him if the two American women had spoken to him. She could see them with their heads together, laughing, as they headed up the *fondamenta*.

"Yes. They wanted the name of an inexpensive restaurant in Venice for dinner tonight. They asked me where I go."

"And . . . ?" Elena asked.

"I don't know any restaurants in Venice, but I warned them to stay away from the tourist areas. Nice women, but a bit silly. One of them giggled the whole time the other one was talking to me. You were probably right when you called me a curmudgeon. I haven't a clue how to talk to women of that age, and I hate it when they giggle."

BEFORE THEY STARTED up the *fondamenta* to look for a man who might have information from sixty years ago, an expedition that Elena thought senseless, she mentioned that she wanted to buy a gift for Piero, and maybe one for his mother. "I have to keep in her good graces," she said, "or she'll snatch him back." Cenni looked at her in surprise. He hadn't realized that once a *mammone*, perhaps always a *mammone*. But he was grateful for the opportunity to visit Serge Cattelan alone. He knew Elena thought his compulsion to solve a decades-old murder foolish, and he wanted to be alone for other reasons as well. He might stop and visit the house where Chiara's mother-in-law had lived. Maybe one of the neighbors might know Chiara's whereabouts.

"Not a problem," Cenni answered. "I don't need anyone to take notes on this one; it's a long shot anyway. Why don't you do some shopping, and we'll meet back here in two hours. Is that enough time?"

"I could buy a house in two hours. But there's a twelfth-century Byzantine church on the island. It's described in the guidebook. Look for me there if you finish early."

Cenni hesitated a moment. "Listen Elena, just in case it takes me longer than two hours, don't wait for me. Go back to the hotel in Venice, and we'll meet up for dinner at eight."

On another occasion, Elena might have asked what he could possibly find to do on an island full of glass shops that could take more than two hours, but he was wearing what she'd once described to Piero as *that obsessed look,* so she agreed.

9

CENNI FOUND SERGE Cattelan taking the sun on the second-floor balcony of a house on Fondamenta Cavour. When he shouted up that Monsignor Dante Tirado had sent him, he was immediately invited up. Only later did he learn that the only fishing Cattelan had done in his lifetime was for his own table and for the occasional fish that he sent down to Rome, to his friend.

"Dante is senile, for more than five years now. I have no idea just how old he is, but I'd say ninety at least. I've never been a fisherman, but I suppose Dante connects the fish I send him with the work I do. Fishing for me is never work. It's my passion."

When Cenni asked why he refused to have a telephone, he looked confused at first and then laughed.

"Of course I have a telephone. I was wondering why

Dante was sending me letters recently." It turned out that Serge Cattelan had taught modern and classical languages at the *liceo* until his retirement twenty years earlier and that he still tutored students who were planning to go on to university.

"So you want to know about *La Resistenza*. You've come to the right person, dottore. Most of my comrades from those days are long dead. The Germans killed my father in 1944, so I took his place. The others didn't think a boy of nineteen could do the job, but they were wrong," he said proudly. "So Marcella Molin thinks she can crown her father king of the heroes by leaving money to a foundation? That'll be a whole lot of money sitting around doing nothing, because it'll never happen. A lot of us are dead, but there are still enough of us around to stop that atrocity."

"You're absolutely sure he wasn't a partisan and he wasn't helping the partisans?" Cenni asked, wanting to be sure he had it right. "Then why did the Germans kill him? The police report says he was found lodged between the pilings under the Fondamente Nove. No autopsy was ever performed. He'd been floating under the pier for some ten days when they found his body. Almost unrecognizable after the fish had gotten to him."

"I'll grant you the fish part, but what makes you think the Germans were involved?" Cattelan asked.

"The family reported that four Germans picked him up and took him away in a police launch. That was the last time he was seen by anyone."

"Dottore, never believe everything you read in a police report. Not all the police in the lagoon were working with

the Germans during the war, and lots of us in northern
Italy speak German fluently. Not everyone in a German
uniform was German. Take me, for example: I taught German for forty years at the *liceo*."

"*You* were one of the four that took Molin away that
night! Did you kill him?"

"*La Resistenza* killed him," Cattelan responded quietly.

"Why? He was one of us," Cenni said censoriously.

"Too many reasons to enumerate. But we picked him up
when we heard from a reliable source that he was planning
to assist the Germans to distribute counterfeit English
pound notes through Italian banks. God knows, we Italians
have very little to be self-righteous about. We were very
quick to change sides when it suited us, and after the war
a lot of our neighbors chose to forget their past. It's not for
me to judge why they did what they did, and for the most
part our fight was with the Germans. But Molin had too
much to answer for, and no excuses. He had position,
money, education; he knew what he was about, all right.
And what he was about was personal profit in wartime. We
met in a warehouse, conducted a trial, and each of us cast
our vote. It was unanimous for the death penalty."

"Did you give Molin a chance to defend himself?" Cenni
asked.

"He made his defense. As I said, the decision was unanimous."

"How come this has never come out?"

"We had nothing against the wife or the daughter,
although the daughter didn't turn out very well, did she?
But you can trust me, dottore; there'll be no foundations

set up in the Veneto to honor Count Molin. That I can promise you!"

"What happened to the money?" In the end, it was the money that Cenni had come to discuss.

"I don't know for sure. Many people played for both sides during the war; toward the end, everyone was jumping ship. Our informer was half English and half German. He did it to save himself and also, of course, for the money. I never knew his name. Our group leader did, but he never broke faith with his sources, not even after the war. We lost two men in that raid and recovered less than a million pounds. But Molin, he had his chance! He denied nothing, just excused it. He did it for Italy, he said. Who knows, maybe if he hadn't said *for the fatherland,* he might be alive today."

CENNI LIKED SERGE Cattelan, so he hesitated only briefly before bringing up Chiara.

"I'm working on something else that you might know about. Not really a case, more a personal matter. I'm looking for a woman who married a man from Murano, a Stefano Tartare. Perhaps you knew him?"

Cattelan drew in his breath. "Stefano Tartare. Yes, I knew him. He was my best student at the *liceo*. A brilliant boy with a brilliant future. He had most of the right stuff to become someone but, unfortunately, not moderation. With his mind and passion, he could have been in the government today with Prodi, in the cabinet, or a Member of Parliament. But he would never temper his views with realism. He wanted to change the world *now*. He used to ask me about my time with the Resistance, but even that he didn't understand. Why didn't we hang all the collaborators in the public squares, he asked? I tried to explain that there wasn't enough rope in all of Italy, and that when the war was over we had to compromise. During the war *La Resistenza* did what it did for Italy, and after the war those of us who survived did what we did for Italy. What good would it have done to try to shake every collaborator out of every tree? There would always have been another one waiting."

"Did you ever hear anything about him getting married?" Cenni asked.

"I saw the woman he married on a few occasions, but we never spoke. Stefano never came back to visit his mother; he sent his wife. I suppose he was afraid of being arrested. But I saw her twice. A beautiful woman. But then Stefano was a beautiful man."

Cenni explained his plan to speak to the neighbors about Chiara, but Cattelan discouraged him. "You're not Muranese, dottore. They'll never talk to you. Tomorrow, I'm off to Milan for a few weeks to visit my granddaughter. Come back when I return, and I'll help you."

THE STORM THAT had threatened on the western horizon arrived while Cenni was visiting with Serge Cattelan, and he found himself caught in a fierce downpour. He had intended to look for Elena in her twelfth-century church, which Serge had highly recommended, but he decided instead to duck out of the rain into a small café at the end of the fondamenta. And that's where he found Elena, sitting alone at a table counting her money.

"Problem?" he asked, standing over her. She was so busy counting and recounting, she hadn't seen him come in.

"Only my imminent death," she said, smiling. "Glass here is not cheap. But I found these wonderful wine-glasses, green with gold on the stems, and I bought six of them. I'm wondering now if I should even show them to Piero when I get home. Maybe I should tell him I bought them because they match his eyes. He won't be happy to learn I spent three hundred euros on wine glasses."

"Three hundred euros! That's a lot of money to match Piero's eyes."

"Oh, Alex, I'm such a fool! You know how careful Piero and I are with money. We're saving to buy an apartment, but I couldn't resist them."

"Don't you have a wedding anniversary coming up in July? Perhaps your best man can give them to you as a gift?" Cenni said smiling.

"Really, Alex? I know I shouldn't accept, but I do." She jumped up to hug him.

The two women from the boat had also wandered into the café to escape the rain. The giggler turned to the huntress and said, "See, I told you they were married. That's why he didn't accept your invitation to dinner."

10

WHEN THEY RETURNED to the hotel, Cenni called the Palazzo Molin to say he was in Venice and that he wanted to see Juliet and the countess in the morning.

"I thought you had everything you needed from us," Juliet said, in her musical and fearful voice.

Cenni responded as he always did: "Just a few odds and ends to tidy up. Nothing to worry about."

Juliet Mudarikwa was withholding information. Tomorrow, he'd confront her with his suspicions, suggesting that she could lose her residency permit It was a bluff, of course, but her fear of being sent back to Africa might incite her to talk. In the meantime, he planned to honor Chiara by eating a totally Venetian dinner. When they were finally reconciled, she'd see how much he had changed, that he no longer insisted on having everything his own way.

The couple that ran their hotel was especially concerned to recommend a Venetian restaurant with typical food at reasonable prices after Cenni told them he was a police officer from Umbria. "Too many Italians think Venice is just one big rip-off, and we're here to prove that it's not," the wife explained to Cenni, who was waiting at the desk for Elena to come down. "I know you'll like this place. The food is excellent and the prices are good. Not cheap, mind you. A lot of people don't appreciate that you can't get good fish at pizza prices."

The restaurant was located on the Fondamente Nove waterfront, and he and Elena had secured the last unreserved table. He had an excellent appetite, probably

because he was pleased with what he had learned from
Serge Cattelan. Stefano Tartare had been a hothead and
a fanatic, and Chiara had always been very measured in
her response to political parties that veered too close to
the edge. Her father had been a distinguished jurist, and
his writings were highly respected by leaders on both sides
of the political divide; and in every way Chiara was his
daughter. She hated the tactics of the *Brigate Rosse,* and in
one debate at school had called its members "the new
blackshirts of Italy, bullies who use intimidation and murder
to make a point." He had often wondered if someone sitting in the audience that night had been involved in her
kidnapping. Stefano sounded like one of them, from what
Serge had told him, and he couldn't imagine Chiara willingly marrying a man so opposed to her own values. She
certainly couldn't have loved him.

He'd thought briefly of asking Elena what she thought,
but until now he'd only spoken of Chiara to Renato and
his grandmother. And Elena had been rather distant since
they'd entered the restaurant, although she had been
very excited back at the hotel while she was showing him
the green glasses that matched Piero's eyes.

He had ordered enthusiastically for the two of them,
refusing to let Elena have the only meat dish on the menu,
lamb from Umbria.

"We're in Venice, Elena. When in Venice, you eat fish."

She acceded to all his wishes after he'd rejected her
selection for a second course, pasta with a meat sauce. He
ordered a dinner of Venetian specialties, discussing each
selection at length with their waiter, and he pretended not

to see the glare she gave him when the waiter brought the fish to their table so he could study it in its uncooked glory. He asked if she wanted to pick the wine, but when she suggested a white from Orvieto, he moved her toward a Pinot Grigio. "It's probably best to order a local wine," he said.

They skipped the antipasti. "Let's save our appetites for the real stuff," Alex said, when Elena suggested cold cuts, and they began with a chilled fruit soup that Alex pronounced *superb* and Elena pronounced *ridiculous*. "Whoever heard of making soup from fruit?" The second course was even better than the first, and Alex wished he'd been less lavish in his praise of the soup. It was a rolled red mullet prepared with radicchio and spinach and, after some discussion with the waiter, he decided on a side dish of white asparagus. Alex was so delighted with the sweet, delicate flavor of the fish that he didn't notice that Elena had barely touched hers until the waiter cleared the table. He remembered how stubborn he had been when he'd first visited Venice with Chiara, and he said nothing. Elena passed on salad or cheese entirely, but he decided on two cheeses: Gorgonzola dolce from Piedmont and pecorino di Pienza from Tuscany. He enjoyed the Gorgonzola, which was sweet and mildly spicy, but he was particularly intrigued by the musky flavor of the pecorino, which was studded with truffles. He tried offering Elena a small sliver on his knife.

"*No, grazie,*" she said, without an accompanying smile.

When the waiter asked if they wanted something sweet to finish, he said *no* and ordered two coffees.

"*Scusi,*" Elena called after the waiter. "No coffee for me, and bring two orders of tiramisu, *per favore!*"

"You never have dessert, Elena, and I don't like tiramisu," Cenni said. "If you're planning to bring that back to Piero, it'll never last that long in this hot weather."

"I intend to savor every morsel myself," Elena said. "I'm starving." And that's how she began her after-dinner review of his faults.

"I appreciate your offer to buy the wineglasses, Alex, but I must decline. I'll take the money out of my clothes budget. It will be a good lesson for me to resist impulse buying in the future."

He protested, but she was adamant. He tried again, "There's something else going on. *Dimmi!*"

"Didn't you even notice that I hated the food? Everything that we ate and drank was chosen by you, for you. And who the hell ever heard of fruit soup? You didn't even ask if I wanted dessert, and on top of all that you ordered me a coffee. I never drink coffee after six o'clock."

"You could have said something, Elena. You're not usually so retiring," Alex protested.

"Hah! That's how I show my gratitude for the wineglasses, by refusing to eat your fruit soup? As you told Piero, one favor always leads to another. Speaking of which. . . ."

He knew from the ferocity of her expression that she was on a roll.

"Give me a minute, Elena," he said, and ordered another coffee.

* * *

EARLIER IN THE day, when he had defended his actions to Elena on the efficacy of getting information from reluctant witnesses by pointing out minor lapses in other areas, like not paying their taxes, he hadn't seen any irony, but then he wasn't thinking of his recent run-in with Piero. Elena had seen it, as Piero told her everything, and she pointed it out to Cenni over his three coffees and their two cognacs.

"It's not that I don't agree, Alex. What Piero did was wrong, and you were right to read him the riot act. Believe me, he'll never do it again. But I don't see that what you're doing is a whole lot better. If you really think the car service is cheating on its taxes, call the Finance Police. Don't blackmail the driver. What if he's not cheating, and you scared the wits out of him for no reason?"

That's when they both laughed, and Elena agreed to join him in a cognac.

"Okay, so he is cheating on his taxes; it doesn't change the fact that you blackmailed him, and that's wrong."

Until Elena had openly called it blackmail, Cenni had managed to view his intimidation of witnesses as a bartering system. The police got something they wanted; the witnesses got something in return. Elena forced him to admit that the witnesses already had what they wanted—peace of mind—until he took it away.

"How are you . . . we . . . any different from the bad guys if we break the law to enforce it?" she'd asked.

"I don't know," Cenni replied to her question. "All I know is, we are different."

II

SHORTLY AFTER NINE the next morning, Cenni and Elena arrived at Palazzo Molin. "Get a load of this place!" Elena said, as they waited for someone to open the gate. "Don't tell me things have changed in this country when an old lady with a defunct title lives in a palace, and Piero and I have to kill ourselves to buy a one-bedroom apartment." Cenni, who never discussed politics during a case, merely grunted.

"How come the bigger the place is, the more I whisper?" Elena asked, as they followed Molin's servant up a wide arc of stairs to the *piano nobile*. "Shouldn't it be the other way round?"

"Because it feels like a church," Cenni responded distractedly. He was thinking about how to approach Marcella Molin. Her servant had just informed him that the countess was dying.

She was propped up on a mound of pillows and was so frail that she barely made a presence in the bed. She might easily disappear into the linens and never be seen again, Cenni thought, as he entered the room. He made his decision right then not to question her any further about Baudler's murder, but she proved uncooperative.

"Dottore, I was missing you and now you're back. I want to know more about who killed Jarvinia," she said, patting the side of her bed with her claw-like hand. He went to take the chair that the servant had placed next to the bed, but she patted the bed again. "Please," she said. "It's too difficult for me to talk if you sit so far away."

Cenni sat where she indicated, and in an unthinking gesture covered her hand with his own. When he realized what he'd done, he pulled it back quickly.

"Sorry!" he said.

The dying woman started to laugh, which set off a fit of coughing. Her servant, a wizened ancient, barely alive herself, lifted the countess, took her in her arms and held her until she'd stopped coughing, then gently laid her back on the pillows.

He waited until the countess caught her breath and asked himself for the umpteenth time why he did what he did, and, even worse, why he was good at it.

"We can do this another time, *contessa*," he said, addressing her for the first time by her title.

"There isn't going to be another time," she snapped. "Let's do it now. Why are you here?"

He didn't answer.

"Dottore, I'm dying! Whatever you say, or don't say, won't make a particle of difference to the end game. A few days, a few hours! It's not as though I have a child winging his way across the Atlantic to say goodbye to Mamma. More power to me," she added.

She was hardly the prototype of the sweet dying old lady one reads about in novels, but he admired her spirit anyway.

"You don't like me!" she said, throwing the words out as a challenge.

"I don't know you well enough to like you or dislike you, *contessa*. I like you well enough" he added, after a moment of silence. "Not sure why, though."

"Good, then tell me how Jarvinia died. Did she suffer?"

"Probably not. She was hit once and died of a heart attack. Anything that happened after that was gratuitous."

"I'm glad," she responded.

"Why?"

"I loved her once, and she made me laugh."

"She was blackmailing you!"

"I see you're still pushing the blackmail theory."

"I'm not pushing anything, *contessa*. She did the same to your cousin, only for the opposite reason, and with the same letter. I'll give her this; she was economical."

"So you found the letter! Tell me, dottore, is Saverio going to get this pile of stones after all? Be frank," she said, suppressing a cough in her anxiety to hear his answer.

"If you persist in making your father a hero, I'm afraid he will," Cenni said.

"You're *afraid* he will. Then you've met the pious hypocrite," she said and fell into another fit of coughing. When the coughing subsided, she held out her hand in farewell. "Since you're not planning to arrest me, dottore, I'll say good day. My lawyer and I have a new will to write."

As he got up from the bed, she said in a hoarse whisper, "Leave her be!"

"Who?" Cenni asked.

"Juliet. She's not your killer."

JULIET WASN'T LYING, at least about the murder, Cenni decided. And he didn't base this conclusion on what the countess had told him. The African was afraid, but mainly about losing her residency permit.

"Why didn't you tell me you visited Jarvinia the day of her death?" he asked at the outset, deciding not to play cat-and-mouse. Perhaps Elena had made an impact after all.

"I was afraid," Juliet responded. "I never saw her, I swear. I called out a few times, and when she didn't answer, I just packed my clothes and got out of there in a hurry. You can ask the countess if you don't believe me."

"I prefer to trust the driver on this one. He said you returned to the car in less than fifteen minutes."

She sighed in relief.

"You had an appointment to meet her at four o'clock. Why?"

"She wanted me back, and I wanted my clothes."

"You could have sent the driver in for your clothes."

She looked down at her hands, which were folded in her lap.

"Juliet," Cenni said, speaking her name softly. "Tell me the truth. It's better for you to be completely honest. I'm looking for Jarvinia's murderer, I don't care about anything else going on between you."

She looked up and searched his face. "All right," she said. "Jarvinia said if I didn't show up, she'd have me arrested and sent back to Zimbabwe."

"How could she? You already had a permit to reside in Venice." He held her eyes, making it difficult for her to look away. "Juliet, I want the truth."

She looked toward the America room. "The countess can't know," she said.

He nodded in agreement.

"It was all Jarvinia's idea. We met Marcella in the Caffé

Inglese when we were visiting Venice four months ago. Marcella was very excited about a foundation she was setting up for her father. That's all she talked about, mostly how it would destroy her cousin if he didn't get the palazzo. 'Remember what a weasel he was,' she said to Jarvinia. At one point, I went to the toilet, and that's when she told Jarvinia about her cancer.

"'She has more money than God, and I'm going to get some of it before she dies,' Jarvinia told me afterward. She had information about Marcella's father, but she wouldn't tell me what it was. When we returned to Paradiso, Jarvinia wrote to Marcella. 'This should bring in a tidy sum,' she said while sealing the letter. She instructed me to deliver it personally. 'I can get in big trouble if this goes through the mail,' she said."

"What did the letter say?"

"I don't know. She didn't tell me."

She stopped talking and fiddled with the bracelet on her left arm.

"So far, I don't see any problem. You were the postman, a disinterested party."

"She wrote another letter, to Count Volpe, which I also delivered."

"I still don't see any problem."

"Jarvinia said she'd go to the police if she had to, confess everything and say I was in on it from the beginning."

"What did she think that would accomplish?"

"She said I'd be kicked out of the country."

"What did she expect would happen to her?"

"She didn't care. She also said she had diplomatic immunity."

Cenni looked skeptical, which drew an immediate protest.

"I'm black and African. Do you think the police would believe me over her?"

"No, I don't. How did you wind up in Venice and not back in Paradiso with Baudler?" he asked.

"When I brought her the letter, Marcella offered me a room. It was too late to go back to Umbria that night, and the next day she asked me to work for her, doing some cooking and other things, for a salary. It's not what you're thinking," she added defiantly. "She's very sick, and I've been a real help to her. But she doesn't care about me. She wanted to get even with Jarvinia, and I was the means."

"You have no idea what I'm thinking," Cenni said in response to her earlier statement. "Was it 'helping her out' to meet with her cousin behind her back?"

Two red spots appeared high on her cheeks. "Nobody will take care of me but me," she said defensively.

"And what was Baudler's reaction?"

"She was furious. In the beginning, she phoned two, three times a day, trying to speak to me. And then she showed up here a month ago. She was drunk and she threatened all kinds of things. Finally, to get rid of her, I promised to meet her, but in a bar, not at the house."

"You met her in Assisi," Cenni said, remembering the story Orlando had told him."

"She threw a drink at me! Afterward, Marcella's driver

took me back to Paradiso, so I could collect my clothes, but she refused to let me inside. Ten days ago, she called again and threatened me with the police if I didn't meet her at the house. Marcella thought she was bluffing. But I didn't. And now she's dead!" She looked at him defiantly. "I'm glad she's dead. She promised me an exciting life in Rome, and then stuck me in that horrid town. I was better off in South Africa."

"So, you knew Jarvinia was blackmailing the countess and her cousin, but you didn't know about what, or for how much," Cenni summarized. "I don't see how that's possible, but I'm not here to arrest you for blackmail. Who else?" he asked.

"Who else, what?" Juliet responded.

"Jarvinia Baudler had the blackmailing habit. Who else was she blackmailing?"

She stared at him for a moment, wondering what it would take to make him go away. "I know she was desperate for money. She talked a lot about what idiots most people are, but it was always general talk, no details about why they were idiots."

"That's all?" Cenni asked.

"A man came to visit her. She sent me to the third floor, but even up there I could hear angry voices. They spoke in German, so I didn't understand."

"What did he look like?"

"He was older, in his sixties."

"Thin and balding?" Cenni asked.

"I think so."

"The same man who gave her the key to the back door?"

"Yes, that's him. A lot of help, he was. It only opened the door from the one side, so Jarvinia threw it away."

SHE STOOD ON the landing, looking down on the two police officers as they left the palazzo. "Juliet, tell me the truth," the policeman had said softly, holding her gaze like a lover. She was seduced, coming that close to telling him everything that he'd wanted to know about Jarvinia and her blackmailing schemes. Nannette had saved her. The old woman had come into the room soundlessly during their interview. Her shriveled face hardened with hatred when she saw Juliet, but when Cenni turned to acknowledge her presence, her expression softened into an ingratiating smile. Until that moment, Juliet had almost forgotten that she was the outsider, the African. "Juliet, I want the truth," Cenni had said again, but the time for seduction had passed.

The commissario was right: she had known about Jarvinia's blackmailing schemes. "Queenie will pay whatever I ask," Jarvinia had told her when they'd returned from Venice. "Count Molin was never a leader in the resistance, and she knows it. Her father was training her to take over the family business. He told her about the notes and their shipping date; she told me; and I told Fritz."

"They took you into their home; they befriended you," Juiet had responded, although not in censure. She had wanted to understand why Jarvinia had betrayed the count to help Fritz and her mother, when she'd claimed repeatedly to hate them both.

"Blood counts," Jarvinia had responded. "We needed

money to get out of Venice before the Allies arrived, lots of money. What was the count or Queenie to me?"

"Does Queenie know that you betrayed her father?"

"Does she know, or does she *admit* to knowing?" Jarvinia had responded with contempt. "Where else would Fritz get English pound notes to pay for my boarding school in Switzerland? She never asked and we never talked about it, but she knew."

"So what do you think?" Elena asked Cenni as they were driving back to Umbria.

"About what?"

"For starters, Juliet's statement that the key to the basement door never worked and that Baudler threw it into the garbage."

"It's probably true, as it agrees with Reimann's story. We can check Reimann's key tomorrow. And let's not forget when we wrap up this case to return Juliet's key to Signora Tangassi. It'll save her at least ten euros."

"Do you think she was telling the truth?"

"About not murdering Jarvinia Baudler, yes. For the rest, mainly lies. She'll go a long way.

"What did you think?" Cenni asked in return. "You didn't ask any questions."

"You were doing okay without me, except toward the end."

"How's that?"

"You practically handed her the description of the man who came to the house."

"I did, didn't I?" Cenni said, not at all concerned.

"One interesting point," Elena added. "She insisted that Anita Tangassi entered the house when they were away, that their cleaning woman saw her go inside a few times, but Tangassi told us that she never went inside after she rented to the German."

"A landlord with a key? Not likely!" Cenni responded.

12

THE NEXT DAY was rainy and cold and matched Cenni's mood exactly. His visit to Venice had eliminated suspects, but he still didn't have a murderer. Elena hadn't yet visited Signora Cecchetti to find out about Lorenzo and Anita's relationship, so he decided to do it himself. The woman who answered the door looked somewhat different from Elena's description. She was not old—in her late sixties rather than eighties—and quite glamorous in an old-fashioned way. Her hair was piled high on her head, held in place with tortoiseshell combs, and two long strands of pearls were draped around her long, soft neck. She was wearing a print silk dress and high heels and was made up for the evening. But when he asked if he was interrupting anything, she assured him that she no plans that day other than to water her plants.

The police gossiping with the neighbors raised a delicate issue, and he approached it with finesse. "I'm concerned about the stress you must have experienced, having a neighbor murdered. I called to be sure you're all right, no aftereffects," Cenni said with his brightest smile.

She grabbed her pearls with her right hand. "Do you

think I'm in danger? I do worry so, being alone at night. I was married, you know, but my husband died very young, leaving me alone in the world. I've dedicated my life to his memory, which is why I've never married again." She smiled flirtatiously. "I've had my chances, but Antonio was my life."

Cenni smiled in return and asked if there was any chance of a coffee.

SIGNORA CECCHETTI'S ABILITY to remember everything that had ever happened in her life and everyone else's life, from her earliest recollection of an older sister wheeling her about in a stroller to the story of her next-door neighbor stealing rosemary from one of her pots at night, when she thought no one was looking, was remarkable. She was a lexicon of neighborhood scandals, secrets, and grudges.

"Whatever you want to know about that family, I can tell you. Marta was my dear friend, and she told me everything. *Everything*," she emphasized. She lowered her voice when she came to the part about the rape. "Yes, commissario, *rape!* Orazio raped his own sister, in the dungeons. She was stacking firewood when he grabbed her from behind. He raped her twice. The father found them and had to pull him off. Shocking, and one of our oldest families too. We live in a wicked world, commissario." She blessed herself and asked again if he would like biscotti. "Almond," she said. "I make them myself."

"*Malata mentale* from the time he was a little boy. We were in school together, and he was always fighting, with the other children, the teachers, his cousin Lorenzo, but his mother worshipped him. Nothing was too good for her darling Orazio. Marta was a late child and was always an afterthought to her mother. After the rape, the mother blamed Marta. Both Marta and Orazio had their bedrooms on the second floor and the parents had theirs on the third. The mother accused Marta of walking around half naked, tempting her brother into sin. Well, I never walked around him half naked, and he attacked me, in the walkway that runs beneath this building. Antonio caught him and gave him a permanent limp, but his mother begged us not to go to the police." She shrugged. "Antonio didn't want people talking about me."

"How does Anita fit into this?" Cenni asked.

She shook her head with regret. "Anita is the baby that Marta had nine months after her brother raped her. The father found a shepherd from Sardinia who was working in Castelluccio to marry Marta. They paid him off, and he disappeared a few months after Anita was born. The woman policeman, she told you about Anita?" she asked, turning away from him to get the coffee pot, and also to avoid looking at him. Cenni said, "Yes," and she continued. "Monsignor Lacrimosa told Marta that Anita's deformity was the price of original sin. Marta's parents were killed three years after Anita was born, in a car accident, on that terrible curve as you come into Paradiso. If you ask me, that was the price of original sin, bringing that monster Orazio into this world."

"Did the priest know that Marta had been raped?" Cenni asked.

"Oh, yes! Marta told him. She was devoted to him . . . and the Church. When Anita was four, Monsignor Lacrimosa insisted that Marta take the child to Rome for surgery to fix . . . you know," she said, coloring deeply. Cenni nodded to indicate he understood, and she continued: "He said it served as an occasion of sin to the child. Marta was always very careful with money, and Orazio refused to contribute any money toward the operation, so Marta had a doctor in Perugia do it. She said Rome was too expensive." She picked up the coffee cups and moved toward the sink, again avoiding his eyes. "The surgeon cut too deeply, and Anita continues to have problems—back and forth to Rome all the time—and she can't have children. When Anita was old enough to understand what had been done to her, she blamed her mother. They never got along."

"Is that why you told Inspector Ottaviani that she killed her mother?"

She got flustered. "Did I tell her that?"

"I believe you did," Cenni said.

"I think she misunderstood," she responded. "But it's strange, you'll have to admit. Marta was fearfully afraid of heights and never went near the edge of that terrace." She paused, and the lines in her forehead deepened. "I completely forgot about it until now. Marta told me that Anita was just like her—terrified of heights. Perhaps she didn't do it."

"You also told Inspector Ottaviani that Anita killed her uncle, the one who died from eating poisoned mushrooms."

"That isn't just me talking," she protested. "Plenty of

others say the same. Orazio paid Anita to cook for him. She'd leave his meals at the door, but she never went inside, not while he lived there. It's true that she was in Rome when he died, but she could have left the food for him before she left. I even said to my sister that it was very strange. If you want, I can call her and she can tell you exactly what I said."

Cenni declined the offer. "What about the priest? It appears that he died in the same way."

"Doesn't that prove what I was saying? The police said Orazio shared his supper with Monsignor Lacrimosa, and they both died from eating the same stew. Orazio never gave anything away, certainly not his supper. Marta found him. She was heartsick."

"She was heartsick about her brother?" Cenni asked, surprised.

"Good heavens, no! She hated Orazio. I meant about Monsignor Lacrimosa."

"Did Orazio have anyone besides his sister? A woman friend, maybe?"

"No woman would have anything to do with him. Marta was his only family, and when he died she got it all: the other half of the house, the store, and the apartment building. Anita's a rich woman, although you'd never know it to look at her. She actually cuts her own hair!"

She was shocked when he asked her about Anita and the Lanese murders. "Anita was just a little bit of a thing back then. Everyone in town, and I mean everyone, felt for the child and the horror she experienced when she found her friend's bloodied body. Commissario, we are not monsters!" she asserted. "No one in this town ever made such a suggestion."

She was as informative about Lorenzo Vannicelli as she had been about the others, and he didn't come off a whole lot better than Orazio. "If you want my opinion, the whole family is crazy. Lorenzo is a staunch Communist, yet he wouldn't give a heel of bread to a starving beggar if he could get a coin for it. That house of his also belongs to Anita, and to Marta before her. Lorenzo helped with Anita when she was growing up, taking her to school and doctors, but only so he could live rent-free. And he treats that cat of his like it's his child. A few days ago, I saw him carrying it in his arms like a baby. They were coming out of Dottor Rotondi's office. That cat sees the doctor more than I do."

"You don't like cats, signora?"

"Hate them! They're always doing their business in my flowerpots. I've gone to town meeting after town meeting to complain about the cat problem. Keep them indoors or get rid of them, is what I say; but nobody listens."

Cenni wondered if her dislike of Lorenzo Vannicelli was stimulated by his affiliation with *Rifondazione Comunista*—she had crossed herself four times during their conversation—or by his cat fetish. He'd rather liked the man himself.

"Life in Paradiso must be rather uncomfortable for Signora Tangassi," Cenni observed, "with everyone knowing she's a hermaphrodite and, also, that Orazio was her father."

"Anita doesn't know that Orazio was her father. No one

would tell her that. Marta never did. What kind of people do you think we are?"

When he was ready to make his escape, equipped with a small bag of Signora Cecchetti's almond biscotti "for later," Cenni asked one last question:

"Signora, why didn't you tell all this to Inspector Ottaviani when she was here?"

"She didn't ask," the signora replied. "And I don't like to gossip."

13

ELENA WAS SITTING in a darkened office when he returned to the Questura toward the end of the morning.

"As my mother always says, you'll go blind reading in the dark," Cenni told her, hitting the light switch.

"I wasn't reading," she responded icily.

"Okay, tell me what's wrong." He read her moods as easily as she read his.

"Yesterday, you told me to visit Signora Cecchetti, and when I arrive here this morning—at eight o'clock too!—Marinella says you've already left for Paradiso. You couldn't wait for me? Or better yet, let me do my job as instructed. I asked Sergeant Giachini, who lives in Spello, to meet me in the café in Paradiso at nine o'clock. It was a good training opportunity for her. Lucky thing she carries a cell phone, or I would've had that long drive to Paradiso for nothing."

Cenni was tempted to say that everyone in Italy carries a cell phone, usually two, but he thought better of it.

"Sorry, Elena! I had nothing planned for this morning, and I took off without thinking. Where does the sergeant sit? I'll apologize to her as well."

"Never mind. I caught her before she left home." He was looking at her with concern, so she added, "Okay, forget it. But next time, remember when you tell me to do something, and don't go off and do it yourself."

"Tell you what, Elena. I'll buy you lunch and give you the lowdown on Piazza Garibaldi and its residents, straight from the horse's mouth. And for after, we have biscotti." He held up the paper bag.

Elena laughed. "Signora Cecchetti, of course. Where to for lunch?"

"Across the street, where else?"

"Sorry! Piero made me a better offer. He's taking me to the trattoria in Piazza Dante. The first place he ever took me," she added.

And every woman he ever dated!

"Anything else happening that I should know about?" he asked.

"I almost forgot," Elena said. "Dottoressa Falchi came by. She left the final version of the postmortem report. She got tired of waiting for you. Said for you to call her. Some dodgy findings, I gather."

"You didn't read it?"

"Of course not. It's on your desk. It's marked *confidential.*"

"Never stopped you before," Cenni shot back.

Two copies of the official postmortem report were inside the envelope. The final report included the identity of the deceased, time of death, nature and extent of

internal and external injuries, cause of death, circumstances surrounding death, and a review of existing and
former diseases: coronary heart disease and polio. He
glanced over the information quickly but saw no major
changes from what he'd previously discussed with Falchi.
But on the report copy, she had highlighted one line in
yellow: Baudler's blood group was type *O negative*. A footnote indicated that two different blood groups had been
mixed in the blood samples collected at the crime scene.
The second was listed as *type unknown*. A handwritten note
on the side margin said, "Call me."

He got through to Falchi immediately. She'd been waiting for his call.

"I asked you to call because I'm not sure what to make of
the blood groupings. The blood samples we collected from
the floor and by the steps definitely are mixed. The *O negative* is Baudler's blood. I'm not one hundred percent sure
on the other blood group, but we don't think it's human.
Possibly it's from the neighbor's cat, but let's be sure. You
never told me that the cat that found Baudler's body was
injured. It helps, you know, if you give us all the facts."

He was staring off into space, putting two and two
together and probably coming up with five, when Elena
looked in to announce she was off to lunch. "Sure you
don't want to come with us?"

"Yes, very sure. And you'd better call Piero and cancel.
We can grab something later. We're off to Paradiso."

ON THE DRIVE, he told Elena what he'd learned about
the Vannicelli family. Elena, who had an amazingly negative

view of human nature, was not in the least surprised to hear that it was probably Orazio who had killed the Lanese mother and child. He had raped his sister, after all. What seemed to bother her most, though, was his refusal to pay for Anita's surgery. "Such a prick!" she said. "He deserved to choke on his own supper and so did that priest he took with him. Male chauvinists!"

No greater sin!

By the time they reached Paradiso, Alex had decided on a course of action. "Listen, Elena, and don't blow up! I'm going to see the vet as a private citizen, and not as the police, so I can't take you with me. Wait for me in the café and, if you can, get some of the locals talking. You never know what you might learn. Have lunch on me," he said, handing her ten euros. "And park the car. I'm going to walk."

Dottor Rotondi's office was on a hilly back street overlooking the valley, and no one else was hanging about when Cenni rang the bell for admittance. He hoped he'd be as lucky inside the clinic, and he was. Just one patient was waiting, a rabbit carried by a young girl of twelve years or so. "He has indigestion," she said, picking him up so Cenni could get a better look. "It would appear he doesn't like carrots," she said in a very grown-up manner. Cenni was rather interested in the rabbit's digestive problems and was disappointed when the vet invited the girl and the rabbit into his surgery before he could learn more. They were inside for twenty minutes, and when the girl and the rabbit emerged, she was carrying a small vial of pills. "A bad stomach," she said as she was leaving, "two a day for one week, and we'll keep our fingers crossed."

Cenni's story to the vet was very simple. He had a cat that was ailing. It wouldn't eat and wasn't having regular bowel movements. His own vet didn't seem to have any idea of what was wrong, and Cenni had come to make an appointment with Dottor Rotondi, who had an excellent reputation, especially among cat owners. Lorenzo Vanni-celli had recommended him.

"Of course, Lorenzo and Tommaso, one of the great love stories of our age," Rotondi said, laughing. "Lorenzo loves that cat more than himself."

"Yes!" Cenni agreed. "Lorenzo was in a great deal of distress this past week when Tommaso hurt himself. How is Tommaso doing, by the way?"

"You know what they say about cats having nine lives. Another week off that leg, and he'll be fine. A bit gimpy afterward, but he'll still have the stuff to terrorize the neighborhood. Nasty wound, that! Looked more like it had been caught in a trap than on a fence, but Lorenzo knows best. He found him. And now they have a new member of their household. Tommaso's not too happy about that!"

"So, WHAT DOES it all mean?" Elena asked. They were sitting at a back table in the café, and Cenni was telling Elena what he'd learned from the vet.

"I'll start with the facts, without drawing any conclusions," Cenni responded. "Some type of animal was loose in the basement before, during, or after the time Baudler was attacked, and some of the blood recovered from the crime scene belongs to that animal. We know of two animals that were in the house the day Baudler was killed: her own cat and the neighbor's cat. My visit to the vet confirms that the neighbor's cat was injured around the time that Baudler was murdered. No one has seen Baudler's cat, so it may also have an injury."

"Do you think the killer attacked the cats?" Elena asked.

"If that were the case, I'd have to wonder why Vannicelli didn't tell us. What reason would he have for concealment? And if he was the killer, why would he attack his own cat, or even Baudler's cat? He's a cat lover. I don't know what it means, Elena, but I have my suspicions."

"What exactly did the vet say?"

"The cat had a serious injury to its right front leg and paw when Vannicelli brought it in the morning after the murder. Vannicelli claims his cat injured himself on a barbed-wire fence. Dottor Rotondi made it clear without stating so directly that the cat's injury doesn't match Vannicelli's story."

"And you didn't threaten him with the tax man to get the full lowdown?" Elena asked.

"Since I had sold myself as the owner of a cat with a shitting problem, I could hardly have done so. I'll leave that to you if it becomes necessary," he responded, not provoked. *Elena hated it when he left her out of things.* "Right now, I want to talk to Vannicelli about his cat's health. I took a walk around town after visiting the vet, looking for barbed-wire fences, and discovered only one. It's eight feet high and encloses the property behind the olive oil cooperative. I suppose a cat could climb to the top, but it wouldn't be easy, particularly for a cat that's overfed. From what the vet said, Tommaso is no lightweight."

"You can't accuse Vannicelli of a crime just because he didn't tell the police that his cat was hurt climbing a neighbor's fence," Elena asserted. "We have too many laws in Italy, but, thank God, that's not one of them!"

"How about misleading the police in their investigation of a homicide or removing evidence from a crime scene? Those are just for starters," Cenni responded calmly. "Don't forget, I asked Vannicelli if his cat had climbed back through the cellar window the day after the murder. He responded that Tommaso was too occupied entertaining the German's cat. But the cat couldn't even walk, according to the vet; he was hardly up to entertaining the ladies. And what cat lover, unless he's got something to hide, wouldn't mention that his cat was at home with a serious injury?"

"So, draw some conclusions," Elena said. "How does the case of *The Cat Strikes Again!* relate to Baudler's murder?"

"I can think of a few possibilities, but someone who doesn't like cats could never appreciate them," Cenni responded, finally provoked.

14

LORENZO VANNICELLI'S HOUSE stank of cat urine, and Cenni looked around to see what kind of litter he used. The box was in the corner of the kitchen, filled with shredded newspaper. Signora Cecchetti had been correct on that point: the Vannicelli family hated to part with its money.

Vannicelli looked very sheepish when Cenni asked to see Tommaso. He responded that Tommaso was out, roaming the neighborhood, a difficult lie to sustain when Tommaso, no longer threatened by a strange voice, came crawling out from under the couch. He looks pathetic, Cenni thought, as he watched the cat hobble over to his owner and rub against his leg, begging to be picked up.

"Please do," Cenni said, indicating to Vannicelli that he should pick up the cat.

Elena, who had come with him on the call, made a comment under her breath that sounded like, *Please don't.*

When they finally sat down to talk, with Tommaso sitting on his owner's lap, Vannicelli was apologetic. He admitted that when he found Baudler, he'd also found Tommaso with a terrible injury.

He looked from Cenni to Elena and sighed deeply before proceeding. "This town is totally against Anita. They've made her life miserable, almost from the day she was born. As though she could help what'd happened to her at birth. Everyone knows that Anita hated Jarvinia Baudler and also that she hates cats. I was afraid if you knew of the injuries to Tommaso and made inquiries, you might conclude that Anita was implicated."

Cenni interrupted. "You're suggesting, then, that Anita Tangassi killed Jarvinia Baudler."

Lorenzo looked away from Cenni and down at the cat. "That's not what I said. It's the others in this town I was worried about. You know what that witch across the street said about her, and she's not the only one. Just because Anita always cooked Orazio's supper, they accused her of feeding her uncle poisoned mushrooms."

Cenni said, "You yourself told me that Anita was in Rome in the hospital when her uncle died."

"*Certo.* It's true. But Orazio's body was found only two days after Anita left for Rome. People in town said she could have easily cooked the poisoned stew before she left. I never believed it for a second," he said, stroking the cat.

"You also told me that Anita was with you in your garden when you saw her mother fall from the balcony."

Lorenzo chewed on his upper lip and lifted Tommaso to his shoulder before responding. "I was in the garden, dottore, but Anita was not with me. But she wasn't on the balcony either, or I would have seen her, I'm sure."

"So why did you tell me she was with you?" Cenni asked.

"My dislike of the gossips in this town. They've never had anything good to say about Anita, jealous because she has money and they don't. Some of them even suggested that she'd killed little Bianca Lanese. Can you imagine? Accusing a nine-year-old girl of putting an ax into the head of her best friend."

LATER THAT EVENING, after his interview with Vannicelli and a brief encounter with Anita Tangassi, and then another with Enzo, Piero's uncle, Cenni was in his office preparing the necessary papers to finish up the Baudler case. He had a number of tasks to complete, details the public prosecutor would insist on before he'd agree to ask for a preliminary hearing. Elena was typing up her notes and also checking the hospitals in Rome to find out where Anita Tangassi had had her treatments. "And make sure you get arrival and checkout dates," Cenni had instructed her. He'd also sent the rookie, Sergeant Giachini, over to the medical examiner's office with a set of fingerprints to be matched against those found at the crime scene. Tomorrow, if all went as planned, Jarvinia Baudler's murderer would be in prison.

And then there were the other loose ends. Dieter Reimann had called three times in the last two days, wanting closure. "The ambassador is anxious, and the service for Baudler is Thursday. We'd much prefer to hold the service after the killer is in custody, more satisfying to everyone. Have an end to it and move on," was how Dieter had phrased it. He had also offered up Juliet Mudarikwa as a possible candidate.

If the Germans wanted closure so much, he'd give them closure and make everyone happy, at least everyone on the Italian side of things.

Nothing would make Ettore Hyppolito happier than to secure Leonardo's drawings and notes for the Vatican Library's permanent collection. Perhaps a gift from the German Institute to the Library? The ambassador could make the announcement on Thursday at Baudler's service: a gift from the German government to the Italian people, in Baudler's name, for all her years of service to culture. The Germans might protest a bit when Cenni made this suggestion, but he was sure that if it were put delicately, they'd appreciate the tradeoff. If the British were to learn that the Germans had used counterfeit pounds after the war, they'd want restitution, and at current rates.

What would Elena think of such a maneuver, he wondered? Doesn't matter, he decided. One woman's blackmail is another man's diplomacy. It was a simple matter of returning to Italy what had belonged to her all along. The Greeks need someone like me to get them back the Elgin marbles, he decided, as he dialed Reimann's number.

15

ANITA'S HEAD HURT dreadfully, and Lorenzo had given her some pills to help, some kind of herbal remedy. Two or three before bed with a glass of wine, he'd suggested. A glass of wine always helps before retiring. She definitely needed to take them tonight. Since the murder of her tenant, Anita had taken just the one, two nights ago. It had worked beautifully, stopping the ache in her head and sending her into a deep sleep for ten hours, an entire night without a single visit from her mother. She had no idea what the pills were, or where Lorenzo had gotten them, but she was determined to get some more. But not from her doctor. The last time she had asked for pills, he'd said she was an addict. What does it matter, she thought, so long as I sleep? Tomorrow, she'd call around in Perugia and find a pharmacy that would help her, or maybe she'd call Dottor Ubaldi in Rome. He was always so concerned about her health.

For as long as Anita could remember, she'd had problems sleeping, although her memories didn't go back beyond the age of six, when she began primary school.

Her first day at school was etched in her memory. She wore her favorite dress of pink tulle. Her mother had said "No," that "it was a party dress and not appropriate," but she had cried until she got her way. The other children stared and stared, and at first she thought it was because they liked her dress, but even after she had covered it with a blue smock, and she looked like everyone else in the first grade, the children continued to stare. Signora Taccini gave her a seat at the front of the classroom, and when she'd asked Anita to recite the alphabet Anita could only get to the letter *G*. The other children, who had attended infant's school and already knew the alphabet, laughed. Even her teacher laughed, and Anita re-fused to go back Her mother let her stay home for a while, but then the police called at the house. When she returned to school, Lorenzo came with her and he spoke to Signora Taccini. None of the children laughed at her after that, and Anita made very sure that they would never laugh again. From that day on, she led her class, particularly in mathematics, in which she excelled.

Until Bianca came to Paradiso, Anita never had any friends. Bianca was two years younger, but Anita had seen her standing alone in the schoolyard, and she went over and spoke to her. They became friends right away. Bianca had a father, but he was always away from home, and Anita had no father. They loved playing dolls together, but Anita had just the one doll, an old Raggedy Ann, which some-one had given to her when she was a baby. Monsignor Lacrimosa said dolls were idolatrous, and her mother agreed and refused to buy any others. Anita was desperate for a real doll; she wanted one with hair that grew right out of the doll's head, and it was because of the doll that she'd found Bianca's body. Anita had the idea that they should try to set the doll's hair with bobby pins, and when Bianca didn't show up at school, Anita went looking for her.

The only time that Anita spoke to anyone about that day was to the police immediately afterward. For years, she refused to talk to anyone, including her mother, and she never told the police that she'd picked up the doll and washed the blood from its hair before returning it to Bianca. Bianca would have liked that. She talked to her mother only once about that day, just months before her mother's death. And, finally, this year she'd told Dottor Ubaldi. She had been sitting across from him in his consultation room, and, out of the blue, she began talking about that day, even to telling him how she'd washed the blood from the doll's hair. When she'd finished, he got up from his chair and came around the desk. He knelt down beside her and wrapped her in his arms, pulling her tight to his chest. It lasted just briefly, but some times at night if she thought about that moment, she'd hug herself and pretend it was his arms and his strength.

What she told her mother was a different story, and in a different tone. They'd been arguing, as they usually did before one of Anita's trips to Rome, and her mother had accused her of being secretive and closed. Anita screamed back that she knew plenty of secrets, and she did too. She told how Bianca counted the men who came to her mother at night like other people counted sheep. "One of them was your precious priest and the other was your crazy brother, and just about every other man in this

town, including the carabinieri. *Paradiso hypocrita,*" she'd
said in her best school Latin, taunting her mother. Her
mother had gasped, "But not Monsignor Lacrimosa," and
Anita had taunted her further. "More times than Bianca
could count. She was only seven, you know, and had to
stop at a hundred." She had laughed at the pain on her
mother's face.

That's why Anita's mother visited her every night in
her sleep, because she had lied to her. Monsignor Lacrimosa had gone to the Lanese house just the once, to
threaten Bianca's mother with excommunication if she
didn't stop receiving men. Not that Bianca knew that
word. What Bianca actually told Anita was that the priest
had called her mother "an occasion of sin." Bianca knew
what that meant, as she'd just made her First Holy Communion. It was Orazio who came every night and broke
furniture and threw things. But Anita's mother wouldn't
have cared if it had been Orazio; she hated her brother.

Anita was still considering how many of the pills she
should take, when her telephone rang. It was after ten
o'clock, and no one in Paradiso ever called after nine. She
picked up the telephone gingerly and broke into a smile
when she heard his voice. Dottor Ubaldi. He'd just
returned from a conference abroad and had seen an article in one of the Rome papers about the German's death.
He'd called to ask if she were all right.

On her last visit to Rome, he had warned her about taking too many sleeping pills, and she decided that tonight
she'd try his remedy instead, an aspirin and a warm glass
of milk. It was a night meant for dreaming.

16

CENNI SPENT TEN minutes waiting in line to pay his
admission fee so he could gain access to the streets of
Paradiso. It was the Sunday after the feast of Corpus
Christi, and Paradiso was celebrating the festival of flowers.
Lines were long, the sun was hot, tempers were flaring,
and the woman directly behind him had asked twice if he
would mind holding her child while she looked for wipes
in her carryall. A commissario in the *Polizia di Stato*
shouldn't have to wait, or pay, but Cenni had decided not
to identify himself to the man at the front gate. He had no
desire to announce himself or his intentions to anyone but
Baudler's murderer; even on a day like this, news of a
senior detective's arrival in Paradiso, all the way from the
Perugia Questura, would spread like wildfire.

It was not the sort of day on which to arrest anyone, and
Cenni had considered waiting until evening for the
tourists to go home, but he was afraid that Baudler's murderer had a pathological conviction of invincibility. He'd
seen the signs yesterday, and he had to be careful. A neighbor might drop a careless word or indicate by a sideways
glance that the killer was no longer safe. Signora Cecchetti was not the only person in Paradiso who saw and
remembered things, and Cenni feared that the killer
might strike again.

Yesterday, Cenni had promised Lorenzo Vannicelli that
the police would give him advance notice if they planned
to arrest Anita so he could be on hand to assist her. He
had also promised Vannicelli that an arrest, when made,

would be quiet and dignified: the police would not come at Anita with sirens whirring or officers brandishing guns. He never made promises he couldn't keep.

Vannicelli had expressed extreme guilt when he realized it was due to his unwitting slip of the tongue that the police now viewed Anita as the prime suspect, and he was quick to point out that Anita was a special case, deserving special consideration. "She's suffered enough without having the neighbors looking on as she's led away in handcuffs. Her mother was my cousin, but she was a fool like most women. It was that priest who stirred her up. Every time Anita did something that Marta thought in the least improper, she'd run to him for advice. Marta spent more time in confession and at the rectory than she ever did at home with Anita. If she could have, she'd have left her money to the Church, but thanks to Garibaldi we have laws to prevent that kind of thing. I'm glad Anita poisoned that frock-wearing hypocrite. It would have been more fitting, though, if she'd laced his communion wine with cyanide." At the end of his diatribe against the priest and his idolater, he added, "You need to be very gentle with Anita. She's tried to kill herself once, and I worry that she might try again."

ANITA, THE HYPOTHETICAL poisoner, awoke that Sunday morning from a deep and lovely dream to a magnificent June day filled with flowers and celebration. It was *L'Infiorata,* and the streets were crowded with tourists, oohing and aahing over the flower paintings that carpeted the streets and squares of Paradiso—although not

Piazza Garibaldi, which was still cordoned off by the police. The chalk drawings of Jesus, Mary, Joseph, and all the saints were filled in during the pre-dawn hours with sheaves of wheat, dried grasses, aromatic herbs, and thousands and thousands of flower petals of every color and size, gathered from every garden and field located within one mile of Paradiso. Lorenzo said *L'Infiorata* was nothing more than a capitalistic occasion for café owners to charge three euros for a coffee that the day before had cost ninety cents. And every year, he'd point out to whoever would listen that the festival is not even celebrated on the actual feast of Corpus Christi. "Why is this if not to make money, which is hardly a Christian endeavor?" he would ask caustically.

Anita disagreed, although never directly. Lorenzo didn't like it when people disagreed with him. She'd always loved the day of the flowers, and the excitement and the parties, and the anticipation of winning prizes, and the early morning procession with the priest holding the Blessed Eucharist on high for all to see. She particularly loved paintings executed with poppy petals. When she was thirteen, she had participated with the children's group. They painted the blood of Christ in a golden chalice made out of mustard seeds, and Anita spent an entire week from morning until late evening gathering poppies in every field surrounding Paradiso. Her children's group won first prize that year, and her mother, who was very proud, took Anita out for pizza that night to the local café. It was the best memory Anita had of her mother. This *L'Infiorata* will be the best one ever, she thought, still gently dreaming. She'd finally gotten rid of Jarvinia Baudler. When the phone rang, she smiled, thinking it might be Dottor Ubaldi again, but it was Lorenzo, and, as usual, he was calling with bad news.

SIGNORA CECCHETTI WAS humming as she piled her hair high, using her very best combs. Her life had changed dramatically in just twelve days, and it was all due to Jarvinia Baudler. She blessed herself and said a small prayer for the German's soul. First the policewoman had come calling and stayed a full morning, listening to her stories and taking notes. And then the very handsome commissario from Perugia came to visit, not on police business but to check on her well-being. And this morning, she had gone outside to water her plants and Enzo had passed by in a suit and a tie. Instead of ignoring her or hissing at her, as he so often did, he stopped and wished her a very pleasant day. He has a distinguished profile, she decided. And, finally, Anita stopped to compliment her on the quality of her geraniums and to advise her to cut across the olive groves if she wanted to get to town in a hurry and avoid the crowds. Maybe she's forgiven me for being her mother's best friend. It would be nice to have a friend I can talk to, she thought, as she watched Anita cross the square and ring Lorenzo's bell.

ENZO WAS SITTING on the church pew in the belvedere, thinking so hard that he didn't notice Anita and Lorenzo go into the pink house. To anyone who knew Enzo, he was dressed to kill. His hair was combed, his suit was pressed, his shirt collar was clean, and he wore a red-and-blue silk tie, a Christmas gift from his nephew Piero. Even more of a surprise to anyone who knew him, he was sober, and it was already close to noon. Yesterday, he had met Elena and her boss, the one who got Piero his promotion, and they'd talked for more than thirty minutes. He'd confessed to being in the square at the time of the murder. He couldn't remember everything he told them, as he'd been drinking, but Elena was coming back today to take his statement, and he had promised himself last night that he wouldn't disgrace Piero any further. He might even have to act as star witness in a trial, and for that he'd surely have to be sober. Elena and Piero had offered many times to take him to AA meetings, even let him live with them, if he would stop drinking. Maybe it was *doable,* the word that Elena always used. Elena said everything was *doable* if you set your mind to it.

CENNI TOOK HIS time walking up Via di San Giovanni. The main street of Paradiso is narrow and winding, and the flower designs restrict pedestrians to single file. The crowd was appreciative, and when someone stopped to talk or exclaim, the rest of the crowd had to stop too. He was surprised to see how much had changed in thirty years. When he and his brother had visited *L'Infiorata* with their mother, all the designs had had a religious theme. The larger paintings at the bottom of the town were as before; but as they wound their way up toward the Piazza Garibaldi, he noted that many of the paintings had social and even satirical themes, including one that was definitely irreligious: a stained-glass window showing a well-endowed Lady Godiva on horseback. But the mural that stopped the crowd in its tracks was twice the size of the others and featured Harry Potter, Ron, and Hermione. It was difficult for the adults to get the children to move on, and he waited patiently until his cell phone rang.

"*Dimmi,*" he answered, less than politely. He'd been waiting for the call for more than an hour. "You're absolutely sure," he said twice, and then, "Thanks, Tahany, much appreciated." It was the news he'd been hoping for.

Scusi, scusi, Cenni said, pushing past the crowds, incurring a vast number of dirty looks until he finally reached the entrance to Piazza Garibaldi. Two police barriers blocked the entrance, and a young officer, a rookie whom Cenni had seen around Perugia, was standing guard with his back to the square.

"Anyone come in or leave this morning, Sergeant?" Cenni asked.

"No one that I've seen, dottore, other than that old man who likes to nap on the church pew. He's there now, and he's all spiffed up. Must have a new girlfriend," he said laughing.

Cenni smiled in appreciation and walked rapidly across the square. Enzo, as the sergeant had said, was sitting on the bench dressed to the nines. Cenni waved to the old man, but walked directly to Lorenzo Vannicelli's house and rang the bell. He knew the routine; he'd done it a thousand times before, but he was still on edge. There was no answer, and after waiting less than a minute, he rang again, with more force. I hope he's not among the crowd, he thought, or we'll never find him.

Someone called his name, and he turned to see Signora Cecchetti standing in her doorway waving to him. *Damn,* he thought, *I don't have time for one of her childhood stories,* but she was waving at him, and he couldn't just ignore her, so he walked over.

"If you're looking for Lorenzo," she said, without any prefatory chitchat, "I saw him and Anita go into her house ten minutes ago. They were talking rather excitedly, and I thought maybe they were having an argument." Cenni acknowledged her message with an expression that she would later describe to her sister as "one of outright horror."

"Are you sure?" he demanded.

"I'm sure. The two of them went in together."

Cenni raced across the square, but the front door was locked and, of course, he didn't have the key. Elena had it, and she was sitting in an unmarked car a hundred feet below, on the dirt road that abutted the olive groves.

Signora Cecchetti had followed him across the square, and when he found her standing next to him, he pivoted her around by her shoulders and pointed to the black car parked between two large trees.

"Tell the officers in that car that I need them here immediately. I'm going in," he said, yanking at the green iron planter that was attached to the outer wall.

She was looking at him in amazement, and not moving. "You've broken her pots," she said staring at the geraniums now lying on the ground. "Anita will have a conniption!"

"Signora, I mean *now*. Move, pronto," and he gave her a gentle shove in the direction of the car. "Run, don't walk," he yelled, as he simultaneously rammed the planter through the door's window. The glass shattered on the second try, and he covered his hand with his sleeve, reached through the shards of glass, and slid open the bolt.

His first instinct was to check the cellars, and he took the stairs two at a time, but midway down he could see there was no one below. He groaned, remembering the sheer drop from the fourth-floor balcony to the valley below. He raced back to the first floor and up the steps to the second, stopping briefly to search the two small rooms, but they were empty. He went up the next stairway, which was steeper than the first. He looked quickly in the two rooms on that floor—both empty—and started up the third stairway, breathing heavily. His chest was on fire and he knew he was too late. More than fifteen minutes had passed since the cousins had entered the house.

There was no light at the top of the stairs, and he cursed himself for a fool. He should have remembered the door. It was heavy black oak, with a massive iron bar on the other side. "Jesus Fucking Christ! I'll never break through this by myself," he cried, a supposition that proved correct when he injured his right shoulder slamming against it.

"Alex, where are you," Elena called from below.

"Here!" he shouted back frantically. "Grab a log or anything we can use as a battering ram and get up here."

"Let me!" a voice said from behind him. It was Antonio Salani, the Questura's wrestling champion.

Four whacking body blows later and the door came off its hinges. The bolt held.

"*Presto, andiamo!*" Cenni yelled, bursting into the storage room. The door leading to the balcony was wide open, but he saw only empty space and green hills in the distance.

THEY FOUND ANITA Tangassi huddled in a corner of the balcony, sobbing quietly. A few feet away, Lorenzo Vannicelli was lying on his back, legs splayed, arms by his side, his head covered in dirt. He'd been knocked cold by a large pot of rosemary and thyme. Elena, who arrived on the scene carrying a particularly large log, knelt beside the unconscious man to check his pulse and his breathing.

"He's out for the count, but very much alive," she announced in triumph. "Shall I cuff him now, or wait for him to wake up?"

"Cuff him now, *prego!*"

Elena looked up to see who had spoken. Signora Cecchetti was standing in the doorway.

Book Five

Paradise Regained

I

THE NEXT FEW hours were engraved in Anita's memory, more so even than the day she found Bianca's body. Maybe that terrible memory was finally fading. The woman officer, Inspector Ottaviani, whom she'd disliked so much the first time they met, helped her down the stairs to the kitchen and sent Signora Cecchetti across the square to fetch some grappa. She and Signora Cecchetti made her drink two shot glasses before they'd let her talk.

Inspector Ottaviani even held her hand for a short time, while she apologized for not seeing her come into the square. "We were afraid he might try something; he was so cocksure yesterday, and he said a few times that you'd previously tried to kill yourself. We thought we'd covered all our bases."

Anita gasped! "Kill myself? That's a mortal sin! I would never. . . ."

"Of course you wouldn't," Signora Cecchetti said reassuringly to Anita. And to Elena, she said, "Everyone knows the quickest way from Anita's apartment to the pink house is to cut across the olive grove behind my house. Messy, though, especially after a rain," she added, looking down at her shoes. "You parked your car next to the wrong olive grove."

Elena thought briefly of ordering Signora Cecchetti home, but decided against it. The signora was under the impression that Alex had deputized her, and it was hard to fault someone who'd just ruined her best suede pumps fetching the police.

Anita continued, "He phoned late this morning and said lightning had struck my chimney last night. Bricks were raining down onto his garden, and I had to come to assess the damage immediately. I knew it'd rained briefly around eleven. I'd even said a prayer it wouldn't ruin the festival, so I assumed there had been lightning also. Why would he lie?" she asked.

"Humph! Why wouldn't he lie?" Signora Cecchetti retorted.

"Signora, I don't want to ask you to leave, but I will if you aren't quiet," Elena said, finally asserting her authority. She continued with Anita:

"What happened when you got upstairs?"

"While we were climbing the stairs, he asked how many pills I'd taken last night. He asked me the same question when he phoned in the morning. He said I looked very fit and must have slept well. It bothered me, all those questions about the sleeping pills, especially since he was the one who gave them to me. And when we reached the top floor, he said I should go out on the balcony and check the damage.

Lorenzo knows I'm afraid of heights, so I thought it strange that he was sending me out alone. As I opened the door to the balcony, something made me turn around. Maybe I heard him slide the bolt. We looked at each other for a moment, and he smiled. I knew he was going to kill me."

"Because of what you knew about Baudler's murder?" Elena prompted.

"I don't know anything about *her* murder. It was because of the money. He's the only family I have. He gets everything if I die."

THE SAME MOROSE Anita Tangassi from whom they'd had to pry information eleven days earlier became a bounteous fountain of information. Cenni, who had joined them after making sure that Lorenzo Vannicelli was safely on his way to Perugia with nothing more than a headache and a lumpy forehead, directed the questioning after that, but first he asked Signora Cecchetti if he might escort her home. For some reason, she took hints from him better than from Elena, and she left quietly after getting Anita to agree to stay with her that night.

Anita told them everything she could remember about Orazio and Lorenzo, her mother and Monsignor Lacrimosa, and even about Bianca's mother and the men she had entertained before her murder.

"After Monsignor Lacrimosa died, my mother decided to sell Lorenzo's house and give the money to the church. Lorenzo was very angry, so I held off doing anything after my mother's death. But a few months ago, I asked him to pay rent, not a whole lot, just 200 euros a month, and he absolutely refused, so I decided to sell. I was afraid to tell him, but my realtor must have told Jarvinia, and Jarvinia must have told him. He screamed at me on the balcony that I'd die just like my mother had, and for the same reason. That's when I picked up the pot and hurled it at him. I've been working with dumbbells to tone my muscles for the last six months. I guess it's helped."

"He told us he was in the garden when your mother fell from the balcony. Is that true?"

"I was in the garden alone, pruning the roses when my mother fell. I have no idea where Lorenzo was, although he told the carabinieri he was working in his basement when it happened. From what he said today, he must have pushed her."

"What can you tell us about the poisoned mushrooms that your uncle and the priest ate? Do you think Lorenzo was responsible for that as well?" Cenni asked.

Cenni and Elena discussed Anita's answer to the last question at length, after they'd returned to Perugia. Elena, who rather liked using scientific terms, even those she didn't fully understand, said it was linear momentum: Anita began to talk and couldn't stop. Cenni was more inclined to think of it as Catholic guilt, and that they had served as her confessors.

"My mother poisoned them both. She confessed to me shortly before she died, and I'd been thinking for years that she jumped because of my lie about Monsignor Lacrimosa. Now I know it isn't so, that Lorenzo pushed her. I'm glad I didn't kill her. Maybe now I'll sleep at night."

2

IT WAS NOT until five days later that Cenni visited the prison. Vannicelli was still denying everything through his lawyer and had lodged a complaint against the police for assault and false arrest. He continued to insist that it was Anita who'd killed Jarvinia, and that it was Anita who'd tried to kill him. Emilio Feduccia, the public prosecutor, was not happy.

"You know, Alex, it would be so much easier for all concerned if he would just confess. You've given me enough so I can move for a preliminary hearing, and I have an excellent chance of winning if we go to the Assizes; but why take the chance, not to mention the wasted time and money? And Carlo's got some idea that Bertinotti will come down from the heights to rescue Vannicelli. I wonder where he picked up such a ridiculous notion."

As prosecutors go, Emilio was one of the good ones, so Cenni agreed to help. He also wanted to close the case in his own mind. Why did Vannicelli kill the German and then mutilate her in such a brutal way? He had theories, but the proof is in the telling. He visited the prisoner carrying a promise of fifteen years, possibly ten if there were extenuating circumstances. "He'll be close to eighty when he gets out," Emilio said, "and only a danger to himself." What Cenni realized as soon as they sat down together was that Lorenzo Vannicelli wanted to confess, he simply hadn't been given the chance. Cenni started off by expressing his assumption that they both knew he was guilty. A confession was merely a formality to tie up loose ends:

CENNI: "I was rather impressed at how well you covered your tracks."

VANNICELLI: "If you were so impressed, how did you find me out?"

CENNI: "You left your prints on the firewood and various other places. We also have a witness who saw you climb through the basement window shortly before three-thirty and come out the front door carrying your cat at four-thirty."

VANNICELLI: "My lawyer says your witness is Enzo. Who's going to believe the town drunk over its science teacher?"

CENNI: "Enzo cleans up very well. And he's very sure about the times. His nephew gave him a new watch for his birthday. And then we have all those official statements you made trying to implicate your cousin in Jarvinia's death and in the deaths of her uncle and her mother. We checked all your statements, and not one of them is true. Don't worry, they'll believe Enzo!"

VANNICELLI: "I went in after my cat. Of course my prints are there."

CENNI: "On the murder weapon?"

VANNICELLI: "I don't believe you can lift fingerprints off unfinished wood, and besides you never took my fingerprints before my arrest."

CENNI: "You can get latent prints off most things these days, even human skin. As for your own fingerprints, weren't you in the National Service?" Securing Vannicelli's prints from National Service records could've taken weeks, or months. Cenni had pilfered a dirty glass, from the twenty or so that were sitting in Vannicelli's sink, while Elena had distracted him by talking about his cat, but that was not for Vannicelli's lawyer to know.

VANNICELLI: "I could say I helped Baudler to stack her wood."

CENNI: "Just the one piece?"

VANNICELLI: "How did you know Tommaso had been to the vet?"

CENNI: "Signora Cecchetti."

THE MENTION OF the ubiquitous Signora Cecchetti seemed to exhaust Vannicelli. All the fight went out of him. The murder had happened exactly as Cenni had theorized, but still it was good to know for sure. They had been fighting over their cats and Baudler always seem to get the best of him, so when he'd heard Tommaso crying in her basement, he decided to get him out by going through the window.

He'd found Tommaso injured and bleeding and also found the traps that Baudler had placed around the cellar. Three of them. He set the cat down on a pile of old newspapers and started going through boxes to find any kind of cloth in which to wrap Tommaso's leg. He accidentally broke two dishes, and Jarvinia, who'd just returned home, heard the noise and came down to the cellar.

"We were standing by the woodpile when I accused her of cruelty to cats. 'You call that overweight scavenger a cat. He's almost as ugly as you are,' she said and laughed at me. And she wouldn't stop. She said Anita was planning to sell my house, the house I was born in. 'You're nothing but a hanger-on,' she taunted me. I picked up a log from the top of the pile and I struck her. I wasn't thinking about it, it just happened. She gasped and stood there with this amazed look on her face, clutched her chest, made a gurgling noise, and fell over. She landed on the woodpile, and I knew she was dead.

"I panicked. All she ever talked about was how important she was, a mover and a shaker in the world of art and culture. If it had been anyone else, someone ordinary, the police might overlook it, just mark it down to an unfortunate accident, but she was the German cultural attaché. I knew I had to cover up what'd happened to Tommaso, and the blood he'd left everywhere, so I pummeled her with the same log a few times, but she scarcely bled at all."

He was unable to meet Cenni's eyes and twisted his chair to the side. "I remembered the letters and the physical threats, and that she'd shown them to the police. Enzo had delivered the letters. He's the town drunk and worthless. Nobody cares what happens to him. I knew what I had to do. I dragged her body over to the stairs to cover up Tommaso's paw prints." He looked away again. "You know the rest."

He continued, "I'd just finished cleaning up, putting the broken dishes back in the box, collecting the traps, when I heard someone moving around upstairs. I held my breath for what seemed like an age, until I heard the door slam and a car pull away. I shoved the traps into my side pockets and one down my shirt and carried Tommaso in my arms. When I left the house, there was no one around.

I hid the traps in my basement and called the police to report her murder." He stopped puzzled.

"But if Enzo was on the bench . . . how did he see me climb through the basement window? You tricked me!"

Fair enough! I did trick you, but not about this.

"*Calmati,* Signore. When you climbed through the window, Enzo was indulging in a bottle of grappa at the bottom of the garden. He stole it from Anita while she was serving a customer. At four-thirty, he retired to the bench, for a nap. That's when he saw you leave the house. I suppose you could call it poetic justice. Your plan was to implicate Enzo in the murder, and it's Enzo's testimony that will put you away for life."

In the end, Lorenzo Vannicelli had collapsed into a feeble old man, begging for mercy. Cenni responded that not charging him with the murder of Marta Vannicelli or the attempted murder of Anita Tangassi was mercy enough.

HE HAD LIKED Vannicelli. Now he had to question if the objectivity that he demanded from all those on his staff had eluded him. From the beginning, he'd gone easy on the man—hadn't even taken his prints—perhaps because they had similar views on politics and religion, or because he liked the man's sense of humor. It was due to luck, and not any skill of his, that Anita Tangassi was still alive. He'd been completely mistaken in Lorenzo Vannicelli. The man hadn't even asked for Tommaso!

3

Cenni and Elena were driving to Assisi the day after Lorenzo Vannicelli's sentencing to investigate rumors of a perfectly preserved body found under the rubble of a building damaged in the 1997 earthquake.

"You never told me, Alex. What convinced you that Vannicelli was the killer and not Anita, even before we talked to Enzo or you'd gotten confirmation on the fingerprints from forensics?"

"Vannicelli said that people in town thought Anita might have murdered Bianca Lanese—"

Elena interrupted, "But at one point, weren't you thinking along that same line?"

"Gossip is mother's milk to Signora Cecchetti. If anyone in town had accused Anita of the Lanese murders, she would have known about it, and instead, she completely denied it. When it comes to gossip, Elena, women rule."

Elena refused to take the bait.

"You'll never guess what Piero told me last night," she said, not actually intending that Cenni should guess. "Anita Tangassi is getting married."

"That's nice," Cenni said. "I'm not surprised. She's a good-looking woman. How did that come about?"

"Enzo told Piero that she's marrying her doctor, from Rome. Enzo says he's an expert on Anita's condition and travels all over the world giving lectures. He's been treating her for close to two years. She sold everything in Paradiso and vows she'll never return. They plan to adopt children—at least five, Anita said— and all of them with physical disabilities. She can afford it, marrying a famous doctor, and with more than a million euros in her own pocket.

"And even more interesting—" Elena continued in her drum-roll voice.

"Yes?" Cenni said, masking his irritation.

"She told Gianluca she's planning to drop her suit against the carabinieri for breaking her periwinkle dishes."

They both laughed

"It gets better. The doctor came to town to pick her up, and everyone in the square was outside to say good-bye. Enzo says she was dressed in pink from head to toe and she looked smashing!"

Cenni asked if there was any other news.

"Guess who's adopted Tommaso and Princess."

He hated guessing games, but he was in a good mood and played along.

"Who?"

"Signora Cecchetti. She told Enzo it's her Christian duty to take them in."

"I knew the signora had hidden depths," Cenni responded. "I think I'll send her a box of chocolates— or, even better, a huge bag of kitty litter."

Epilogue

Flotilla for a Queen

THE BOATS WERE lined up against the quay outside the Chiesa degli Scalzi, waiting for a party of some sort to emerge from the church. It has to be someone high up in the Church or in the government, was Cenni's first thought, judging from the number of boats in the flotilla and the traffic that was being diverted to the other side of the canal. He counted ten boats painted velvet black, all of them with huge blankets of white chrysanthemums draped across their bows. The lead boat was a monstrosity of blue and glossy green with a golden fire dragon some eight feet high dominating the prow. The Pope? he wondered. He'd just missed the direct boat to Murano, where he was meeting Serge Cattelan, and had walked across the Scalzi Bridge to his bank to withdraw money, and like any other tourist he'd stopped in the middle of the bridge to get a better look.

"A saint's day celebration?" he said to an old man who was standing next to him.

"Not yet," the old man responded. "Not until she per-
forms some miracles."

"Sorry, I don't understand."

"It's a funeral," the old man answered. "*La Contessa*
Molin, the richest woman in Venice, some say in all Italy."

She finally died, he thought, and crossed himself out of
habit. Long overdue, according to the predictions of her
doctors, but she was tough. He wondered, though, why she
had fought on for so long. She had no family other than
Count Volpe, and apparently no friends. The last time
he'd seen her, she could barely sit up and every breath had
been an effort.

"It's a big funeral," he remarked to the old man. "The
people of Venice must have loved her."

"People were mostly afraid of her during her life, but it's
different now. She went and left all her money and her
palazzo to Venice: some kind of foundation, they say, to
save the city from sinking into the lagoon. She even left
some money to the boatmen of Venice. I'm a boatman,"
he said grinning proudly. "And a million euros to an old
nanny of hers, a woman in her nineties. Anna says she's
atoning for her sins. Anna's my wife," he added in explanation. "She's in bed with the rheumatism, so I promised
to come and tell her all about it. Women love this sort of
thing."

"Plenty of men here too," Cenni observed.

"You wouldn't have a cigarette on you, by any chance,"
the old man asked, eyeing his companion up and down
for the signs of a smoker. "My wife cut me off, says I smoke
too much."

"Women are like that, aren't they," Cenni responded sympathetically. He had purchased a pack of Players at the station, and it was still unopened. "Take the whole pack. I shouldn't be smoking anyway."

The old man gave him a wide toothless grin in thanks and stuck the unopened pack into his side pocket. "I'm eighty-seven next month, so I don't see why I should stop smoking. Anna says it's for my health, but I know it's because she hates the smell."

"I'll be getting along now," Cenni said, thinking he might pay his respects at the church. He had come to like Marcella Molin, although he'd be hard-pressed to say why.

The old man grabbed him tightly by the arm before he could walk away.

"I was there, you know, the night the Germans came for her father. Four of them, two of them in uniform. They went into the palazzo and brought him out. He walked between them straight and proud, as only a Venetian can. Two doges in the family! I wonder if he knew it was a death boat? Some people are now saying he was a Nazi sympathizer, but I don't believe it. He once helped me lift a crate onto the dock."

The old man's eyes glittered with malice as he continued his story.

"It was that girl, I told my wife. She did it!"

"What girl?" Cenni asked, caught now by the old man's story.

"A fräulein, not more than fourteen or fifteen, with blonde braids and a gimpy leg. She stood in the cold rain waiting for them to bring him out, and when the launch pulled away, she walked to the edge of the quay and bowed. The devil's child, I told Anna, but she scoffed." He held tightly to Cenni's arm. "I know evil when I see it."

As Cenni descended the steps of the bridge, he thought about what had just passed. The old man had answered his last remaining question, *Who had betrayed Count Molin?* He'd probably never know why. Perhaps there is no why, he reflected, as he turned in the direction of the church. A moment of doubt overtook him. What if he never found Chiara? But then he remembered how that old man had appeared out of nowhere.

"I'll find her," he said to no one in particular, and he crossed himself and entered the church.

Acknowledgments

Enormous thanks go to my editor, Laura Hruska, for her great patience and goodwill in editing my manuscript. I am indebted to Kris Peterson for sharing her knowledge of Venice and Murano and for responding immediately to each of my E-mails with the subject line, "Just one more question." *Mille Grazie* to Signor Carlo Cattelan, Kris's neighbor in Murano, for his stories of *La Resistenza*. I owe another debt to Dr. Fraser Charlton, Consultant Pathologist at the Royal Victoria Infirmary in Newcastle Upon Tyne, for instructing me on blood groups and for reviewing my manuscript for errors in forensic science. Thank you to Marco Cioccoloni, Stephanie Ninaud, and Kaitlin Mignella for hunting down misspelled words in English and Italian. And, finally and foremost, I am blessed in having the love and support of my husband, Miguel Peraza, who read each and every chapter, many times, and never once complained.

As an American writing a novel set in Italy, there will be unintentional errors; for these, I have no one but myself to blame.

New York, New York